COMMENCEMENT

JOSEPH LANKFORD

Joe Lankford

PAGE PUBLISHING, INC.
Conneaut Lake, PA

First originally published by Page Publishing 2020

ISBN 978-1-6624-2962-0 (pbk)
ISBN 978-1-6624-2963-7 (digital)

Printed in the United States of America

THE BEGINNING

In the beginning, when God created the universe, the earth was formless and desolate. The raging ocean that covered everything was engulfed in total darkness, and the Spirit of God was moving over the water. Then God commanded, "Let there be light" and the light appeared. God was pleased with what he saw. Then he separated the light from the darkness, and he named the light "Day" and the darkness "Night."

—Genesis 1:1–5

FROM THE BEGINNING of time, there have been four ancient primordial forces charged with maintaining a balance among themselves and Creation. These four forces served the Creator as the creation of the first races came into being. For many eons, Creation was peaceful until the Fall.

The angel Lucifer led his brethren in a civil war leading the four primordials to fight among one another as well. The Creator ended the war and banished Lucifer's army to a dark abyss. The primordials were split and separated, leaving only their influence in Creation and broke their consciousness. Now they wander Creation, barely a shell of their true selves, but for the sake of the Balance, they were kept where they were, as spectators of Creation. For thousands of years, they watched over the Earth when the Creator brought forth humankind.

When humanity was expelled from the garden Eden, they became exposed and targeted by new monsters, creatures born of beasts and malice. Humanity was at the mercy of these many beasts when one of the primordials chose a champion to safeguard humanity. A champion of such strength and ferocity that he was feared by all, even by his charge. Many years thereafter, the warrior faded from existence and memory. They called that champion a Phantom and named his patron Death.

Before the Phantom faded, he took on apprentices from the bravest of humanity and taught them how to fight and defend themselves and others from the monsters of the world. This began the sect that called themselves "Hunters," and they safeguarded humankind as civilization prospered. At the time of the Crucifixion, the Hunters themselves disappeared.

All traces of this group were lost, their deeds were forgotten, and humanity had lost their monsters to mere myth and legend. No one knows of these Hunters who protected their fellow humans from the monsters. No one knows they still exist, that they still fight, that they still keep the evil at bay. This Order is strong, commanded by humans to protect humanity.

This is the story every Hunter in the Order knows and respects. It is the history of our beginning and our duty. We are the Hunter's Order, and we are the nightmares of the things you fear. My name is Dante, and this is my story. It all starts on that morning when I got that assignment that not only changed my life but the way I thought.

CHAPTER 1

A NEW MISSION

I ALWAYS HAVE these nightmares. I'm being tortured and killed. For what reason? I never know. Just before I get any answers, I wake up with a crippling headache.

Last night, I was being burned alive, slashed to pieces, and worst of all was this voice from nothingness seemed to be driving me to madness. The voice screams at me to embrace death and my fate. That's when the nightmare ends, that's when I finally return to consciousness. I woke with a start and grab my head as it begins to throb. Only this time my chest joined in as it began to burn, almost as if it were about to explode. I curl into a ball and try to block out the pain. Every damned time I have one of these nightmares, I wake to throbbing pain, like my subconscious doesn't want me to remember what happened. If any of those dark and painful images is of any indication, I'm better off not knowing.

"I swear to God, these nights are going to kill me long before any of those monsters out there," I said to myself as I worked to get my breathing under control.

The pain passed, and I began to relax. I was in a blank, empty room, no light, no decor, no life. I was used to this. When I wasn't out on a mission, I was at a base. Never there long enough to call a place home, never there long enough to make friends. I was born and raised in the Order, no family, no concerns, and nothing holding me back. I had only one companion for as long as I could remember.

The darkness around me moved and shifted around. There was a pair of crimson-red eyes staring right at me as I became more and more awake. In all my life, this…*thing* was my only companion. He can be described as a living shadow and almost everything about him is an unknown. The few things we do know is that he only stays with the current Phantom, and anyone who hears his voice either goes insane or gets a mild headache. I'm the lucky latter obviously.

"I'm fine, Nex," I assure my familiar. "Just another irritating bad dream. That's all." He glares at me… I think he does anyway, I'm never sure with him, but I doubt he believes me. He can be… difficult to understand. Something caught his attention outside the solitary door in the room, and he started to focus on it. I took this time to get up and get dressed. Just as I got my pants on, I felt a dull throb in the center of my brain.

They are setting explosive charges on the door, he told me. *I'd say about another twenty seconds before they set them off.* Wonderful. Another early morning wake-up call. This is actually nothing new. I'm the Phantom, expected to be ready for anything at any time. That's why a lot of the training measures they give me are designed to get me killed. I moved to hide myself above the door, just enough to be out of the way of the blast, and waited.

The door splintered under the force of the explosion with shrapnel flying every which way. After that, there was a barrage of gunfire that riddled the entire room with bullet holes. As the first guy slowly peeked in to survey the room, I swung down from the doorframe, slamming my knees into his face. When I landed, I continued my assault on the other two near the door, punching and kicking the two guys on the opposite sides. I heard a gunshot and used one of the guys as a human shield. Seven more people were out there trying to kill me, fewer than usual. I grabbed a sidearm from my human shield and unloaded the magazine into four more guys and ran into the open.

"Weapon!" I called out. From out behind me came a pair of tomahawks, straight from Nex's black abyss. Without turning, I reached out and took hold of the handles, solid wood handles with gleaming steel ax-heads. Nice weapons, time to get them dirty. My opponents took out their combat knives and responded. One swung at me, and I hooked his arm in one of my weapons and broke his neck with a swift swing. The other guy was closing in on me, and I slashed his neck open with another swing. Before the last guy got too close, I threw my ax right into his face, and he fell dead. Above me came applause.

"Well done, Phantom Dante." It was a man wearing a lab coat over a dress shirt and dark pants. "Well done. But you missed a couple." There was a growl as something attempted to grab me from behind. I ducked and slammed my elbow into his gut and grabbed his head. I finally got a clear look at those that were trying to kill me. Rotting flesh and trying to eat me. Ghouls, makes sense, not too stupid to learn how to fight like men but still more fragile though, so I snapped its neck. Before the last one got too close, I slammed my foot into his throat and broke his neck too. "Better," the guy above me said.

"I'd be more eager to please if you didn't try to kill me every morning and treat it like a game." I made my way toward a door on the far right. "Nex! Eat your breakfast." I yelled out to the shadow. I see the darkness cover the many bodies in the room and hear the sickening crunches as the corpses are devoured. This is where a lot of my weapons come from. Nex cleans up the remains of people killed and stores many useful things inside his being. A lot of stuff comes from a great many battlefields, and other Hunters that have tried to tame the shadow…it ends poorly for them.

I met up with the man from earlier as I walked toward the mess hall. He was my trainer, went by the code name "Wizard." A master spell caster and wise man. He has been charged with my training for as long as I can remember and has said that extreme situations breed great results. Those who survived were great—didn't mean there were a lot of them.

"Come now, Dante, you have always proven to perform admirably. Or is it that you have no faith in your own abilities?" he asked condescendingly, always playing mind games with me.

"I think that the many dead that you have sent against me is enough to show my skill." He has thrown almost every monster known and forgotten at me in a test of my skills. It has gotten to the point where I am merely annoyed when I have assassins after me.

"Yes, you have proven to be my best trainee out of all the Hunters I have worked with before." A Hunter is always a trainee until after a set number of years and missions. I only have a few more of each before I'm a Master Hunter myself. In my opinion, the sooner I'm rid of him, the better. Nex always stays with the Phantom, the best of the Order, and I'm the youngest Phantom to date. Didn't mean that I bypassed tradition.

"I'm not fighting to impress you, I fight to survive." I never knew anything about my life, I was a Hunter, and I killed the monsters in the world. That was all I knew and that was all I needed, killing just made sense to me. Sometimes I wonder why I do this or what was there before all this. Nex has never talked to me about it, and it's a shame because for some reason, he's the only being I feel I can trust here.

I entered the mess hall to get my breakfast and sat at a table to eat. I had scrambled eggs, bacon, and sausages with coffee. It was a good meal, but to be frank, I don't think I ever had much of an appetite in my life. I had begun eating anyway when I saw someone coming toward me. It wasn't Wizard—it was someone else. She was dressed in a business suit and skirt.

"Excuse me, Phantom," she spoke in a high-pitched squeak. "But your presence is being requested by the higher-ups," she said, and then she ran like her life depended on it. This was actually normal. I was always treated with fear and apprehension. Why? Not really sure, but I did have my theories. Best I had was that Nex Umbra invokes fear and terror in anything less than me. That was the best I had.

I finished my meal and made my way to the special access passage that led to the communications center with access to the council. In there, the top assignments to those that have proved themselves against all odds were given. I'm actually surprised I got called in for a job from the high council. I entered a pitch-black room, knowing

I reached the center when a glyph on the ground started glowing. It was the symbol of the Order: a ring of two intertwining thorny vines with a pair of wings inside, a demon wing and an angel wing. A shining light appeared in the room, and a deep voice sounded.

"Dante, you have been chosen for a special task," he said as I gave my full attention. "Your mission is to scout out this strange energy anomaly and determine if it poses a threat to humankind and whether we should take action." I'm being sent on an espionage mission? Certainly unexpected but not impossible. Just got to see if this is a danger or not. "You may bring your familiar with you, but no one else," he spoke with authority and urgency. "No one can know of your mission, not even Wizard. Do you understand your mission, Phantom?" I nodded. "Good, then go." I turned to leave. "Take this cell phone. We will contact you when there is an urgent mission for you." I was making my way out of the room when I felt another headache, and a strange chill come over me. I ignored it and made my way out, grabbing the cell as it appeared beside the door.

I took a look at the phone, and it was on the GPS map, pointing me to a destination quite some distance away from the base. I was going to need a ride.

CHAPTER 2

JOURNEY TO THE UNKNOWN

I STOOD IN the shower, letting the warm water fall on my body as I calmed myself in the manufactured rain. I took this time to collect my thoughts and think about what was to come. My first major mission for the Order and I had to keep it a secret. How to keep this from Wizard, I wasn't too sure. I got out and dressed myself, my hands and eyes lingering on a mass of scars on my chest, a grim reminder of my harsh training. I try to remember when and how I got this mess, but my headache returns, and I can't focus. I finished getting dressed and gathered my supplies, clothes, and an unlimited credit card. The Order is very well-off and keeps its members well financed for long missions.

I had my stuff and made my way to the base's garage. I surveyed the area and found something that suited my wants and purpose. A black Harley motorcycle, nothing fancy, nothing too noticeable unless you were looking for it. This was also in the stealth area of the garage, so it was a one-man stealth vehicle that had magic runes in the body to hide it. I revved and tried to listen for the engine that roared to life like a lion. I liked it. I'm taking it. I climbed on and rode my way out of the base and into an open field. Underground and inconspicuous, the classics. Ten minutes into my drive, I felt another strange chill, like people were dying close to me...but there was not a single sound to indicate that. Nex caught up to me not long after that.

"I don't want to know what it was you were doing, do I?" I asked as I drove. It was silent, but I could swear I heard its demented giggling. "I figured." I accelerated and continued to follow my map. It seemed to be guiding toward Rocky Mountains, or more accurately, a forest in the mountains. "Yeah, that's not creepy or foreboding at all." I swear, something is going to try to snap at me when I get there. Question is, what?

So what do you think we will encounter there? Nex asked me. This was a five-hour drive, and we only had each other for company. Alone with a psychotic shadow being that causes me headaches when he talks, I've made a terrible mistake somewhere, haven't I?

"I'm not entirely sure. It could be a meeting, some religious thing, anything really. If we're lucky, they're gathering an army, and we have to wipe them out before they grow too great in number." Long shot, but it's smart to prepare for anything. "Entertainment for me and food for you. Fun thought, isn't it?" I was actually very excited—this was my first major mission. I went on hunts before, but this was a full-scale deal. There was a lot of weight on my shoulders to do this right. I'm also jittery and sweaty. Is this what nervousness feels like?

Hours later, we made it to our destination. It was just as dark and ominous as I thought it would be. The trees blocked out any and all light. There were only the faintest sounds, humid, the foliage was so thick I couldn't even see the sky. I'm almost tempted to say it could be worse, but I know how that tends to work. I jumped off the bike, and Nex absorbed it. I'd probably complain about Nex if he wasn't so useful to have around.

"So this is the place, huh?" I checked my map again, and sure enough, this is where it was leading me. "Let's check it out." Silently, I made my way up one of the trees and climbed my way across the branches. After a couple of minutes of crawling, I felt a disturbance in the air. It was…something magical in nature. Strong magic can be like radiation, the powerful energies of the spells would mutate the environment, usually just making things bigger and more aggressive.

11

"What is that feeling?" Dropping down from the trees, I continued my exploration, then I saw spider webbing half the size of my arm. "Oh yeah... I'm being watched," I said as a six-foot butterfly with iridescent blue wings appeared with a shimmering rainbow pattern appearing with every beat of its wings. Looking at this, I couldn't help but think, *At a certain size, some things just stop being cute*, and then it shot lasers out of its eyes, hitting a giant spider and frying it, coincidentally removing the web barrier in my way. We stared at each other for a few moments, then it just flew away.

"Not cute but still a beautiful sight," I said as I continued on my path.

After another five minutes, I found a distortion in the air, like heat shimmers only harder to notice. Nex handed me a blank silver mask that can view most known vision sets and tuned it to see residual magic energy. Previous Phantoms always wore masks, mainly for intimidation and secrecy. Now thanks to development in scanning and communication technology, my mask is an important tool in my arsenal. Magic use is dependent on the user's stamina and how well they can use it to enact the spell chosen or how they manipulate the energy for the spell. I took a look at the magical energy, and it was pretty strong, enough to mutate the surrounding area with size and in rare instances abilities. Fortunately, it requires prolonged contact, months on end at least, which means this portal had been here for quite a while.

"Time to see what's on the other side," I said as I walked into the portal.

In a flash of light, I ended up on the other side, which was the mouth of a tunnel on a mountain trail. I noticed a collection of buildings in the distance and used the zoom function on my mask. The higher-ups were right. There was a mass of the other species. Hundreds of almost every one of the many races have gathered here. Time to see why.

"What'cha doing?" I heard from behind me. I turned and got ready to defend myself. When I saw, I was facing a girl with the most disarming feel about her. She was dressed in black with purple accents, similar makeup, an innocent look on her face as she rested her chin on her hands, riding an old-fashioned broom, and wearing purple hair. I didn't drop my guard, but it was taking an effort. "This is actually my natural hair color by the way." She smiled.

"Okay, not sure what to make of that," I responded. "I heard about this place and came to check it out. What is it?" I asked. Normally, I'd be thinking about how to make her disappear, but there was just something about her. She just seemed so innocent. Might be useful to keep her alive, for now. She gained a sparkle in her eye as her excitement seemed to grow.

"This is SN Academy!" she announced before dragging me on her broom and flying over the campus. She caught me off guard. How did that happen? "This is a safe haven for nonhumans and others ostracized by society. Here, we are safe. Those that attend try to learn how to blend in with humans and live normal lives. Just because we're different doesn't mean we don't deserve a proper education!" She was certainly...energetic.

"So this is just a place to learn how to blend in with humans?"

"Yep! Hunters only really go after those that hurt humans after all, so this is more for the rest of humanity in general."

I would argue, but she does have a point. Hunters are meant to be protectors, not mindless killers. This doesn't mean I'm willing to give them the benefit of the doubt. There's a reason the Hunters still exist to this day.

"So who are you?" I yelled over the rushing wind as she accelerated. I decided to just go along with it for now.

"Name's Monica! Monica Myer! I'm a witch!" Witches, they're not exactly monsters, but their affinity for magic is much stronger than most. While anyone with enough strength and focus can use magic, they can use it much more easily. They also tend to heal faster than normal humans and are just different enough that they are shunned and feared. Never had the best reputation...and that incident in Salem didn't help anyone.

"You sure it's a good idea to announce that so freely?" I asked her as we continued to fly.

An entire school like that is kind of hard to believe. Most of monster kind are little more than mindless beasts, but there are some that can work with people. There is a rather tense peace between the Hunters and a species known as "Incruentatus," or living vampires to simplify it. This entire academy, the meaning of this school, it's a bit of long shot. If it does work out, what does that mean for the world?

"You can know. We're going to be the bestest friends, Dante!" she yelled as she hugged me. I froze when she said my name, which I never told her. While I was still shocked, she let go and counted off on her fingers. "Along with an elf, a skinwalker, a kitsune, a lycan, a succubus, an Incruentatus, and a lycan! I get so many friends!"

"You said lycan twice." I was back on guard again, and this time, I wasn't going to drop it around her. That was certainly an interesting ragtag group of…whatever that would be called. Lycans are basically weaker werewolves, but they have full control of the transformation. Elves are a race deeply in tune with magic and nature, preferably keeping to themselves and usually benign. Kitsune are Japanese fox spirits, can either be guardians or mischief makers. Succubi, demon seductresses, steal your soul, that whole deal. Incruentati are "living vampires," the progenitors of that undead race. A skinwalker, though, that's hard to believe one of them would be here. They're supposed to be shamans who mastered their craft then performed a taboo ritual that corrupts the soul. "Why did you say lycan twice?"

"'Cause there are gonna be two lycans!" She then gasped in a weird realization. "We should get them to hook up!" She grabbed my shoulders and started screaming and begging like a child. "Can we? Please! Can we get them to hook up? They'll be a great couple!" At this point, I was mainly focusing on *not* falling off the flying stick. My initial impression—she's crazy. When she finally stopped trying to kill me, for now, I think, she gasped again. "You still haven't met the rest of the future gang!" She stood on top of the broom and pointed forward. "To the rest of the group!" Then the broom practically shot out from under me, but I managed to get a hold of it. She flew us all the way to a clearing where a tanned black-haired shirtless guy came out of the woods. Monica then made a very sharp turn, and I lost my grip and was thus sent flying into a tree…right next to the guy. How does she keep getting the drop on me?

"You okay?" he asked me. He sounded German. I lifted my head to look at him. Crystal blue eyes that hid a primal ferocity to them. I nodded, and he extended his hand. I accepted his help, and he introduced himself. "Name's Max, Maximilian Wolfgang."

"I'm Dante."

"Oh, you're that guy. Yeah, Monica said you'd be coming," he told me.

"How the heck does she know about me?" Seriously, why does the crazy girl know about me?

"She's certainly confusing, isn't she?" We began walking. Not really sure where, but I'm following him for now. "She acts like a child, always changing interests every few days at worst. One time, she took up fortune telling for a day. Never used the same method twice. She was calmer then." I looked at him incredulously. "Yeah, she got worse. When we asked, all she said was, 'My life's getting interesting!' Then you saw how she is now." He muttered something about how she nearly broke his ribs hugging him.

"So this sugar-high basket case says that we'll be friends and we're taking her word for it?" I asked. He just shrugged.

"I don't know if she was making it up or if she really had a vision of the future. She told me, 'The guys live very close.' No idea what it means, but I suppose I'll have to wait and see."

Okay, this whole espionage thing is going to take some time.

"So how do I get admitted here?" I asked 'cause there is likely a process of getting these "students" accepted.

"Your parents didn't send you here?" he asked.

"I never had any parents. I've been alone most of my life." Not lying, I never had a family.

"That sucks, sorry to hear, man," he said sympathetically. "Well, if you aren't sent here by a parent or guardian…make some noise."

"Elaborate please?" Make some noise?

"Yeah, this a rehabilitation center after all. Some are here by choice to keep them safe. Others are here because they put the rest of us in danger. They are mostly the angry and bad-tempered people here." Just then, my shoulder bumped into a guy that told me to watch my step and called me a rather colorful name.

"So I should get into a fight?" Max was shifting his gaze between me and the other guy.

"Yeah, that should get the faculty's attention, especially if you're new here," he said as he watched me head over to the other guy. "I'd recommend anyone else, though."

"No need. This will do nicely." I began walking toward the other guy. He had a lean build, short black hair, and a smug feel about him. "Give me a good disguise, Nex," I whispered as I felt the shadows creeping up my leg.

"What do you want?" the stranger very rudely said to me. I put my hand on his shoulder and smiled. I cocked my arm back and slammed my fist into his face. He fell back a couple feet, then he got back up and smirked at me. "Big mistake." His hands became talons, his muscles got more defined, his skin changed to scales, and two wings burst out from his back. Seemed to be of the dragon family.

"Maybe for anyone else." Out of the corners of my eyes, I saw Nex's darkness envelope my body. Nex described it to me, horns on my forehead, wings on my back, my arms and legs grew bulkier at their ends, and a tail, all the darkest black. So I looked like a demon… I can work with that.

"Bring it, trash!" Yep, certainly of the western dragon family, prideful. Time to see how badly I can hurt his pride. It devolved into a fistfight pretty soon after that. Just two guys punching each other till one of us goes down. He threw a punch at my face, which I dodged, grabbed his arm, and elbowed him in the face a few times before punching him again and throwing him over my shoulder. He responded by unleashing a torrent of fire at me. Then I was tackled to the ground by a giant stone figure.

"Did anyone get the number of that truck?" I wheezed out. More of these rock figures came forward. They quickly restrained both of us, and someone else came forward. He was dressed in a white button shirt with blue dress pants, glasses, and unkempt hair.

"Now, now, Draco, what have we said about that temper?" he admonished the dragon like a child. Draco just scoffed and looked away to glare at me. "Maybe a few weeks in solitary will cool your head." He gestured to the statues and told them to take him away, and then he turned his attention to me. "You are not from here. So just what do you have to hide?" he spoke lackadaisically like he was interrupted from his nap. "Well, I'll just have to find out." He turned and began to walk away telling the statues to bring me along.

They dragged me across the campus, and I was apparently not the most interesting sight that afternoon because no one spared a second glance at me. Soon I was brought to a room that seemed like solitary confinement. There were dozens of magic seals and a chain-link cage that was electrified. He left me in there for a long time. I think a day passed before the same guy came to get information from me.

"All right, kid, what is your name?" he asked while I was still in the cage.

"My name is Dante."

"What are you doing here?"

"I heard that this was a safe haven, and I would have a better chance surviving here."

"Who told you this?"

"I heard it in some shady circles while I was trying to avoid some unwanted attention. The safest manner possible."

"Is there any reason you can give me to not have you killed?" he asked with a dark, menacing aura that managed to put me a little on edge. I froze with confusion and shock. What can I possibly say in this situation that could get me out of this? After what seemed like an hour of silence, he started laughing. "Calm down, kid. You got admitted in."

"What?" He was messing with me?

"Yeah, there was a meeting, and someone vouched for you," he said as he handed me a folder. "Here's your class schedule and room assignment. You are also going to be watched by the security and sentries. They do have permission to break your bones and cripple you, so I suggest you don't cause trouble."

"Doesn't that seem a little excessive if they abuse their authority?"

"Nah, the head is pretty strict on his officers, and there are some pretty durable people here. Others tend to regenerate quickly." He then dismissed me and snapped his fingers that teleported me outside to another building.

"Great, now where am I?" I asked before I noticed the sign that said "Anansi Hall," emblazoned with the symbol of the trickster deity. Looked pretty modern and sturdy, bricks, concrete, cinder blocks. I checked my folder, and it said my room was 413, fourth floor, thirteenth room. I got into the building and made my way to the stairs and elevators. The floor was cracked, burned, and filled with claw marks, and the walls didn't seem to fare much better. If the base floor was any indication, this was going to get pretty rowdy. I got to the stairs and began my ascent and soon reached my floor and my room.

"Wonder if anyone's in there?" I asked myself and knocked the steel door a couple of times. One minute later, Max opened the door, still shirtless, with a bottle in his hand.

"Hey, looks like you got in," he said happily as we shook hands. "Come on in, I'll grab you a drink," he said as I made my way inside.

For some reason, my stuff was already there. Max grabbed another bottle and handed it to me. It was an unlabeled bottle of dark fluid. I popped the top off and took a swig. It was flavorful yet also bitter.

"Nice. What is this?"

"My own brew, an old family recipe." He took a drink. "Quality beer is good to have." I stopped, realizing what I was drinking.

"You sure we should be having these then?" I asked.

"I'm sixteen and German. It's legal." He took another drink. "Besides, this place isn't bound by human laws, so go nuts."

I thought about it for a second.

"Good point." We clinked the bottles together and drank. "So I guess we're roommates," I said as I unpacked my stuff.

"Looks like it." He began helping me out. "Here are the ground rules—never mind. I can't think of any." We both shared a laugh and agreed we were going to get along. It was late, so we went to bed for the night.

"I'll see you in the morning, Dante."

"Night, Max," I said as I closed my eyes. Once I was sure Max was sleeping, I told Nex to be ready to attack should Max try anything.

CHAPTER 3

GATHERING

I WAS EXPERIENCING another tormenting nightmare until I felt a hand on my shoulder. Thinking I was under attack, I responded very aggressively. I grabbed the person's wrist and throat before throwing him into the wall on the other side of my bed, then I slipped out and got him into an arm lock. I was prepared to continue before I heard Nex telling me to stop.

"Bad dream I take it?" Max asked after I released him. "If so, that was a nasty one."

"Not really...well yes, but also a force of habit," I told him as I went to the bathroom. "But I also wasn't expecting a naked man shaking me awake."

I heard him laugh.

"Yeah, sorry. I forget that people expect modesty. My bad."

I took a quick shower, and Max said he'd take me on a tour since it was the weekend. We got dressed, and just as we left, we ran into two more guys—a slim, lean, and long dark-haired Japanese, I think it's a guy, with fox ears, and a tall and muscular Native American, wearing sunglasses. We said our greetings and began talking as we walked to the school mess hall.

"So this is the new guy?" asked the smaller guy. "The one that sucker punched Draco?"

"Yep, that's me." I have the feeling I brought more attention to myself than I intended.

"Nice! The name's Kashikoi! Pleased to meet ya!" He may have been carrying himself casually, but I could feel he was trying to hide something. "Just don't ask me to tutor you. I need help myself." He started laughing.

"I'm Lance. Nice to meet you," said the bigger guy…and that was about it from him. He looked like a powerhouse but at the same time moved very gracefully.

"My name's Dante. I hope we get along."

The tour proper began. They explained that the school was a blend of cultures from all over—the intelligent monsters and creatures that can blend in with human society came here and enriched the culture of the student society. The place had three major areas, the school that included the dorms and school facilities; the portal called "Gateway" that could take you anywhere in the world as the portals appear at random on the outside; and what they called "the Lands" that actually had every environment—forests, mountains, deserts, lakes, every one of them. Why was it necessary? Don't know, but I had a feeling I was going to learn. While we were walking, we met with Monica again.

"Hi, Dante! I see you've met Koi-kun, Lance, and Max!" She then began to scratch Kashi behind his ears and talking about how cute she finds him.

"I personally find this to be very undignified," he responded while she crawled on him.

"Maybe if you ignore her, she'll go away," I said before she jumped on my back, screaming, "Piggyback ride!" We just kept walking around as they showed me to my classrooms. Turns out, I had science and magic, which were mixed into one class apparently, with Monica whose lab partner was there waiting for their study session.

"Sorry, Zoe," she whined after "Zoe" scolded her. Zoe was tall with fair skin that had a golden undertone and green eyes. Monica then perked up and introduced me. "Zoe, this is Dante! He's gonna be our new lab partner in class!" She presented me like a game show prize.

"I don't get a say in this, do I?" I asked.

"You get used to it," Zoe replied. "I look forward to working with you," she said before grabbing Monica by the ear and dragging her away.

"Oh! Dante, head for the language classroom right now! Go, but be alone!" Monica yelled after me while the guys and I left.

"So do I ignore that or what?" I asked while moving on.

"Hard to say," Max mumbled.

"She acts like that, but she's also the smartest person in school," Kashi informed.

"Where have I seen that before?" I mused.

"It tends to aggravate the people that put forth the effort," Lance said.

"One time she substituted for a teacher," Max said.

"How did that turn out?" I asked, and they all froze like they were triggered.

Apparently, it was a traumatic event that no one talks about. The rest of the tour was kept in an awkward silence until we reached the classroom in question; apparently, they cover every language curriculum. "Well, guys, as much as I think it's in my best health to ignore that crazy witch, I'll be going in alone." I opened the door and walked in. It was empty with the exception of one person. She was beautiful with long shining dark hair, tanned bronze skin, deep brown eyes, with a body that seem made for seduction. We just stared at each other for a bit until I finally noticed I had another headache.

"Sorry, I was checking out my classrooms for the year," I said, switching to a different language. She seemed to snap out of her daze as well.

"Then it looks like we're going to be classmates. My name is Lucrezia Giovanni," she spoke in a hypnotizing tone as she walked up to me, using flawless Italian. Times like this made me glad for the charm, "gift of language." If I had to warrant a guess, this was probably the succubus that Monica said was going to be a friend. This could be interesting.

"I'm Dante. A pleasure." I held out my hand, which she took and curtsied.

"I haven't seen you before. Are you new?"

"I just got accepted yesterday."

She took a smile while examining me. "Well then, why don't I take you on a tour?"

I could almost feel the demonic charm of her activating. "I already have a few tour guides," I told her.

"Then you can take me to dinner," she responded.

"Oh, can I?"

"Your way of apologizing for interrupting my reading." I noticed the book at her table. "Or not if you're afraid."

"I am not afraid," I said confidently.

"Okay then, when?"

"How about next weekend?"

She took my chin in hand and whispered in a sultry tone right in my ear. "It's a date." She then kissed me on my cheek and went back to her desk, and I left the room before I paused.

"What the hell just happened?" The guys just stared at me, wide-eyed, and shrugged. We kept walking until Max ran into a girl who was tanned, had gray hair, and was wearing a tube top and very short shorts.

"Watch where you're going, you filthy mutt!" she yelled.

"I must have been too distracted to even recognize your stench, you runt!" Max replied. They then devolved into a pretty childish fight of yelling back and forth.

"So what is this?" I asked.

"This is how Max and Andrea talk," Kashi said. "Andrea Kain and Max always fight like this."

"They like each other," Lance said.

"Really?" I asked.

"Yep, it's all a matter of tension," Kashi elaborated. I personally doubt it, but I do see some subtle hints. "When that breaks…" He started giggling. After a few minutes of watching, we got tired of the argument and began to leave. Lance had to go back and grab Max and carry him back to us.

Max and I were back in our dorm room just passing the time when there was a knock on the door. I opened it and was face to neck with a tall Russian man with pale blond hair and thick muscles.

"Dante, I am your parole officer. My name is Volk Gulski. You will refer to me as 'sir,' and you will report to me at the end of the day every two days. You will also be watched continuously by the rest of the safety committee of the school." He handed me a folded piece of paper. "Here is a map to find my office. If you are late, you will be brought to my office for your report of the two days. Your parole will end when I see fit." He then turned and left. With that, I shut the door and sat back down with Max who handed me a fresh beer.

"This should be an interesting year," he said.

"Yep."

CHAPTER 4

THE PRINCESS OF BLOOD

A WEEK HAD already passed, and I had acclimated to the student life-style. I went through the opening ceremony and attended my classes. I made my reports to both my parole guy and the Hunters who gave me the standing order to stay and monitor the place, hanging out with the people I've met. And then there was my date with Lucrezia. She showed me how the Gateway worked by taking us to a restaurant in Venice. We talked about some interests, how I was doing at the school, standard first date stuff. She did bring up something interesting, though.

"You know that one absent student in class?" she asked as we returned to the school and made our way to her dorm.

"Saya, right?" She told me she was supposed to have a room-mate named Saya Shizuka, but she had an excused absence for the past week. "What about it?"

"Whatever business she had is finally over, and she'll be back at school soon." She latched onto my arm and began pressing her breasts against me and gave me the puppy eyes. "Could I get a big strong man to help me move her in?" She doesn't play fair apparently.

"Yeah, I guess." She smiled cutely, and I escorted her to her dorm. After we bid our goodbyes, I headed back to Anansi Hall. I got to my room to find Max.

"Good date?" he asked, sitting on the couch and watching television.

"Yeah, I actually enjoyed myself." I sat down to join him.

"She called not too long ago and said to tell you 'Never mind, Saya's already here.' Wasn't that the absent girl?"

"Yeah, looks like we finally meet the mystery girl."

"Should be fun. Wonder what kept her?"

I shrugged, and we left it at that. The rest of the weekend went by uneventfully except for the camping trip announcement where we had to survive on our own in groups, which would be assigned. In class, the teacher announced Saya had come to school and told her to give an introduction. I saw her and froze, pale as the moon with hair like a stream of glittering silver and had eyes like shining rubies. The weirdest thing is that she seemed familiar to me for some reason. I never met her before, but there was just something about her that seemed so familiar.

"Hello, everyone," she spoke with a mix of nobility and pure-hearted kindness as she did a little bow. "My name is Saya Shizuka. I hope we can all get along." The teacher then told her to go sit next to me. She sat next to me and asked for my name.

"Dante. Nice to meet you." I know I met her somewhere before, but where? Damn, this is going to bug me as bad as trying to remember a song. The rest of the class went by pretty normally, except for this weird electricity in the air coming from Lucrezia toward Saya. I wonder why. Time went by until we had lunch, during which I made my way to the roof and just lay down. Thoughts of Saya playing in my head while I tried to remember her.

"Dude," said Kashikoi, showing up to join me, "heard that girl that was absent finally showed up." He took a seat and began eating some flavored bread before handing me one. "What's her name again?"

"Saya Shizuka." I tore into the flavored pastry. "I know her from somewhere, but I can't remember."

"I know that feeling. I remember the name, but what is it?"

"Maybe you met her before?" said Lance as he and Max joined us.

"Possibly, but even then, I should have recognized her in some way," I told them as they sat. "Man, this is going to irritate me to no end!" I let myself fall backward until I was looking up to what should have been the sky, but Lucrezia and Saya were standing in the way. "Ladies."

"Hello again, Dante," they said with a smile, "nice to see you again."

I sat back up as the girls joined us with Lucrezia taking a place a little too close to me.

"You've met *my* boyfriend, Shizuka-chan." I recognized the emphasis that meant to remind me that I was dating her for now. "The one that's next to him is Kashikoi, then Max, and Lance."

"And those are just *our* guy friends!" I heard Monica's voice coming from my girlfriend's chest. I pulled on her blouse and looked down to see Monica, shrank to an inch tall, nestled between Lucrezia's breasts.

"What are you doing?" I asked the crazy witch girl.

"Taking a nap! These are so warm and soft!"

I reached in and pulled her out. "Quit it," I said before bringing her up to my mouth and blew. For some reason, she inflated like a balloon till a pop sounded, bringing her back to normal. I'm still surprised that worked, honestly.

"Did you know that was going to work?" asked Kashi.

"I didn't really think anything would happen." Monica was dazed before shaking it off. "I was just winging it."

"That was neat!" said Monica with a grin as she threw her hands up. "Let's do that again!"

Then Kashi whacked her on the head. "Sit down and eat already," he said as she curled up to Lucrezia, whining that "Kashi-kun is mad."

"You people are so much fun!" Saya said in a fit of giggles. I just kept watching her, racking my brain with trying to remember who is she. This pale complexion, those red eyes, those fangs in her mouth…fangs?

"Hey, aren't you going to eat?" Lucrezia asked.

"I'm just thirsty," she responded, taking a juice pouch and drinking from it. I was able to pick up the distinct hint of copper. Fangs, bloodred eyes, and she's most likely drinking blood or a blood substitute. I am an idiot. Saya Shizuka, of the Shizuka bloodline of the Incruentatus families, also known as the vampire nobles to most. Hunters are to know each one of the families for reasons of either protection or assassination. Shizuka stands out a bit more in my head, but why?

"So *you're* an Incruentatus?" said Monica, completely out of nowhere, while looking at Saya in the face.

Saya apparently gasped and started choking on her drink. Lucrezia and I were helping Saya from choking while Kashi was scolding Monica about her lack of manners.

"Yeah, sorry about her. She's American. No manners," Lucrezia said when Saya finally caught her breath.

"You learn to get used to her...apparently. I still haven't," I told Saya.

"It's all right," she said before the air around her seemed to change. I didn't feel like I was looking at a teenage girl. I was looking at a highborn noble. "I wasn't expecting someone to just announce that out loud. Not that I was hiding it exactly."

"So as a member of a noble family," Kashikoi started, "why would you be here?" He had a point as this did not make much sense to them. It is known that the Hunters and Incruentatus are on non-aggression terms, but the relationship is still shaky at best. Most of the nonhuman creatures think the two are on good terms and they are impressed and disgusted with the Incruentatus for even *speaking* with the Hunters, never knowing that it was an unpopular decision among both groups. "Shouldn't the *Hunters* have a place for your kind?" He growled out Hunters.

"No such place exists, Kashi-san. The Hunters only focus on training their people. This place, Supernatural Academy, this is one of the few places my father would allow me to go." After a while, the mood somehow returned to an easy atmosphere.

"So you used to work as a fashion model part-time?" asked Monica as the girls had their talk.

"So that's where I recognized her from," spoke Kashi as lunch was ending.

"How would you know her from that?" I asked as we all began to walk back to our classes.

"I'd rather not say, Dante."

We just left it at that and proceeded with the rest of the day. Word had apparently gotten out that Saya was nobility. So on top of beauty, she also has status. It was only a matter of time before some idiot would try to reach beyond their grasp and things would only go downhill from there. Also, speak of the devil, and he shall send his idiots.

"Why don't you ditch these nobodies and get with someone more your rank?" Draco Carlac, now trying to make a claim on Saya. There was the ego at work, but then again, he is a western dragon—greedy, prideful, and arrogant to a fault.

"Don't waste my time or your disgusting breath," she told him. "I am already engaged, and my fiancé is leagues above you."

"Oh yeah?" He roughly grabbed her wrist and pulled her right to his face. "What's some loser got on a dragon?" He developed a malicious glow in his eyes, and smoke began to pour out his mouth.

"A reputation of terror and a legacy that few can hope to match. I'm engaged to the Phantom," she said, and everyone practically jumped away from her. This raised all sorts of questions: One, what? Two, who? Three, when? And four, *what*? "Now unless if you really want to try your luck, you'll back off." For a moment, it looked like Draco was going to back off, then pride happened, so I decided I should step in.

"If he is so terrifying, why doesn't he show up and prove you're his?" He was still trembling slightly, but it was evident he wasn't going to back down.

"Because that is a death sentence for all involved," I said, getting in between the two. I noticed a gleam on Saya's neck. *Nex, can you grab me whatever that is?* I asked him using the mental link, and he began to move. "Do you really want to risk bringing the Hunters here? To this dear sanctuary?" There were some murmuring around us.

28

"Dante." His fear disappeared in favor of anger. "You know what? I still haven't paid you back for that sucker punch you gave me last time."

"It is strange to see you without a bandage on your face. Wanna fix that?"

That clinched it, and he threw his fist toward my face. I grabbed his wrist and his upper arm and threw him over my shoulder. I didn't let go and jumped as he went over, taking the quick chance to grab the medallion that Nex handed me. The moment we landed, the sentries were on us and took Draco away as I was "protecting" Saya.

"Thanks for that, Dante," she said as she visibly relaxed. "I was really getting annoyed by that idiot."

Everyone began to leave for their dorms. I had other plans.

"Well, I'm off," I told her before waving my hand goodbye.

Her eyes widened as she recognized the secret signal only known to the Hunters and the Incruentatus, "Meet me later," and I made my way to a quiet place to think and examine what I was holding. I walked to an open field on the border of the Outside and climbed a tree branch. I took the medallion and gazed into it. Polished silver so clear I was looking at a mirror, an etching of the Hunter's sigil invisible to anyone not looking for it. There was only one thing left to confirm her identity. I got it opened and saw the proof, a pattern of polished rubies in the form of a heart and set in such a way that it looked like it was bleeding.

"The Bleeding Heart." Symbol of the heir or heiress to the throne of the royal family, made as a gift from the Phantom that made the peace treaty possible. Saya "Nosferatu" Shizuka Dracul, daughter of the current lord, Kaname Nosferatu Dracul. The next in line to the throne is always raised in obscurity for security reasons, only people that know the truth are the higher-ups of the kingdom, very few Hunters, and only a scarce few of both can recognize that medallion. So not only is she likely the one Monica was talking about as one of my "friends," but she's the crown princess. Wonderful.

"How do you think people would react if they knew that the Hunters know about this place?" Saya asked as she made it to the field.

29

I closed the medallion and threw it back at her, which she caught with a casual ease.

"Probably worse than if they knew who you really were, Princess." I jumped off the tree and walked up to her. "So you want to explain about this whole engagement thing 'cause I heard *nothing* about my needing to marry the princess of blood." She began to giggle before laughing out loud.

"Just a ruse and nothing more I assure you, Phantom." She explained that it was a lie made by her father and my bosses to keep unworthy suitors from courting her with an added benefit that it seems that the two sides were on friendlier terms with each other. "I hope you don't mind."

"It doesn't affect me, or at least it hasn't yet, so I don't see why not."

"Thank you, Dante. So why are you here?"

I shrugged my shoulders.

"My bosses apparently found out about a magical disturbance and wanted me to check it out. After I told them what I found, they told me to stick around and observe. Maybe they're hoping that this helps human/monster relations." I didn't tell her how little faith I had in this institution and its goal. Humans always hate what they don't understand, and monsters will always be monsters.

"I share that hope," she said as she looked down. "All this hiding, this fear, this paranoia, it's sickening! Are we not living sentient beings? Do we not have a right to live as well?"

"Saya, our two sides have been at peace for the past two centuries, and they *still* walk a knife's edge from going to war with each other. I can't imagine that this engagement, lie, though, it may be, was a popular decision. You remember hearing about all the attempted coups on the first Blood King?"

Every other day, there was another attempted assassination and rebellion, ended by Hunters and Incruentatus, and still the relations were rocky at best. I again must express my lack of faith at this school accomplishing its goal.

"I'll hold on to hope. Maybe a better world is on the horizon. Someone simply needs to make it seen," she said, bringing her head up with a determined steel in her eyes.

"And while you do that, I'd hold my breath, but I'd rather not suffocate," I said as I made my way back to my room in Anansi Hall.

I got into the room and saw Max packing a suitcase.

"Is there an explanation?"

He pointed to a paper with a note on the table. It talked about an upcoming camping trip where the students would be broken into groups in an effort to learn teamwork. The note told me my group: Max, Lance, and Kashikoi.

CHAPTER 5

EMBRACE THE BEAST

It was the day of my group's turn into the woods. We were trekking across a steep mountainous area, searching for a proper campsite. It didn't help that instead of letting us keep our stuff, they left us with "bare essentials," which were knives—two of them. Considering that I'm the only human, this made sense. Most other races have capabilities to survive on their own, even those that tend to band together. So now I'm in a group with three unknowns and an insane shadow demon. I'd say it could be worse, but I know better than to jinx it—also not the worst situation I've been in. Let's just skip ahead to that night because all that happened was, we found a cave, and it was night. We decided to rest and recover our energy for tomorrow. Now the important stuff. We were each finishing our beds of leaves when I noticed Max had a distracted look to him. He wasn't looking at the setting sun, more at the moon, which was in its full moon cycle.

"Hey, Max, you all right?" I asked, shaking him out of his stupor.

"Wha...?" was his intelligent response. "Oh, yeah. I-I'm fine Dante," he said before looking back at the moon. "Hey, could one of you take first watch? There's something I need to do."

"Tradition thing?" Kashi asked.

"Something like that," he said before walking off.

It was almost an hour before we talked about what happened.

"Something's obviously up," Kashi broke the silence, knowing we weren't asleep.

"Yeah, but it's not our problem," Lance said from his viewpoint. "This seems like it's a personal issue. Not something we should poke our noses in."

"Normally, I'd agree, Lance," I said, getting up from the leaf mattress. "Unfortunately, this is a group activity, so let's go get him."

We all set out into the woods to try to find our wayward teammate. The only light we had was that of the moon and the sense that something was watching us, following us. "Hey, guys?"

"Yeah?" they responded.

"Do we know what Max is?" There was a pause, silently making our guesses. "There's apparently something about the moon that's affecting him."

"Werewolves aren't accepted here," Kashi told me. "They're not exactly a species, more like an affliction. A person with an illness."

"We do have lycans, but they aren't affected by the lunar cycle," Lance said. "They're in control of the 'beast inside.' Werewolves may be stronger and more vicious, but lycans are smarter." The debate continued until I remembered a rumor I heard sometime ago.

"Guys, do you know the oldest myth about werewolves?" I was answered with silence. "It dates back to ancient Greece when a king angered the gods of Olympus and they cursed him by transforming him into a wolf. I bring this up because of a rumor I heard a long time ago. Some people have said that once every few hundred years, a lycan will be born as that same ferocious beast. A lycan alpha, born with the strength of a werewolf and the intelligence of a human."

"You're saying Max is this alpha lycan?" Lance asked. "If he is, then why did he run?"

"Well, I think there was something about overcoming the beast to prove one worthy of the power, but your guess is as good as mine," I said as I ran into a solid wall of muscle covered in fur as black as the new moon. I backed up a little and was staring at a snarling wolf face with a maw of pointed teeth dripping with blood and carrion. Two yellow eyes, burning with anger and hunger, glowing the darkness.

The beast rose to its full height, a staggering ten feet of sinew and aggression, and let out a deep primal growl.

"Did anyone remember to grab the knives?" I asked in a hushed whisper. There was the sound of clothes rustling before they answered…no. "Bummer." The beast swung his massive claw at me, which I narrowly dodged as the three of us tried to surround the beast, but he was moving too fast and slammed into me before biting onto my shoulder and bolting into the darkness once more, dragging me along with him. In the matter of seconds, we ended up a few kilometers away from where we started before he threw me against a tree. "Again with the trees? Really?"

I slowly stood back up and glared at the beast before me. It definitely looked like a werewolf, but it was bigger and faster. Werewolves usually are two feet taller than their human form with lycans just being one. This hulking beast was bigger than any of either I've seen in my life. I brought my hand to my shoulder as I glared at the monster, noticing that I was not bleeding. He began stalking toward me, and I got into a readied stance. He charged at me, and I flipped over him, seeing his claws tear into the tree, practically ripping it down. He kept making lunges at me, and I kept narrowly dodging his attacks. It was a little confusing. He seemed to be moving more slowly than before, so I had just enough time to avoid him. I ended back at the same tree that was swaying slightly. He charged at me again, and I readied my trap.

"What are you doing, Max?" I asked as he was just about to attack, making him freeze.

"When did you figure it out?" he asked, standing back and relaxing.

"Not once did you seem like you were deliberately trying to hurt me. Plus, you seemed a little smarter than the usual werewolf." We tore down the tree and sat on the massive trunk. "So tall, dark, and savage, you wanna try to explain this?"

He stood up and began to shift back into his human form, which was fine, except he didn't have his clothes with him—not something out of the ordinary when this happens.

"As you now know, I'm a lycan. A rare one known as the 'alpha.' When a lycan comes of age, there is a struggle of control between the man and the beast. This happens on the first full moon after the twelfth birthday. When you first change, you are just a mindless beast unless you manage to overcome your own instincts." He paused and took a shaky breath. "Alphas are far more dangerous, and when I first turned, my older brothers tried to help keep me under control. I ended up killing my oldest brother and almost killed the other two. Afterward, they tried to convince me that it wasn't my fault." He began to cry. "We are like wolves, Dante! Pack animals, nothing more important than your pack, and I hurt them!" He began sobbing, digging up some old wounds, so I went to his side and gave a... rather awkward hug.

That's what I was supposed to do, right? Once he calmed down, he explained that every full moon since then, he goes into the wilderness and lets the beast back out so he never forgets that night. His penance for his crime.

"That's very noble of you, Max," I said, patting him on the back a few more times. Then I cracked him on the skull. "Your brother isn't here, so I'll do it in his stead."

"Do what?" he yelled, holding his head.

"Help you get over it. Do you really think he wants you to be sad? He gave his life so his little brother could be safe. The best way for you to honor him to protect yourself and your pack in his stead."

"But—" I bonked him again.

"No buts, you dork. Now Mom is worried sick about us, so let's go home. Sound good, little brother?"

He let out a chuckle.

"'Kay, bro."

"Good, now either change or put on some pants."

He turned, and we made our way back to the campsite, bringing along firewood. The rest of the night was peaceful with Max on duty.

CHAPTER 6

CLAN TROUBLES

THE MORNING CAME quickly after that. Max and Lance went out to look for something we could eat for breakfast, leaving me and Kashi to get a fire ready, something neither of us had either the patience or skill to do. Seriously, how long is someone supposed to rub sticks together to get that spark? Wish I had some flint at least.

"Those two will be bringing back a full-grown deer by the time we get this ready," I said after the stick slipped out of my hands for the fifth time. "Not sure how people figured this worked." I was about to try again before Kashi put the kindling into the firepit.

"Dante, do me a favor and don't make a big deal out of this." He closed his eyes and from the base of his spine came four long orange foxtails. He put the tips of them in the pit, and then there was a loud click of electricity before he pulled his tails back. I leaned in to the budding flames and gently blew, and sure enough, the fire was starting. I sat back down and looked at Kashikoi who was grinning sheepishly.

"Care to elaborate?" I asked.

He sighed before adopting a sad smile. "I'm Inari Kashikoi of the Inari clan of kitsune."

"That matriarchal clan of fox spirits?"

"The very same."

"I imagine there's more?" He nodded. "Look you don't have to say anything if you don't want to."

"No, it's okay. I should probably talk to someone about this. If you can help me like you did Max, then I should be golden."

"One thing, no promises."

"Deal," he chuckled out. "As you said, the Inari is matriarchal, and my mother is the head of the clan. I'm also an only child as my father, the head priest of my family's temple, died before I was born. Mother is very traditional and refused to remarry. She also refused me as her son and tried to pass me off as a girl."

"That could not have been comfortable."

"Meh, I was cute." He shrugged before showing me his wallet, and I saw him dressed as a girl. He actually pulled it off really well.

"Any reason why you keep these?"

"Probably to make Mom feel better," he said, putting his wallet away. "So yeah, for years, she tried to make it seem I was a girl, but when my cousin was brought up for succession rights, the truth came out. Mother was shamed, and I was almost banished."

"What prevented that?"

"Well, I always had a crush on my cousin, and it was my aunt who demanded the challenge, stating that I was gay and would not birth a daughter."

"In actuality, you were straight and a boy."

"Kinda funny in a way, isn't it? Anyway, I said that I would take her as my bride when she comes of age for humans. Mom refuses to acknowledge me as her child till then, and I had to leave home till that day comes."

"Okay, that's a little off. There's more isn't there?"

He hung his head. "I will have to challenge the priests of the family temple who are trained in fighting yokai and spirits. They have always been strong."

"Okay. You have to fight for your potential fiancée so you can remain a member of that family?"

"Oh no, I hate my clan, and my mother drives me crazy. I only love Shigure-chan. But they are my family so might as well make the best of it."

"How long ago was this?"

"Ten years, been here ever since."

"The plan? Train yourself?"

"Trying, but I was always the weak one. Born weak, lived weak, I was born with only one tail, the first one-tailed fox in a hundred generations."

"Big deal," I told him.

"Huh?"

"You had one tail, but you managed to get up to four. That's progress."

"Yeah, but it gets harder and harder to get more tails," he told me as I threw more wood on the fire.

"So? I would prefer to earn my strength than be born with it." I stood up and pulled him with me. "Think of it like this, you have less, so you worked harder to earn more, you gain more experience with more strength. That means you know more than how to fight with training, you know how to fight with experience. You'll unconsciously adapt and improve. It's better for hard work than raw talent." He thought about what I told him before smiling.

"Thanks, I'll work harder then." He held out his hand.

"I'll lend a hand if you ask." I grasped his.

"Hey, don't forget us!" yelled Lance while Max was carrying a deer.

"How much did you hear?" Kashi asked.

"Enough to say that your family sucks, and we want to help," Max said as he changed back, and Lance got the deer ready to cook.

"You are not alone, pal." I put my hand on Kashi's shoulder. "We're here."

CHAPTER 7

IDENTITY CRISIS

THE REST OF the week was passing by relatively fine. Each of us either sparred with each other or went out hunting and foraging, and now it was mine and Lance's turn. Ironically, this was the first time that we were alone together, and he never once took off his shades. We were hunting for prey of some kind when I decided to take a chance.

"So Max had a traumatic past, Kashikoi has a personal mission, I'm haunted by nightmares for whatever reason, you want to continue this trend or be the exception?"

He turned to me and without missing a beat with an obvious sarcastic tone. "Out of all of us, I am the only normal one." There was a pause before we began to laugh. "Dante, do you know what a skinwalker is?" he asked in a hushed tone as we found a trail of a boar.

"The Navajo witches that use their skills for purely selfish reasons after committing some kind of terrible taboo. Now they can change their form to that of any animal. That right?" I asked, following his lead as we stalked our prey.

"Pretty much. My uncle was very respectful, and obsessed, with the old craft, and I was his apprentice. One day, three years ago, my uncle tried to use me in a ritual sacrifice to obtain the power of the skinwalker. I managed to escape my bonds and fought back." We climbed a tree and ran along the branches when the boar came into sight. This pig was huge with big daggerlike tusks and could easily feed us for the next few days. "I ended up killing my uncle in self-defense, but that is still murder of one's blood, and I was not as trusted as my uncle. So I pleaded for help of some kind when the spirit coyote gave me a chance to flee. He apparently staged this to punish my uncle for his greed and gave me the power." We were on top of the pig when he handed me his shades. "Now I can do this," he said, dropping from the tree, swiftly peeling off his clothes while turning into an even bigger bear and landed on the boar's back before clamping down on his neck and began shaking it.

I dropped down to join him, the massive bulk of his new form keeping the boar pinned. I grabbed onto the tusks and jerked the head in opposition to Lance's shaking, and there was the loud crack of the beast's neck, and its struggle ceased. He changed back to human form and continued his story.

"Yee Naaldlooshii are generally not trusted, and to look one in the eyes is a death sentence apparently. Never tried to test it, never wanted to risk it," he said, putting his sunglasses back on before I took them off and stared him in the eye.

"Tough luck, I don't fear death." We just stared at each other for a few more seconds before realizing nothing was happening. "Maybe that whole death thing is a hoax," I suggested before returning his glasses. "Besides, you are just a Yee Naaldlooshii in name and ability. I can see it in your eyes that you are not lying."

"Thanks, Dante," he said with a smile before returning his glasses to his face. "So how are we getting this back?" He pointed at the pig.

He turned into an ox to drag while I pushed—it was heavy.

CHAPTER 8

TOGETHER FOR THE FIRST TIME

IT WAS THE last three days, and we were told to meet up with the other group that was doing survival training in the forest. We left the safety of our cave dwelling and proceeded through the forest. Max was in front of us, trying to pick up a scent while Lance was above acting as look out.

"Is it really necessary for you to be crawling like that?" Kashi asked.

It's been hours, and we had no trail to yet follow.

"I'm trying to catch the scent. Getting in touch with my inner beast, Kashi. How else am I supposed to do it?" he responded.

"For starters, *transform first!*" I yelled. That was the reason we've been walking for hours; with no luck, he was in human form right now.

"I'm just as capable like this."

"Yes, but I doubt you really need to be crawling around like this," Kashi said.

"Yeah, if there are other people here, then the scent should be relatively fresh, right?" I asked.

"Not necessarily." Lance came down to join us. "They might not have passed by this way at all, or there is just a lingering scent."

"Well, you two are the best trackers, so we'll defer to your expertise."

"Yeah, but should we keep going?" Max asked. "The sun is setting, and these woods are thick enough that without the sun, it might as well be night."

I took a moment to think.

"Kashi, would it be too much trouble for you to keep a sustained light?"

He seemed to ponder the idea himself. "I could try, but what color do you want?" He extended his tails, and each one took a ghostly light of blue, green, white, and purple at their tips.

"Let's go with the one that will be the least draining." There was a silence. "There's not really any difference, is there?" He chuckled a little.

Now he was in front of us with his tails burning blue and nursing a lump on his head. The fires had light but no heat. As it was magic, it wouldn't become physical until it left him. The next few hours passed by uneventfully until I heard a rustle in the darkness.

This seemed to wake Nex. *Are we going to play?* he asked.

"We're surrounded," Lance whispered as we stopped.

"By what?" asked Max as he got ready to pounce.

"Let's find out," Kashi said before we ducked, and he spun his tails, throwing the fire to the trees. This gave us the light to see what we were up against—trolls.

Trolls are an unseemly race. Only two things were consistent with these brutes, ugly big-nosed faces and dull minds. What they lacked in intelligence, they made up for in size and strength. We had a variety of them surrounding us, big, small, bulky, skinny, hairy, bald, multiple heads, and there were maybe over a hundred of these freaks. Wonderful.

"Well, this is unfortunate," Lance said as the brutes were thrown into a frenzy because of the fire. Many of them fled out of fear, but others decided to focus on eating us.

"Maybe, but we have no other choice now, do we?" Max said before transforming and attacking a troll twice his size. It was over just as it started as Max ripped the beast's head off and jumped at the next one. Lance, Kashi, and myself looked at each other before grinning. Lance began to charge at the smaller trolls before turning into rhino. Kashi turned into a man-sized fox as he began to spew fire and lightning at our foes, setting more of the forest on fire and turning it into a caricature of hell.

Well, this is certainly a thing, I thought as the chaos ensued. *We should probably get involved, Nex. Got anything to make it seem like I'm not human and can still fight?'*

This will hurt, he said as I felt him creep upon my body till I felt my arms get heavier and heavier till they were covered in shadow before I felt them getting pierced and my shoulders had spikes being dug into them. I looked at the both of them and saw they were now huge and covered in spiked bones and claws. In between the chinks of the bone armor was shadow. He was right—that really, *really* hurt. A troll came charging at me, and I punched it, which sent it flying back with holes in its chest.

"I like this," I said with a grin before groaning in pain. "Too bad, these are damaging me." I was then grabbed by another troll that was trying to eat me. As it brought me to its gaping maw, I punched the roof of its mouth, making it recoil in pain before I slammed down on its arm, breaking it off. As it began to stumble around, I grabbed the severed arm and swung it like a club, smashing it in the troll's face and making it fall. "I'd give these a six out of ten."

From there, it was chaos. The four of us were tearing the trolls apart with relative ease, teaming up on some of the much bigger ones. The smoke and fire kept building before it began to blind, burn, and choke us. Kashi managed to burn a hole in the canopy above, letting the smoke escape and free up our sight. That was probably what led them to find us.

The battle just kept going on before a very sudden deluge of heavy rain came down on us, practically extinguishing the flames and soaking everything. All activity just froze after it happened. I shook my head until I was able to open my eyes again, and Monica was right in front of me, giving me a disturbingly innocent smile before closing her eyes.

"Thank you for using my delivery service!" She held out a clipboard. "Sign here to confirm delivery." Getting dragged into her pace, I ended up signing the paper.

"What did I order, Monica?" I asked hesitantly.

She just beamed before grabbing the hem of her skirt and throwing it over her head...and was wearing a red vest with a white undershirt and biker shorts with a Gibson guitar in her hands.

"A nice big can of whoop-ass!" she yelled before bashing a troll in the face and sending it flying, laughing like a crazy person and charging into the madness. Kashi walked up next to me as we watched the psychotic witch have her weird fun, shooting off a spell every now and then.

"She watches a lot of anime, doesn't she?" he asked.

"I would not for the life of me have guessed," I said dryly.

The other group turned out to be the girls' group, Saya, Lucrezia, Zoe, Monica, and Andrea. Andrea revealed herself as a lycan and joined Max in his assault, along with Zoe, whom I had to guess was an elf with how she moved, Monica was helping Kashi with the magic artillery, Saya and Lucrezia came up to me while the others fought. Lucrezia wrapped her arms around my neck and smiled.

"Hello, lover," she said in a sultry tone. "Did you miss me?" She began to lean in closer to me before Saya began to pull on her ear.

"Flirting later, killing now," she growled like she was annoyed.

This trip must have been wearing on her. Saya proudly displayed her kind's strength and ability by swiftly, gracefully, and brutally tearing the beasts apart with sheer strength and speed, occasionally tearing into a few necks and taking a drink. Lucrezia was charming some of the trolls into attacking their own, somehow, and started using magic that fel...dark.

"So my girlfriend really is a soul-sucking-demon-temptress... bummer," I said as I watched my succubus join Monica in spell casting while continuing to charm the trolls. We eventually managed to clear out the beasts, leaving us alone with each other. "Well, Monica, is this the group you were talking about?" She was smiling and shaking so much she began to blur, almost like a chemical reaction just before—

"*Finally!*" she exploded. An actual explosion of multicolored sparks, confetti, and smoke. "*Everyone's together!*" She then turned into a mini version of herself and started teleporting all over the place near instantly. "Zoe the Elf, Kashi-kun the Fox, Lance the Shape-Shifter, Saya the Incruentatus, Lucrezia the Sex Demon, me, the witch, Max and Andrea the Lycans, and Dante, our leader!" she screamed gleefully, holding onto my waist, now normal... I think.

"Let the record show I did not support this claim," I said before Monica shrank to the size of a cat and appearing on top of my head.

"Come on, Dante," she whined with a pouty face and kitty ears. "You'd be a great leader." I tried to grab her, but she was apparently between Max and Andrea, pulling them closer together. "Besides, now we can focus on their puppy love and get actual puppies!"

Max and Andrea blushed before smacking Monica, who was crying into my chest saying that the "doggy couple" was angry. I think I understand how she always gets the drop on me—she never wants to harm me.

"Gee, I wonder why," I said before the ground began to shake. "Oh, bloody hell, what now?" I asked before we went into a clearing and saw a mountainous troll, a few trees still clinging to his shoulders. "How have we not killed every single one of these brutes yet?"

After that many, it was hard to imagine any were left. He began to lumber his way toward us, most likely looking to crush and eat us.

"So...do we fight or do something new?" asked Zoe as the giant seemed to have caught our scent.

"Dante can beat him!" Monica exclaimed.

I was beginning to think she could be on something.

Let me feed. I heard Nex whisper in my mind. My head was throbbing with every word spoken, trying to keep my sanity together.

"If he does, then he might as well be the leader," Kashi said.

"Go get 'em, babe," Lucrezia said, smacking my butt in the process.

I just sighed and began walking to the behemoth.

"I still want it known that I did not want that title!"

The troll seemed to have spotted me through the haze and smoke, our only light being the moon and a scarce few fires and embers. *So what are you going to do?* I asked my dark familiar. I looked at the ground and saw a giant toothy grin that I was standing in the middle of. "That answers that," I said before darkness erupted around me. I jumped through the swirling shadows and ended up between the troll and Nex's growing form. Before long, it developed thousands of glowing eyes around a giant smiling mouth, a sideways mouth. Nex towered over the troll who began to realize the danger and run for its life. That was in vain when Nex opened his mouth and bone claws burst out and pierced the giant before dragging him into Nex's hungry maw. "I should really be used to this by now," I said as Nex ate the troll. The darkness began to descend, and I walked to where the shadows concentrated until it returned to being my shadow. "But I'm not."

"Okay, who else isn't getting any sleep tonight?" I heard Kashi say as I walked back to them.

Everyone raised their hands. I shrugged as I walked by.

CHAPTER 9

THE CURSED BLADE

A FEW DAYS passed after that incident. A few days of apprehension from my new friends, except for Monica who acted no differently. In time, it all became water under the bridge, and they once again relaxed around me. They were still wary around me, but they calmed down immensely. I thought it was better for them to think that I was the eldritch horror instead of them knowing about Nex. He's worse. I was beginning to get used to life here when I felt a strange electricity in the air.

"So you think Nex is going to be a problem?" Saya asked as I finished my report to the Hunters. "Watching him do that was pretty disturbing."

"Nex is bound to the Phantom. He won't do anything I don't allow him to." I pocketed my phone and began walking toward the dorms. That's what I heard anyway. Nex had done what I asked and had never lied to me once. I did some research, but there were few records of the shadow creature. He was just there, and for some reason, only the Phantoms could control him. To this day, there was no answer as to anything about Nex. "Besides"—Nex sent a shadowy serpent up my leg and wrapped around my arm—"I like him." I affectionately patted the thing's head.

"So this is just what you're going to do?" she said, walking next to me. "Report every week, 'no change, program making X amount of progress'?"

"Eh," I said, shrugging, "might as well enjoy the downtime," before feeling this weird buzz in the back of my head. It was a mild irritant, but it seemed like Nex noticed it. If he did, he said nothing about it.

* * *

The next week passed by normal. Every now and then, I get those buzzes in my head but continued to ignore them. Until one day the next week, it burst into a crippling migraine.

"Dante, maybe you should stay in bed today," Max said while we were having our breakfast.

I couldn't even hold my head up, and it just kept throbbing, the pain increasing more and more each time.

"Yeah, that sounds good," I somehow managed to groan out.

He got me back into my bed while I kept clutching at my skull, almost pleading for the pain to stop. Soon enough, I began to drift in and out of consciousness as my headache persisted. In my waking periods, I could swear Nex was outright furious at something, but what? During my blackouts, I dreamed…not my usually nightmares, something…else. I saw an island fortress that was filled with an odd mix of all sorts of yokai, Japanese native monsters. There was a massive, rotting gate that was facing northeast and letting more of the yokai enter the physical plane and a castle with a lone occupant. A human, dressed in a black robe, kneeling with a Japanese katana that was sheathed in a bleached white scabbard with bloodred lines and a matching crisscross-cord pattern on the hilt. I felt an intense rage and bloodlust emanating from the blade. The man's eyes looked empty and focused—and that worried me.

I woke up one more time and my headache was completely gone. I held my head, and the throbbing was completely nonexistent. I sat up and noticed that it was night. I saw Max sitting at my side, along with Monica. Lucrezia was sleeping next to me.

They were worried for you, Nex told me. The window by my bed opened up, and Nex gestured me to follow him. I managed to crawl my way out from my bed without causing a stir and joined Nex on the rooftops. *Are you all right?*

"For the most part, I guess," I told him before gazing into the sky. "I don't know what caused that migraine, but it's over now... hopefully."

Nex's shadowy form was shifting and swirling furiously. He was mad about something, but I couldn't tell what, and I was afraid to ask. He then froze before sending me my phone. I was receiving a call from the Hunters. I answered and put the phone to my ear. "What is it?"

"Phantom, we have another mission for you," a filtered voice told me. "Our sensors have picked up a lot of foul energy somewhere on the island Megijima. The only other thing of note is a supposedly cursed sword that has a trail of murders linked to it. Sending you coordinates of the latest victims. A team will meet up with you for debriefing. Good luck."

They hung up, and I gave the phone back to Nex.

"Japan, huh?" The island in my dream had a feudal Japanese castle and was inhabited by Japanese demons. What the hell is the connection? "Come on, Nex, we have a job to do."

What are you going to tell the others?

I paused, trying to think of something to say. "Let's tell them, 'My migraine was feeling better, so I went to an old acquaintance to pick up a herbal remedy to get rid of it. Might be gone for a few days, don't worry. Please take notes for me.' Now we have to remember to get some tea."

Do you think they'll buy that? he asked as he produced a paper with the message written down.

"I hope so." I dropped down to my window, catching onto the ledge, and slipped the note inside before shutting the window. I continued to drop myself from window to window before hitting the ground. Then I broke into a run toward the cave I first emerged from when I came here. I was told the Gateway responds to your thoughts on a location, whether specific or general area. I got to the tunnel, and Nex gave back my phone to check the information I got. With that, I ran through the portal and to my next destination.

The instant I was out, I noticed it was nighttime, and I came out from a Shinto shrine gate. The temple itself seemed abandoned, but I didn't stick around. I ran for the road and tried to get my bearings. After running for a few minutes, I had enough to get an idea. An old road leading to a small coast town. If my location was right, then this was along the inland sea of Seto. Sure enough, I saw Megijima in the distance, and it had a dark cloud over it. I started running down the road to reach the town, heading for the address included in the coordinates I was given.

The town itself was quiet, some lights still on in some of the buildings, and the house that I was heading for was taped off. I managed to stay out of sight by climbing to the rooftops and above where people look. I took out my silver mask again and tried to scan the building to find whatever I could. No signs of forced entry, and the police already did their cleanup. The only thing I managed to find was trace amounts of malevolent energy, and I was picking up more on the other side of town.

"Well, that's lucky," I commented as I bolted to my new destination. I soon came upon a moderate white two-story house, nothing out of the ordinary. I got in front of the door and was about to pick the lock when I noticed a line of salt in front of the door with a warding spell carved into the frame. Salt is a natural purifier of corrupted spirits, and most warding magic is to repel those same spirits. There was a very small list of spirits that could get through this kind of barrier, so I checked the door, and sure enough, it was unlocked. I entered the building and began looking for any clues. The air was so thick with malevolent energy that my scanner was practically useless, aside from one thing shining with a purifying light. I deactivated the scanner and found myself looking at a katana in the hand of a dead body.

He looked to be in his midthirties, tanned and weathered skin, and just recently killed, with a swift cut on his neck. Looking closer, I saw the crest of the Order just under the collar of his shirt. I bowed my head in silent prayer to a fallen comrade before turning my attention to the sword. The sword did have power to it, but it wasn't a cursed blade. Something else was involved with the sword, and it was time to get answers. I reached down to grasp the hilt, but the second I touched it, a voice cried out in my head.

Behind you! I immediately grabbed the hilt, turned, and stabbed, resulting in me impaling a short elderly man in a lavish robe with a gourd-shaped head.

Nurarihyon? I wondered, letting go of the blade as the yokai stumbled to the ground. This particular yokai would've definitely been able to infiltrate, but they usually only target lavish buildings with expensive pleasures. More importantly, they aren't known for killing. My window of interrogation was closing fast as the yokai lost more and more of his life.

Onigashima, he whispered, struggling to breath. *Stop...the summoning... Keep the serpent...sealed.* He fell limp before disappearing into a breeze.

That explains the dark cloud over Megijima—it's in the same place as the Island of Ogres in the spiritual plane. If what that spirit said was true, than something terrible was about to happen. Worst case is that the barrier between planes break, which is the last thing the Hunters want. My only problem, how to enter the spiritual plane and stop this?

Maybe you can do it. I turned back to the sword as it began to glow with a small figure appearing on the blade. A silver-eyed woman in a black kimono with long black hair. *Quick, I've been searching for a skilled warrior to take me up and go to the Demon Island to stop the summoning of a most horrid demon, the Orochi.* Wonderful, someone is trying to bring back the eight-headed serpent. Big as a mountain range and one of the strongest in Japanese lore—well, only if he had that Kusanagi blade in him, which is one of the few relics with enough power and a link to actually summon him. This just keeps getting worse. *We need to hurry and get to the island!*

"And I'd love to hear your suggestion," I responded while fastening the sheath to my belt, "but we'd still need to cross into the spirit realm." I then went in the kitchen to find some spell ingredients to banish the demons on the island. "And I don't really have a way to transport us there anyway." I found a calligraphy set and a scroll, opening to find a complex sealing spell already on it. "At least I have a way to seal them now."

I already have a way for us, she told me as I sheathed the blade, pocketed the scroll, and grabbed some rubbing alcohol, salt, and two lighters. *Take me to the sea, and I will summon the dragon guarding these waters. He's agreed to help anyone stop the resurrection of Orochi.* I sprinkled the salt and alcohol on the Hunter's corpse.

"May your spirit find rest, for your fight is now over," I said, breaking a lighter and pouring the fuel on his body. "Goodbye, my brother in arms." I lit the fuel on fire, and the body was quickly consumed before disappearing, leaving nothing behind—not even burns or ashes. "Very well. Let's go," I said after finishing the ritual and began walking out of the building and running for the coast, sending a message to any nearby Hunter for backup. Upon reaching it, I unsheathed the blade and stuck her in the water. There was a pulse of light that rang throughout the water, followed soon after by a massive blue serpentine figure with a wolfish head and two long whiskers, rising in front of me. "Neat."

You reek of death, warrior, the dragon said to me, immediately putting me on guard to fight back, *but, perhaps that is what is necessary for this.* He leaned down and opened his maw. *Climb inside, and I will take you to Onigashima.* I looked at the dragon hesitantly before sighing and going inside. Oddly enough, it smelled like a fresh sea breeze, and the sword's glowing blade gave me plenty of light.

"So what do I call you?" I asked the sword spirit, figuring that I would be keeping the blade when this was over.

I am Yawarakai-Te, the Masamune sword of purification.

CHAPTER 10

A HUNTER'S MISSION

THE TRIP PASSED in minutes, and the next thing I knew I saw a beach blanketed in red light. I exited the mouth of the dragon, who quickly swam away and scanned my surroundings. The moon was glowing an ugly red, and the air smelled foul of disease. Further inland was a feudal Japanese fortress with the central building looking like some horned face, along with a wooden gate that was made of rotted wood. The same gate from my nightmares and releasing more yokai by the second. I decided to aim for the mastermind behind all this first and made my way to the fortress wall. If I went for the gate first, whoever this person was may be able to escape and try again.

Upon reaching the walls of the fortress, I began looking for any way to climb or crawl through to get inside. If that failed, Nex had plenty of tools I could use, and I'm just looking for the most silent way to infiltrate. Despite the rot of age that seemed to cover the area, I found no way to climb up or any gate, at least until I found a perfectly clean and normal section. It was out of place because of how perfectly normal it looked, but upon closer inspection, I found a pair of eyes.

"Nurikabe." I sighed, partly in relief and partly in annoyance. These wall spirits usually allow no passage by them in any way, but every defense has a hole, and I know this one's. I took Yawarakai's sheath and tapped the very bottom of the spirit, where his body met the ground. Releasing a deep, rumbling laugh, it disappeared, and I was facing a much more degraded wall. This time, there were hand-holds that I could use to climb up. I did as such and got a full look inside the fortress grounds. Wheels of fire patrolled the grounds, various Oni of different sizes wandered about with spiked iron clubs, a spider with an ox head, and an eyeless old man running straight at me.

"Too slow," I muttered as he came within blade's reach, and I slashed him in two. I checked the hands, finding a single eye on both. "This might have been a sentry and was probably trailing me since I got up here."

The tenome's hunger for bones must've overridden its sense, Yawarakai added as the yokai's body faded. I turned my attention to the demonic tower that held the darkest energy. *I can feel him. My darker counterpart must be there. Only he could have an energy that foul,* she spoke in rage and disgust. Again, I thought back to my dream, to the bloodthirsty sword and the empty soulless eyes of the man. I sheathed the sword and continued my way to the tower, trying to keep out of sight as much as I could. More than a few times, yokai with a strong sense of smell seemed able to pick up on my presence, leading to my needing to quickly kill before they could alert the rest of the fortress. Soon I reached the tower itself and climbed the outside to the top and the uppermost room in the building. Just like in my vision, I found him sitting there. Waiting with that white-and-red blade in front of him, radiating bloodlust, while the man himself felt empty.

"Have you come to kill me?" he suddenly asked, looking in my direction.

Dropping any pretense of stealth, I slid through the open window and stood across him. He was exactly as I saw in my vision, black GI, short-cropped black hair, clean-shaven, and empty dead eyes. The blade in front of him was radiating rage and bloodlust, and I could feel Yawarakai-Te shaking, eager to fight it.

"I'm more interested in stopping the summoning going on over there," I responded, trying to stop Yawarakai's movements while turning to the demon gate. "If left unchecked, it'll rain devastation across the world. If you can still fight through that possession, you'd help me." I heard him stand up and walk toward me. "I can feel it. You are trapped. Held under the thumb of this foul being." I immediately spun around, knocking the blade he tried to stab me with aside and slammed my palm into his chest. "You, on the other hand, you want to unleash this damned monster." He glared at me before catching his breath and getting into a ready stance just as I did.

"We humans are ants," he growled, letting some of his anger through. "I will be the one to resurrect the age of the gods and demons!" He charged forward for a downward strike that I deflected and countered with my own swing that he jumped away from. "Yes, the world will be engulfed in a sea of fire as mankind is reminded of their place. And through the fires of chaos, a new era will be born. Brought back to before, we all got swept up in our own arrogance!" he called out as a red aura grew from the sword in his hand.

I dashed forward, making him raise his sword to block, then I kicked him in the knee.

"Here's the problem with that," I started as he tried to swing at my legs, making me jump back and let him get back to his feet. "There are people like you ready to sell your souls to demons. They'd betray the rest of their friends and family for power or magic. And that's not even getting into the fact that there are other beings that would tear the planet apart in an attempt to claim dominance of the entire world." He charged at me with another series of swings and stabs that I blocked and dodged until the building started shaking. I looked out the window and smiled beneath my mask, watching as a squad of fifty Hunters stormed the island. "And then there's us, the people that keep the monsters at bay."

"You!" he growled as I turned back to see him filled with fury. "I will not—!" he roared, getting ready to fight again, only for his blade to shift in such a way that it cut his arm clean off. Ahhhhhh! He howled in agony, gripping the stump of his arm. "You useless piece of scrap!" he roared at the blade, reaching down for it before I kicked him away and grabbed the sword for myself.

"I figured you would help," I whispered to the sword, earning a red glow from the blade. I turned back to my opponent, who was growing paler from the blood loss. He'd soon be dead whether I did anything or not, but a good rule is to always make sure an enemy is dead. As I took the first step toward him, he raised his hand.

"It's clear that I lost and that my life will soon end," he said, pulling out a small dagger, "but I would not go with this dishonor. I will do this, so be my second. At least." He got into a kneeling position and readied a dagger to kill himself.

"Fine. I'll grant you the—" I said just before he cut me off.

"I give my life to your freedom, Master Orochi." He swiftly disemboweled himself, flashing with a purple light, which flew from his body and to the top of the demon gate, and in turn produced eight massive snake heads.

"Ah crap!" I exclaimed while the Hunters nearest to the gate created magic barriers and began to push against the snakes. "That won't last long." I quickly grabbed the blade sheath from the corpse and fastened that to my side before running to the balcony. *Where is the catalyst he was using to summon Orochi?* I wondered as I scanned the towering gate, finally seeing the brightest point at the top of the gate. "Let's pray, that's it. Nex, give me a launch!" I told my familiar as I sheathed my sword and ran with a shield rising from the darkness. The moment my foot touched the round metal shield, Nex launched me off, jumping at the last second to fly toward the gate. I did end up bouncing off one of Orochi's heads and did not have a graceful landing, but I made it to the top and not that far from my mark. A blade hilt that was firmly planted in the wood of the gate.

Remove the sword! a distinctly male voice yelled out from my new sword. *Without it, Orochi will stay in the demon realm!* As he said that, one of the serpent's heads squeezed through to the top of the gate, glaring at me with intense hate. Our eyes locked and shifted to the blade in the wood before going back to each other. I bolted to grab the sword while Orochi sprayed a cloud of poison gas at me. I managed to grab hold of the sword and shut my eyes just before the venomous cloud of green hit me. I stopped breathing and tried to free the blade from its confines like it was Excalibur. My skin burned from the toxic fumes, but my grip did not lessen until I heard the cackle of electricity, and the blade slipped free from its confines. The cloud of poison disappeared, freeing me to open my eyes just in time to see Orochi dissolve into black smoke and back into his prison. I took the chance to breathe a sigh of relief, and I knew I jinxed it.

"An army approaches!" one of the Hunters that was holding Orochi's back yelled out. I made my way to the edge and looked into the gate to see a massive army of yokai demons storming toward us. Five magi began chanting a sealing spell while the rest of the Hunters protected them from the rest of the yokai on the island. I jumped off the edge and landed behind them just as they finished chanting.

The spell on this scroll better be strong enough, I thought as I pulled out the ofuda scroll I got earlier and threw it into the gate as all the magi said the final phrase. "Evil spirits, begone!" I yelled with them with a massive kanji character for seal appearing in the air. The very next instant, a vortex appeared, sucking everything back into the gate. Buildings, the yokai, even the black cloud of malevolence was being absorbed. When everything was done, the gate began to collapse and fade while crowds of people were manifesting. I and the other Hunters were slowly returning to the physical plane. As per protocol, we all made sure to make it so no one would notice our sudden appearance. One even cast a spell to disguise my swords so as not to arouse suspicion. As soon as we returned, I was heading for a bench with a lone, stocky, and bald man who had glasses and was smoking a pipe. I sat next to him, and he began to speak in English…for some reason.

"We've known something was happening here for some time but were told not to get involved until you arrived." I turned to look at him while he simply blew out a smoke ring. "Not entirely sure why, but orders are orders, I suppose. Call me Genbu, the leader of the Hunters in Japan's southern region."

"That does makes very little sense," I admitted, trying to figure out why the Order was ordered to stay their hand until I got involved. "If I was any later, Orochi would've returned."

"The snake would've been beaten back," he said with a chuckle. "The only difference would be the number of dead. As of now, seven were lost in the fight."

We took a moment of silence for our fallen brothers before I continued with my questions.

"How did he get his hands on the Kusanagi blade?" I asked, holding up the relic blade. "I thought it was under protection in that one shrine."

"A cursed replica, nothing more. Meant to protect the sword and stop fools from abusing its power. Though, him finding the blade was indeed worrying," he admitted, snapping his fingers and wrapping the blade up in protective charms. I slid the blade back onto my hip. "Now you should go to Mt. Kurama and bury it at the peak. The Tengu promised to protect it." I looked at him in shock, completely disbelieving he had said what he did. "Meanwhile, me and the other Japanese leaders need to find a suitable heir for Nurarihyon."

"You make it sound like we deal with monsters," I said to him as he stood up and extinguished his pipe. "I figured a few less would be a good thing, especially the heads of the yokai."

"Your education seems to be lacking, Phantom. That is troubling," he told me as he stretched himself out. "It's always been this way. We can't keep the normal and the supernatural separated without cooperation on both sides, especially with divine relics and organizations. That is the mission of the Hunters. Now get that blade to Sojobo's mountain. They're trustworthy." He walked away, leaving me with my thoughts. I made my way back to the mainland and toward Mt. Kurama in Kyoto with nothing but my thoughts.

We're meant to keep humanity safe from the various monsters, but we do some diplomacy with certain factions. I guess I could see that with the Seelie fairies. Many magic users almost always have familiars to help them, something I could attest to with my own familiar, but the treaty with the Incruentatus is strained at best, and a lot of other supernatural beings are often too violent to tolerate. More often than not, even the good ones are filled with corruption from rage and resentment in some form or another. As for the Tengu that Genbu was talking about, they are often monastic and train in near complete isolation from the public, which made them unpredictable. Sojobo himself is considered the king of Tengu for his strength and wisdom, though there was a rumor that he ate children that got lost in his domain. Hours passed, and I reached the mountain, passing underneath a few Shinto gates and returning to the spirit realm—probably the Kusanagi sword's influence. The eerie red light was gone, and the only other indicator was a stronger sense of magic in the air and a weird tranquility.

"Well, here we go," I said as I kept moving, eventually coming upon a clearing. I stopped moving when I got the uneasy sense that I was being watched and confirming such when I scanned the treetops.

"I have with me the divine sword, Kusanagi. I was told to bring it to the realm of the Tengu King, that he and his people would protect it," I called out in Japanese.

Within the next instant, I was surrounded by them. Redskinned, wearing thick beads and ascetic Japanese monk robes, feathered wings, and long noses, all set and ready to attack me. The one in front of me, a nose longer than the rest, marched right up to me, and I presented him the sword. He looked it over before taking it from me and bowing, the rest of the Tengu warriors dispersing as a result. I was about to leave when he grabbed my shoulder, sniffed me, and seemed to cast a spell, creating a portal in the air, before disappearing himself. I put on my mask and scanned the portal, which matched the signature of the one leading to the school. Did the Order know about this? Did they create the school? Questions swarmed in my head as I put my mask away and walked through the portal.

CHAPTER 11

THE NOBILITY OF THE BLOODLESS

I DID RETURN to the academy—well, deep within the forest, but that was close enough—and returned to the others. I told them that I did as I wrote in the note with Monica poking my head repeatedly and that I got my new swords as gifts. Kashi was freaking out about authentic Masamune and Muramasa blades being in my possession while the others told me that I needed to see Volk because I left the school unsupervised. He was not happy. I spent the next week under house arrest and a near constant watch. That made looking into the other issues that much more difficult, not that I was going to be making much progress while I acted under my cover at this place.

I always understood the mission of the Hunters Order to be the protection of humankind, something that could be assured if we did wipe out the more malicious factions. The peace with the Incruentatus was because one Phantom established it, though I never knew why. Now I learn that the Hunters have done more with more creatures, arrangements with Japanese demons may just be the start of the rabbit hole, and I don't know how far it goes. Did they know about the school before sending me here, and if they did, why send me here in the first place? Nex wouldn't tell me anything, and when I tried to think about any hints I may have missed growing up, my head felt like it was trying to implode. Something that I should know is going on, but something else seems to be trying to prevent that.

The week ended after what felt like an eternity, and I was finally able to return to my business. The first thing, maintenance of my new swords.

"Okay, so you two are the swords from the myth of Masamune and Muramasa as master and apprentice who had a challenge to see who could forge a finer blade," I clarified while wiping down the Muramasa blade, now known as Juuchi Yosamu. The spirit of this blade was a scarred and gruff man with cold steel eyes and white hair. "You were taken by that psychopath because it'd be easier to pin the blame on a Muramasa blade since they were notorious for their bloodlust."

Yep, he responded, keeping his talking to a minimum as I cleaned his real body.

And I tried to find someone to help me stop him, Yawarakai continued, sitting atop her blade. *The rest, you know.*

"Indeed," I acknowledged as I finished the cleaning process and returned Juuchi back to his sheath. "Sorry about this, but I shouldn't have weapons like you two out in the open," I told them as Nex concentrated beneath them and slowly absorbed them into the massive armory of my predecessors. They gave their consent before disappearing as I fell on my back. "This has been so boring," I groaned, getting nowhere in anything, only learning what I already knew and doing the only thing on my to-do list.

* * *

A week went by, and I was actually itching for something new—something to answer my questions or just some excitement at least. I was actually asking for another possible catastrophe, just out of boredom, asking for that was a dumb thing to do, as my prayers were soon answered when Saya showed up.

"This is a sight that one should not expect to see in regards to someone like you," she said, looking down at me. "Your house arrest is over, so where is everyone else?" Something I noticed was that she had none of her previous cheer—what she was doing here was something that demanded her focus.

"I told them I actually needed some time alone, that I would see them when I figured some stuff out." I sat up and stretched out. "Is something going on that I should be aware of?" I asked, figuring we'd might as well get down to business. Certain stuff should be done sooner rather than later.

"There's been an incident with one of the noble families, one that might lead to a vampire outbreak," she said, making me tense up. Incruentatus, they are the normal-looking bloodsuckers that possess extra powers that pop culture think of when certain groups hear "vampire," except they were born that way. Actual vampires are the transformed beasts that result when Incruentati improperly disposes of their victims, shunned by the light, and driven by their need to feed. Starting out as normal-looking humans with a mouth full of fangs, transforming into a more bat-like beast as the decades passed, until they can transform at will and grow evermore dangerous. They can become like a plague, and the single most important stricture of the treaty is that the vampires are either contained or wiped out—failure to do so results in the deaths of the nobles responsible for the failure.

"When did this happen?" I asked, sending a mental command to Nex to ready the supplies I'll need.

"Late last night," she answered as we began making our way to the Gateway. "The initial reports claim that one of the patriarchs of one of the UK nobles was assassinated and was fed on." That was very unsettling. Rogue vampires were bad, but a rogue Incruentatus was worse. "I volunteered to handle this matter with you as my partner. The Hunters insisted you be there."

"Probably to be your bodyguard," I returned as we reached the gate, Saya explaining to the new gatekeeper (which was the result of my leaving without consent) that we had business in the outside world. She got the pass because she's royalty while I was being glared at. "You'll handle the talking, I take it?"

"Of course," she returned, checking her ID to make sure it was the proper one for the situation. "You just put on that mask and stay silent once we get there." As we were passing through, she put on a pair of rounded dark sunglasses and a hairband that turned her silver hair into a more natural shade of blond just in time for us to appear somewhere in Westminster, England. I kept silent as she led the way to where the nobles were located. Took us about two hours through cities and towns to an out-of-the-way, secluded property that was very well-maintained, perfectly manicured lawn and gardens surrounded by a tall iron fence, nice Victorian-style building, and a heavy sense of sorrow and depression over the entire place—fun.

"Let's hope they're willing to talk," I said, placing my mask over my face as a pair of guards approached Saya. She flashed them her ID, and after a few seconds of verification, we were let in. I'll admit to expecting glares and scowls, but everyone, literally every person, looked like they were still struggling not to cry. "Their head is gone, but they continue their work," I remarked, watching as decorations were put up for a kind of festival. "I know this is callous, but shouldn't they be preparing to mourn?" I asked as we entered the building.

"I'll find out what happened," she assured me as we were led to a single room through the halls of the manor. I ignored the decorations and all else, trying to focus on the task at hand. Any distractions would not be tolerated. I needed to focus. We entered the master bedroom to find a woman of icy pale skin, golden-brown hair, piercing red eyes, and sitting in bed with a presence that still spoke volumes of her age and experience. "Lady Elizabeth." Saya greeted with a nod. "We're—"

"I only care that you bring my husband's murderer to justice," she said quickly and fiercely, wishing nothing but pain on the one that took her other half. Guess the "blood bond" among the Incruentatus really is soul-binding. "He was one of the servants of the house. I found him at the edge of despair and took him in as a butler. He apparently grew quite infatuated with me, or rather with what I am." I noticed her hand move to rest above her stomach. "When news of my pregnancy reached him, I fear he snapped." She reached for a plate piled high with blood red balls, like apples, except I caught the heavy scent of blood as she bit into it. "My husband overreacted and insisted that I should be getting all of the nourishment for our child, neglecting his health in the process. Then that traitor slashed his neck open with a silver dagger and drank his blood. He exposed himself when he tried to claim me for his own and the guards forced him to flee."

"One of your human servants did this?" Saya asked, deeply concerned about the situation. For good reason too, vampires were animals, rogue nobles are clever, but the last time a human drank the blood of a noble, that person went insane while building an army without a care in the world. If that incident is any indication, our mission became much more severe. "Do you have any idea where he went?" Saya all but demanded.

"There is a farm to the east of here," Elizabeth answered. "It should take half a day to reach for a vampire. I'd give you some of my guards, but none are willing to leave."

Saya nodded in understanding, getting up and facing me. We nodded to each other as we rushed out of the building and ran eastward. The sun was already setting.

CHAPTER 12

DANCE OF BLOOD

THE RUN WAS a pain…literally. Because of the danger that our target represented, Saya was running at full force, which was enough to make everything around us blur. She carried me because I don't run over two hundred miles an hour. Her claws kept digging into my legs, and I felt like she'd pull my hips out of their joints on more than one occasion. The point is that we made it to the farmhouse just in time to find our prey, and he was being productive in the worst way for us. To vampires, blood is blood, and the only limit is how diseased or decayed it was. All around the property were the corpses of cattle, fowl, and other livestock. The house was just a pile of debris with the barn being the only standing building.

"It's still fresh," Saya said after smelling the air. "What do you see?"

I scanned the area and activated one of the scanners. Blood was everywhere, as was obvious, but I got visual on targets. Over twenty newly made vampires—mindless beasts that know only their thirst and obey their sire like a colony queen, inhabited the large two-story barn. Brown wood and gray stones with covered windows smeared with blood. All seemed like normal people if you ignore the mouth full of fangs, the claws, and the red eyes.

"A little under thirty vampires. Most are still feeding on a few deer with a few patrolling," I said, having Nex bring me Juuchi

Yosamu. "No sign of our actual target, and I think there's about five sets of footprints heading for town." I turned to her as she cut open her wrist with her thumbnail.

"*Thirsting blade*," she said in Latin, throwing her arm out with a flick of her wrist and making a red-and-white blade appear in her hand. A conjuring spell of the Incruentatus, using their blood as a catalyst to form a blade of hardened blood and fangs formed by magic. Saya's took the form of a Chinese Jian, a thin double-edged straight sword with a red hilt and guard in the shape of bat wings while the blade was tooth white with a seemingly straight edge that was actually serrated like a shark tooth. These blades were made with the idea of draining the enemy of all their blood as the sword itself was just as thirsty as its master, a true weapon for the lords of blood-suckers. "Then we'll have to leave some of them alive for an interrogation." She turned to me while licking her lips, indicating her own hunger. "Shall we hunt, Phantom?" I was already moving when she started, but those last two words lingered in my head.

Hunt, Phantom.

Why did those two words ring in my head? It wasn't even in Saya's voice after the first time but a multitude of others. None of which I recognized, but each one felt familiar in some way. I didn't even notice that I had already beheaded one of the vampires with another charging right at me and another letting out an earsplitting shriek, signaling the rest, just before Saya impaled her. I watched the vampire turn into a dried-out husk before Saya ripped her blade free. My attention turned to the barn as the vampires swarmed our position, all unleashing bloodcurdling screams. I'm starting to get a little sick of the blood theme.

"We needed to form a plan!" Saya hissed as she charged at the swarm of thirsty undead.

I joined her in the attack, but my own body felt like it was on autopilot, not in the same way as adrenaline or muscle memory or even instinct. It felt like something else, and I didn't like it. Still, I wasn't in the market to complain as of yet. As of now, the two of us were carving our way through the vamps. Saya was pretty much dancing her way through, moving like the water as her blade cut through the undead. My own process was messier, severing body parts with every slash and deep wounds on others.

Now I know what you're thinking. You're not stabbing them in the heart. You don't have holy water, no sunlight. Honestly, the only consistent lore of killing vampires is chopping off their heads. But the truth is that it's all about the blood. Blood carries the life energy that gives the turned humans their unnatural life, but they need it almost constantly. Think of it like a battery, when that drains, it dies. They don't have the healing ability to stop blood loss and eventually drop as their bodies suck themselves dry. After that is a simple matter of removing the remains—that's where the sun comes in. There's never been a case of a vampire not drinking blood yet coming out fine. They usually turn to dust instead.

That very need for blood was the crux of my strategy. Saya's blade can transfer the blood of those she cuts to herself and keep her in top shape. Me? Well, when blood starts pouring from over a dozen able bodies while surrounded by those with a constant thirst, they were bound to turn on each other soon enough. I had cut off another vampire's arm when I noticed that one had begun to feed off the remains of one of my kills. One became two, two became four, and I think you see the pattern.

"Nex, mimic," I quickly ordered my familiar as I reached out to Saya, whose eyes were glowing red with a feral grin as she continued to cut and feed. Nex mimicked my actions as shadows wrapped around Saya before I ran out of the feeding frenzy, bringing her with me. We got out of the swarm and turned to see the hideous display. Saya glared at me, most likely because I interrupted her dinner but soon calmed herself as the vampires continued to tear each other apart for a drop of blood.

"Just beasts at this stage," Saya reiterated, apathetic to the display of gore. "They can be trained, but that takes decades, and they're only interested in quenching their thirst." I did a quick scan to find that half of the vampires were now dead, and another set of ten footprints were coming here before running off. "What idiot thought vampires were the ultimate paranormal romance and started that damn trend?" she growled while I sighed in aggravation.

"I think that was Bram Stoker with Dracula," I answered, still studying the footprints...that were leading back to London. Damn it. "A little odd since he was a Hunter, but enough history. Our target's on the run," I told her, getting her attention off the dwindling vampires. "Looks like he was on a recruitment mission, saw what we've done, and is now on the run." I heard her growl again as she turned her attention back to the vampires.

"When I'm done, stab me in the leg," she quickly ordered, opening her pendant. Before I could ask what she was planning, she bit through her lips, dripped blood onto the ruby heart, which began to glow, with Saya's eyes turning white as she spoke in some language I didn't recognize. "*Feed my hunger.*" The ruby heart shined an ethereal glow on the remaining vampires and the bloodstained ground that soon created a thick red fog of what I assumed to be blood. Saya's mouth went from humanoid to some form of lamprey as she took a deep breath, which was sucking in the fog of blood. I watched as all the bodies, dead and still struggling, quickly shriveled up and turn to dust. When all in front of us was a big pile of dust, I impaled my blade through Saya's knee and made her drop to the ground. She stopped and screeched in pain, but the bloodred returned to her eyes. And this was the only time when that was a good thing.

"You good? Are we finished here?" I asked, twisting Yosamu a bit and earning a pained grunt from her.

"Are there any survivors?" she asked, making me double-check before confirming as such. "Then we're done here," she said, ripping the blade out of her knee and quickly healing. "Come on. We're not done yet." She grabbed my shirt and charged off at full speed, throwing me on her back again as we made our way back into the city. Pretty sure, my face would've peeled off from all the air friction from this running. I'm glad I have my mask.

Just like last time, everything was pretty much a blur as we returned to the city. The city lights were still on for those who were still out and about...at four forty-five in the morning. That had to be a small list, but there were still people about and doing their business. No one paying any heed to the two teenagers in the alleyway, both armed and looking like odd cosplayers. I'm a little surprised we didn't raise any sort of alarm yet.

"Any luck?" Saya asked as I searched for prints while she tried to catch their scent. I was about to say we lost them until I saw some bloodied prints and scratches ascending a wall.

"Rooftops," I said, making her look up. Without any hesitation, she grabbed me and jumped to the top of one of the buildings. I would've taken the time to appreciate the skyline, but I saw our target. He was accompanied by nine others, and they were running in the direction of the Thames River. "There!" I yelled, pointing at the group as they seemed to be forced to a human's run. "Why are they moving so slow now?"

"They're still not used to their abilities," Saya returned as we gave chase, maneuvering across the rooftops with grace. "I'd say they can manage a straight line at best." We were reaching an edge with the next building across a two-lane road gap. She got ahead of me and laced her hands together, giving me a foothold, and the moment I put all my weight on it, she threw me across to the next building. I landed on the rooftop exit and rolled onto the roof itself, landing on my feet and continued to run. Parkour was such a useful skill to have. I continued without concern for Saya to catch up, she would eventually, but I needed to get to these vampires before they reach the Thames. They reach that then they could disappear in any number of ways, and we can't let that happen.

Hurry! Hurry! I thought to myself, urging my body to move faster. I removed all other thoughts from my head and focused on that one task of catching up to my prey. I jumped, rolled, swerved, and ran through the rooftops of London, along and around rails, generators, vents, and air-conditioners until we reached the same building—Westminster Palace. Could've gone around the building, through the brush on one side or the bridge on the other, but they jumped to the top of the London's Parliament building instead—literally jumped and climbed up to the top of the palace. *That seems like a poor choice*, I thought as I passed a pair of guards and started to climb up the walls as fast as I could. After a few seconds, I reached the top to find that Saya was already there and in a standoff with the other vampires. I unsheathed Yosamu and got behind them, soon joined by the very same pair of guards I passed earlier, both wearing black jackets, pants, and vests carrying their various gear. On their thigh was a single handgun while they carried SMGs with suppressors on the barrel. One was white with a British police cap while the other was Indian with a black turban.

"Need some help?" asked the weathered White man in his forties as he and his partner took aim. Saya said nothing she just blurred with speed as she grabbed the man in the middle and disappeared, leaving me and the guards with nine other vampires.

"Just don't die," I told them as our two sides waited for the other to move.

CHAPTER 13

RED SUN RISES

THE WAIT WASN'T even that long since, in pretty much that next instant, Saya's clash with her quarry began. That prompted the vampires to move. My allies immediately began shooting, the muffled clicks replacing the otherwise loud bangs. The first vampire came at me with a swipe to my head while the others charged to my comrades. I raised my sword to block, bracing the spine against my forearm and letting the beast's claw meet the edge of my sword. The legendary sharpness of the Muramasa blades lived to their reputation as the vampire lost all his fingers as he met my sword. I felt the blood splash against me as I made a quick swing to the creature's neck, nearly decapitating the beast.

The guards that were helping me got a few shots in on the vampires, but they were all in the limbs and grazing shots. None were actually debilitating, before the vampires closed in, claws out and jaws ready to bite. What I saw next earned my respect for the guys, though, because the moment the vampires got that close, they pulled out blades. The Brit threw his arm into one vampire's jaws and shot another in the chest, directly into the heart, before shooting the one, chewing on him in the throat. With his knife hand free, he threw his blade into the back of a fleeing vampire while shooting the other in the spine before going over to finish the job.

The other was faring much better, almost dancing through the vampires with his hand flashing about wildly. Didn't think I'd see a Kalaripayattu practitioner here. A push dagger going through a throat, into a chest, under a chin, while his body twisted and spun around his attackers. Soon, all nine were dead and bleeding. The battle was quick and should be expected. Hunters go in prepared, and this prey was still young and ignorant of their abilities.

"Was it really okay for you two to leave your position?" I asked as we cleaned off our blades and gathered bullets casings. Their response was to smile while the Indian threw me his badge. One side was the expected emblem, the other was the Hunter's crest.

"Mankind first, queen and country second," the Brit said as I returned the badge. "Word was that something went down with the nearby Incruentatus family. Then we see you blokes come running through."

"Anyone in the Order can recognize that mask on sight, Phantom," the other guy returned as I shrugged. "We can finish up here. You should help your companion."

"Yeah. In fact, why haven't you gone yet?" I pointed to the top of Big Ben to reveal that Saya already had her quarry by the throat, hanging over the side.

"If I had to guess, she's waiting for a painful execution via sunlight," I told them. I said earlier that the sun is part of the "cleanup" process when dealing with vampires. It's a fun little chemical reaction. See, as it turns out, the Incruentati inject a venom that turns normal human blood into something else and causes slight mutations to humans. That result is the monster known as vampire, and that new blood is highly reactive to UV rays, evaporating in an instant but catching on fire when inside a body. The Incruentatus are immune to that weakness to light because their skin is able to deflect UV rays. Humans...they tend to bake.

"Good luck with that," the Brit said with a chuckle in his voice. "London isn't exactly known for her sunny days."

As he said that, the sun's light pierced through the clouds and directly onto where Saya and her prey currently stood. The person in her grasp began to struggle and smoke wildly, but Saya remained impassive as the man burst into flames. It was an odd and disturbing sight, watching a figure wreathed in flames clawing for vengeance or relief, letting out a chilling scream of pain and suffering as it slowly died. Saya gave the creature her mercy, piercing her own clawed hand through his chest and crushing the heart in her grasp. "That was... that was disturbing."

"It's the job," I told him as I began walking toward the clock tower. He wasn't wrong that, as Hunters, you see some pretty horrific things. All the things that haunt the dreams of mortal kind, mythical creatures, otherworldly beings, their feasts and the results after, and sometimes their own deaths and the cleanup afterward. How are you supposed to react when you find a room painted in blood, when you find someone with their guts torn out, a child drowned in a river, and those were the people that died. Those become sights that are normal if you're too late. I left them to finish up the cleanup as more sunlight bathed the rooftop of Westminster palace as I went over to Saya, who descended from the tower like an angel. Not as much of a compliment as you'd think.

"We're done here," she announced as her feet touched down. "We're heading back to the family," she quickly ordered.

I didn't even have the chance to ask anything. She just walked off. I made sure to follow as we returned to the noble's house. There were more decorations up now, wreathes of green and white roses hanging off the walls and posts, deep red banners bridging gaps in the space overhead, and a group of maids sewing a message onto one more red silk banner. Other than that, and one other thing, the trip through here was pretty much the same. The one other thing were some odd visions I started having with that same damn phrase echoing in my mind.

Hunt, Phantom—I'm hearing that again and again, and as I'm walking through the garden and through the halls of the noble's home, I'm seeing death and carnage. Every few steps and I'll get a flash in my mind, snapping a neck, stabbing into a heart, cutting off a head, just a trail of blood and death as we made our way through. They were memories, that much I was sure of, but I don't actually remember any of them. From the looks of it, I was killing an entire clan of Incruentatus. There are only two reasons why I would do that: one, they broke the treaty with malicious intent; or two... I really wish it wasn't the second option. The visions ended as I realized that we were back in front of the Incruentatus that sent us on this mission.

"May peace be upon you, Lady Ivy," Saya said as she bowed to the smiling noble, happy that justice was done.

But that joy was hollow, that smile was just inches away from lifeless. Saya grabbed my arm and pulled me away, getting us out of the manor and off the property. As soon as there was an appreciable distance from the manor and into a field with a lone tree, she punched that tree so hard it splintered and collapsed.

"Should I ask?" I asked, aware that I'd be walking on eggshells with an angry vampiric noble. She turned to me with glowing red eyes and fangs bared, taking those aggressive breaths that were between hissing and growling. Eventually, she calmed down and stood straight up, the primal fury from earlier almost gone...almost.

"When my kind marry, it ties our souls together," she explained, walking back to Westminster Abbey. "You know of the 'blood bond,' Dante, but just try to imagine feeling the loss of someone your very soul is linked to. When that bastard killed her husband, it almost killed her as well. The shock is that powerful."

"Is it because she's with child that she's still alive?" I asked as we slowly made our way back into the city.

"Yes," she answered, so quietly I almost missed it. "Some might say that it's a good thing. That she was lucky, that nothing is more precious than life. Humans can be so naive," she hissed with a sense of disgust. "They live such fleeting lives that every day is precious, and they usually waste it at the same time. Beings like us, we can live for eternity, but what use is that long life if the most precious person in that immortal life is gone." She stopped to look back at the manor, shrinking to a dot in the distance. "She'll continue to eat those fruit of the Jubokko, carry, birth, and nurture her child until he is old enough to take over as the family head. Wishing for her death the whole time until she can be with her beloved."

"I wasn't aware that the Japanese 'vampire trees' actually bore fruit of their own," I said as we continued our walk.

"Cultivating them is *not* easy," she returned, seemingly calming down. "But the results are undeniable. The freshest and cleanest blood that anyone could drink. Saved for when an Incruentatus is pregnant, offering all the necessary nutrients needed for a healthy child."

We walked in silence as we reached the city and went to the portal, still hidden inside the Abbey.

"Hey, Saya?" I started, keeping her from leaving just yet. "Can you think of any nobility that was wiped out recently? Hunter or otherwise?"

She paused to think for a moment. "There was the Flor Roja family in Spain," she finally answered, reflecting on the loss with a sense of melancholy. "They were completely wiped out in a single night. They never did anything to justify it…but they were just gone. Hunters and Incruentati have been unable to figure out anything."

That's what I was afraid of.

We went back through the portal, into the school's dimensional space again, and back to the dorms. While we were doing that, my mind went back to what was going on with me since last night. I hear that phrase replaying in my head like a twisted mantra, pushing me to kill mindlessly. I get visions of people dying en masse, an entire Incruentatus clan, probably by my own hands. Getting the confirmation that one such clan was indeed killed but with not a single trace of evidence gave a troubling implication for me. One possibility was that it was because they broke the treaty and needed to be dealt with. The other was that I killed them and cleaned up the mess but have no recollection of doing such. I really, *really* hope this ends up as being nothing.

CHAPTER 14

ALONE WITH MY THOUGHTS

THE NEXT COUPLE of months passed by with little incident for me and everyone else. September became October, October to November, and November to December. The only hitch was the way Monica celebrated "All Hallows Eve," raising the dead and getting everyone attacked by monster pumpkins because of an error in her spell work. Apparently, that was one of the more boring Samhain celebrations she partook in. I didn't want to know what counted as a "fun" one. Other than that, Kashi got another tail, which means our training with him is paying off. Lucrezia and I had a few dates, and that was pretty much it. It was nearing the end of the year, and everyone was getting ready to leave, each one doing their own holiday celebrations.

Most everyone was going home. Kashi and Lance were the exceptions due to being in exile until the former earns the right to return to his clan and the latter because he's a skinwalker, not exactly welcomed among his people. Monica celebrated Christmas, not for any magic, magic reasons, but she just loved the concept of togetherness and goodwill. Andrea and Max went back to England and Germany respectively, lycans being pack animals and family emphasis around the holidays and whatnot. Saya's going to a ball that the royal family was hosting, nobility obligations and such. Zoe said something a summons from her "fair king," whatever that meant. Also, to my surprise, Lucrezia was going to her family in Italy to celebrate Christmas. I found that out on our date, sitting by a lake and just enjoying the scenery.

"Of course, I celebrate Christmas," she said when I asked, almost shocked that the words came out of my mouth. "It's one of the most love-filled holidays, and love is *very* close to lust," she said, licking her lips. I guess it shouldn't surprise me too much. During the Ancient Roman times, Christians would partake in the pagan holidays to avoid being killed by the Romans. Guess nonhumans adopted the same policy, and for some, it just stuck with them. "But enough about me," she said while sliding next to me on the bench we were sitting on, "what are you planning for Christmas? Am I going to be in those thoughts of yours?" Her succubus nature was certainly shining through as she pressed her chest against my arm and fondled my chest.

"Maybe," I responded, "never really celebrated the holidays." She gasped as she pulled away with a look that clearly said that she couldn't believe what I had just said. "Never had any reason to." I looked up to the sky, reflecting on my life. "No family to celebrate with." My only constant companion was the demon in my shadow. "No traditions to call my own." No family or nationality to cement anything resembling the festive times. "The holidays are just another day. The difference is that people actually try to get along, if only for a few hours." I felt a wetness on my arm and saw her crying.

"Dante," she said, pulling me to her in a comforting hug. Well, I'm sure she thought she was being comforting, but I was uncomfortable. "No one should have to be alone during this time of year." She then immediately brightened up. "If you want, you can come with me to Italy. I'm sure my mother would *love* to meet you," she said in a rather sultry tone before leaning in to my ear. "Maybe make some *hot* memories together." Some would say this was a moment killer, but she's a succubus. It'd be weirder if she *didn't* imply sex in some way.

"I appreciate the offer, Lucrezia, but I'm going to have to decline," I said, gently pushing her off. "Something came up, and I could use the alone time." She had a flash of disappointment that was replaced with concern as I looked ahead, hoping my expression would stay calm enough for her to leave me be without worries. "Nothing bad, just some…memories I need to sort out."

The same excuse I've been giving when I needed some time to think, the same damn one for weeks. It was clear to the both of us that this was the end of the date as we got up to leave, and I escorted her back to her dorms. She gave me a kiss on my cheek and said that the offer was still open until six, then she'd have to leave. I hope it wouldn't disappoint her too much when I don't show up. I continued on my way toward the boys' dorm, where I saw Kashi and Lance packing.

"I thought you guys didn't have any plans."

"Uh, well, there is this one cake shop back in Japan that I've been meaning to get to," Kashi said, looking a little nervous. "I made a special Christmas order, and it's going to be a bit of a trip to get there and get the cake before the sale ends."

Must be a pretty popular bakery. Unfortunately, I didn't exactly believe him since he seems to be packing for an extended trip, and I doubt any cake is worth that.

"Also, Monica talked everyone into doing this worldwide scavenger hunt that some ancestor of hers made some centuries back," Lance said, Kashi looking at him with disbelief and shock. "What? I think it's strange that out of everyone that 'supposed' to be in this group of friends, this mysterious ancestor of hers made this hunt and *solely* for the benefit of this one guy," he said while pointing at me before looking at me with an apologetic look. "No offense."

"I'm guessing another divination/fortune-telling incident within her family?" They both shrugged, the usual response to when Monica is getting us to do anything. No idea how or why, but it always seems like the best call is to trust her. In this case, it seems like I'm the only one that isn't going to be involved until the end. Probably for the best, I can have some time to think, but I might be distracted by wondering about whatever this whole "scavenger hunt" thing is about. "Well, I wish you guys luck. I'll be here…just relaxing." I think they knew I wasn't planning on that, not that I'd be able to, but I didn't give them time to ask. I went to my dorm room and locked the door before throwing myself onto the bed.

Time seemed to slow to a crawl until I heard them leave, finally putting me in solitude. This whole year and mission is messing with my head and what I knew about the Hunters was being tested. What I know and what still holds true is that we fight back the monsters, the creatures that only create pain and chaos, death, and destruction. What I thought is that we kill or exorcise the dangerous ones, not make deals with them. Going back to Japan with Nurarihyon, but they are more of an inconvenient kind that commands many more dangerous beings, Tengu tend to be isolationist, and some are active helpers to a human household. Most of Europe has the faerie folk who are split between the Seelie and un-Seelie courts—helpful/benign and mischievous/malicious. There's that treaty with the Incruentatus, and that's to control the vampire population. Just how much do I actually know about the Order? I've been with it my whole life, and now I feel like it's becoming a stranger to me.

And that brings me to this school, this school for inhumans. Did the Order not know about this place, and if they did know about this place, then why send me? I'm the guy they send in to *kill* monsters, not do diplomatic missions or espionage. I can understand some concerns about whether this place is really helpful to our goals of protecting humanity, but then why take chances? What do I have to do with any of this? As I think about that, my mind returns to that vampire hunt when Saya said that one phrase that kept reverberating in my head.

Hunt, Phantom.

Just thinking about those two words in that order gives me a migraine, and the more I think about it, the more my head throbs. Am I subconsciously trying to hide something from myself? Was it part of a secret that I'm not supposed to know about? Doubtful actually, since after hearing Saya say it, I immediately went on an offensive strike and killed a group of vampires before I got out of the trance. That meant only one thing; it's a trigger phrase.

The question there is, Why did I have a trigger phrase? Was it to make me enter a state of mind where I was a better combatant and a more effective hunter? But then why would I have memories of killing an entire Incruentati clan? I managed to do some digging on the

Flor Roja, and they were clean, no reason for the Hunters or the royal family to go after them. They were wiped out in a way that seemed like they disappeared from the face of the earth for what seems to be no reason at all.

Leading to another question there, Why did I have memories of attacking that family, and how did they essentially disappear as a result? Was it important to keep hidden, and did they know something that threatened the world? Was it just an incident of senseless murder, and why was I the one that did it? I kept thinking to that phrase and trying to figure out what was the reason, the meaning behind any of it. That was a decision I soon came to regret.

Mentally powering through that migraine seemed to get me closer to something. That something brought my nightmares to my waking world, and I was feeling every bit of it. My skin was burning, I felt blades and saws cutting into my body, dozens of needles shoved into my veins, and pumping these various drugs into my system— okay, that was new. My outside felt like I was being burned alive while my insides were turning to ice and that I was being carved into some new shape. The difference from this and the usual nightmares, no voice screaming at me to "accept my destiny" or to wake up. Instead, I heard multiple voices discussing…something. A line about "the conditioning," another about "rejecting the serum," but one overpowering one cried above all others, *"Get him under control!"* The pain was getting too severe, and my focus was shattered all I could think about was stopping it. I stumbled to my feet, dragged myself to a wall, and bashed my skull into it until I hit a stud, and everything went dark.

When I finally came to, I found that three days had passed and Nex was wrapped around me like a cocoon of shadows. My head still ached, but the worst of my pain was gone. I also was nowhere near as hungry as I think I should be, but the hunger was definitely there. It was a struggle, but I managed to pick myself up and stumble into the kitchen area. I could feel my familiar looking at me with worry the whole while. I was making myself a light ham-and-cheese sandwich, something easy and simple to make and eat, when my eyes drifted to a butcher knife. The voices from my dreams returned as I pulled the blade out.

The experiment shows to be a success, one of the voices said. *He now has regenerative abilities. As long as it's not life-threatening and he has the energy, he should no longer worry about injuries.* Was that it? Was that why my memories might be sealed and I was probably tortured? Trying to boost the chances of humanity in the eternal war? But then why was I never informed that I had that ability? Although, thinking back on it, I supposed that does explain how I survived that cloud of poison from Orochi. Well, only one way to really check.

"I'm going to regret this," I whispered, just before plunging that steel blade into my hand. I roared in pain as it cut through my flesh and felt my blood pouring out of my wound. Just as quickly as I stabbed myself, I tore the blade back out and watched my hand. It was like time was slowly being reversed. My hand was healing, and all the blood that spilled out was being sucked back into my hand. I felt the afflicted area, and it was like I was never injured in the first place. As another test, I singled out my left pinky finger and swiftly chopped it off. Again, the pain was severe, but I powered through. As soon as I moved the blade, strings of blood went from my hand to my finger and reattached itself.

"Maybe all those drugs they pumped into me were spell catalysts to make sure this was constant and sustainable," I said, though it sounded like I was trying to justify what had happened to me. That what I went through served a higher purpose and that the Order wasn't keeping secrets. I could tell myself that all I wanted, but a part of me knows that my trust in the Order was damaged, and it probably won't get fixed anytime soon. With nothing else to do, I grabbed my sandwich and began eating it while heading for the couch. Any number of Christmas movies should be on by now, that's what you get on TV on Christmas Eve. Maybe one of them will serve as a good distraction. Before I could even hit the power, Nex shot my phone at me. My cellphone for when the Order has a mission, and just my luck, it had a call. I picked it up and answered.

"Phantom, we're getting reports of people disappearing in the mountain forests of North America. The Appalachian Mountains of

West Virginia." There's a short list of people that don't get the holidays off. Hunters are on that list. "We sent a team earlier, but all they managed to send to us was that the evidence pointed to a werewolf." Must have been a pretty powerful one if it took down a team already, but now I'm getting involved. And *nothing* survives an attack by the Phantom. That's the reputation of my predecessors and a legacy I must live up to.

"Understood. I'll set out immediately," I returned before hanging up. Werewolf, one of the oldest of monster kind, known for strength, agility, and hostility. Silver is highly lethal to them, burning upon contact and causes the heart to stop upon contact with the muscle. A straightforward and simple hunt, just have to be careful and one step ahead of the beast itself. "Nex, get me an M1911 with a couple of magazines with silver bullets and silver knife." I ordered as the shadow familiar obeyed. A sleek black pistol appeared with two full clips of silver bullets and an eight-inch silver knife with a round black grip. I slipped the gun into the back of my pants and pocketed the clips along with the knife and got ready to go the mountains of North America. I was about to leave before I stopped myself, looking to Nex in my shadow.

"Hey, how about I deal with this alone?" I asked, getting a look of concern from the shadow creature. "I know, but I wasn't kidding when I said I wanted to be alone. And you've never really left my side. I want to do this hunt on my own." If it was possible, I could've sworn that he was giving me some form of puppy eyes. "Don't worry. They think it's a werewolf. I'll be fine." Before I could turn to leave, he shot a few red rods at me. Turns out, they were road flares. "Thanks, that's a good idea," I said, pocketing them as well. I said one last goodbye and swiftly made my way past the security guard at the Gateway.

This was supposed to be a simple hunt. It did not turn out to be a simple hunt.

CHAPTER 15

HUNTING ALONE

THE COORDINATES PUT me deep in the mountains and away from civilization; the closest trace was an old hiking trail that went to a pretty decent campsite. Reception was pretty much dead, so the only other method of communication would be through spells. At least my mask still worked, providing me vision in the dark forest. There was a thin blanket of snow on the ground, and most of the trees were now decorated in the powdered ice. I myself was in camouflage hunting jacket and pants, might as well since I *am* hunting, with my gun in one hand and my knife in the other. I was wandering the forest, looking for anything that could point me in the direction of the werewolf when I finally noticed something odd.

What is with this place? I wasn't hearing anything. I wasn't seeing anything. There was *nothing* alive in these woods. Even werewolves mingle with actual wolves, more on that if it ever becomes relevant, but I felt nothing here. Just emptiness and death, and that is *always* bad news. I saw some claw marks on a couple of trees as I went deeper into the woods.

"Help! Somebody help me! Please!" I heard a voice calling out from deeper inside the woods. Anyone else would have the first impulse be to run toward it and try to help—well, mostly the good people. Others would turn around and try to run, either the cowards...or the smart ones. Christmas in the United States, most people would be at home celebrating. Add to that the fact that according to the people I actually managed to talk to, I was nowhere near any cabins. I did hear that someone built a bunker here some years back, but that person vanished. Some said he went crazy and disappeared in the mountains. Since then, people sometimes end up missing after taking that hiking trail and began to believe it to be cursed.

"Please, for the love of the Creator, don't be that," I muttered under my breath as I progressed deeper into the forest, running toward the noise but completely on guard. Werewolves would howl, growl, be territorial, and let you know you're trespassing. They aren't known for being chatty, and the more time I spend in these woods, the more I'm convinced I'm after something much worse than a werewolf. I followed the sounds deeper and deeper, examining each tree for claw marks until some seemed familiar. It was leading me around.

"Damn it!" I cursed, slamming my fist against the tree. There was the rattle of branches and falling snow. That was when I finally noticed the putrid smell of rotting flesh and snow crunching beneath feet. I immediately turned and was slammed against the tree. Two large gaunt, near-skeletal hands wrapped around my head, ready to twist it off, as I frantically kept my pistol from slipping out of my fingers. Before it could snap my neck, I shot three rounds into the creature's stomach, making it cry out in pain as it released me and backed away. I fell to my hand and knees, but I immediately pushed myself up and took aim, being unable to get a clean shot as it fled. "Wendigo," I growled, getting a good look at the thing. Tall, gaunt, sunken in eyes, needlelike teeth, near rotted skin pulled taut over the skeleton.

All the evidence pointed to it being a wendigo, but that just made no sense. For starters, this was too far south since wendigoag are native to the Great Lakes region in the United States and Canada, the furthest confirmed presence was in Minnesota. And they only existed because of the curse by the Algonquian spirit by the same name when someone commits the taboo of cannibalism. Nothing good ever comes from humans eating each other, especially in this case. They lose all their humanity and are constantly hungry, always craving human flesh. But I have to wonder, how did whoever that thing was get cursed when the Hunters sealed away the Wendigo spirit some centuries back? Unfortunately, now wasn't the time to ask questions. More like running for my life until I can figure out how to permanently kill a nigh invulnerable and near-perfect hunter. I immediately started running.

I didn't really have any idea of where I was running I didn't have a set goal in mind. I got so focused on finding the damn thing that I let it lead me around until I lost all my bearings. Meaning, I have no idea where I am or where I'm going, and I'm being stalked. I heard the branches above me snap, prompting me to turn around just as the monster fell on top of me. I felt my dagger stab into its stomach, causing an unearthly screech of pain to ring out from its throat and into my ears. Keeping a firm grip on my blade, I tore it through the wendigo's decaying flesh as much as I could and causing the beast to flee once again.

Thank the Creator that silver's the bane of almost all monsters, I thought as I got back up and continued running. Silver can hurt wendigoag, so can fire, but unless I can get at the thing's heart, then it'll just heal and come after me again. I needed a way to cripple its movements so I could do that. Question is, How can I possibly pull that off? All I have is a knife, a pistol with a couple magazines of silver bullets, and a couple of road flares. This thing is stronger than bears, faster than the eye can follow, and smart. Unless I was very, *very* lucky, I wasn't going to pull this off with what I currently have. After two minutes passed of me running, I heard the beast howl again. It sounds like it *really* wants me dead for hurting it so much. And now my legs started to burn—luck has not been on my side.

I heard another snapping of branches, but I didn't turn around. Instead, I assumed the plan of the wendigo was to trick me and dove to the right. Turned out, I was right that it was trying to trick me. I was just wrong on the direction, and I rolled between the creature's legs. Before I could attack it, it swung one of its arms and sent me flying. I slammed against a tree and very nearly blacked out, somehow keeping a hold on my gun but dropped my dagger—arguably the more important tool for when I finally beat this thing, if I can, that is.

I tried to get up to fight, but the wendigo was already right in front of me. It lifted me up by my neck and speared a clawed hand straight through my gut. My eyes widened in shock and pain as I felt the hand pierce into me. That's when the adrenaline kicked in, and I wasn't sure if this meant I was lucky or unlucky. As it got ready to take a bite out of me, I shoved my pistol right into its neck and started shooting. The wendigo let go of me, grasping at its neck like it was choking or just in intense pain. Again, I love silver.

On my side, I felt the hole in my stomach close itself up as it reversed the damage. I didn't examine the process and instead pointed my gun at the wendigo again, shooting it as much as I could. I seemed to have gotten a lucky shot while it was flailing about as it fell onto a tree. I think I got its spine, but it could still move its arms and thus climbed the tree. I had to reload and did such while scanning for my knife before finding it a few feet behind me. I forced myself up and learned just how much it cost to heal that hole the wendigo made in me. I felt like I had run a marathon after a two-week diet of junk food and no preparation, not a good feeling in general.

I had to force myself to look strong and still able, so as to keep the wendigo off me for as long as possible, but my body was aching, and I needed to lie down, not something I could afford at the moment with that thing out there. The moment I reached my knife, my mask scanner picked up some magical energy. It looked to be a spell of healing, coming further in the forest. A wendigo just naturally regenerates, and I'm supposed to be the only other person in these woods that's supposed to be alive at least, unless it didn't yet kill the team of Hunters that came here before me. If that's the case, then I'd have to risk my luck. Ignoring how tired I was, ignoring the protest in my body, I started running again and directly toward the source of magical energy.

If I had made that wendigo mad by shooting and stabbing it, then it was livid now. That probably means that I was heading directly for its lair, and it *really* didn't want me there unless I was dead. Fortunately, it must have still been healing from all the bullet wounds I gave it because there was no other way I could've gotten as far as I did. I found an open hole in the ground with a bunker hatch standing up, the magic energy flowing out of it like smoke. I got to the hatch, grabbed its wheel, and then jumped into the hole. It almost shut, but a clawed hand caught it. I braced my feet against the ladder and pulled, struggling as much as I could against the cannibal, but the hatch was getting pried open. I felt something slipping out of my pockets and saw the road flares, giving me a bad but desperate idea. I freed one hand to grab the flare, the wendigo getting another hand under the hatch, pulled my mask, and bit onto the cap of the flare before pulling it off. I tucked the flare under my chin and turned the cap, still in my mouth, till I could pull the lid off and expose the scratch surface.

This is a horrible idea, I thought to myself one more time before grabbing the flare and striking it, creating the geyser of flame. I did burn my face, but I ignored that as I freed my feet from the ladder and let the wendigo tear open the hatch. It reached out to grab me while roaring in my face, which was exactly what I was hoping for, as I shoved the flare directly into the creature's mouth. Its head caught on fire as it let go and fled again, letting the hatch fall shut with me hanging there. I turned the wheel until it locked before grabbing my knife to start drawing a circle of Anasazi symbols around the opening, ensuring my protection from this entryway. I breathed a sigh of relief before letting go, forgetting that I was hanging upside down. The ground didn't forget to be soft and gentle concrete, though.

"Ow!" I groaned out as I slipped my mask back on to get night-vision back. I wanted to move, but I felt too exhausted after everything that happened. I didn't think I was going to make much progress against the wendigo in this state and almost blacked out. The only reason I didn't was because I learned that I was not alone in that bunker.

"Hey, you still alive over there?" a dry, gasping voice called out. I managed to twist my head enough to see a bloodied and bruised man in similar gear to mine hanging by his chained hands. "It's too dark for me to see," he said again before coughing. I forced myself up and examined the rest of the bunker, using the wall for support. The layout seemed intended for survival, not comfort, with a touch of paranoia. Smooth concrete on all sides, a HAM radio setup that had an ax buried in it, maps that seemed to point to hunting spots for game and other foraging purposes with security monitors that were left off, a cot with several animal skins, a furnace that hadn't seen any use for a couple years, shelves full of dry preserve foods and water, a closet and chest full of guns and ammo, a gas generator in the far room that seemed connected to the lights, and the whole place was littered with bones and blood smears. Some were human, most were animal, but I think I got the picture.

"Give me a moment," I told the guy, stepping around the bones to avoid tripping as I went to one of the shelves and grabbed a water bottle. The water itself was frozen from the cold, but that was an easy fix. "*Let this liquid life flow freely once more,*" I spoke in… Gaelic, I think. The language charm removes any sense of identity of a language just to let you speak it, even magic spells are subject to it. But it gave me what I wanted as the ice turned to water, and I started to give it to my fellow Hunter. He took slow and careful sips, managing to ignore the impulse of drinking too much too fast as I examined his chain shackles—simply wrapped around and locked in with a hook while he was hanging from a meat hook. I lifted him off, and we both collapsed—I really should've taken care of myself first. I rolled him off me, snapping some bones beneath him, as we pulled the hook off and just lay there.

"Backup?" he asked, proving that he was one of the Hunters that was sent in first. I merely grunted in response, not having the energy to form actual words. "Sorry, this is all my fault. I just didn't think it was possible for another wendigo to appear." No one did. That was the point of sealing away the original wendigo spirit—to prevent another one of these things. I could admit the use of certain inhuman beings throughout the world, but wendigoag are nothing but destructive, driven to madness and hunger by the spirit before becoming its vessel from the act of cannibalism. Even other wendigoag hate them. They're very territorial and antisocial. There was a loud bang on the hatch, followed by a screech of pure fury. Looks like it healed and was angrier than before, but so long as that ward circle remains and we stay here, then we should be safe.

"Is there another way in here?" I asked, wanting to be sure before realizing how stupid it was to ask that.

"None that I know of. Haven't had a chance to look," he responded. Should've figured as much. I was feeling better, just a bit, so I forced myself up and examined the rest of the bunker. First stop was where the generator was. The good news was there was a ventilation shaft in there, and the shaft was too small for anything bigger than a raccoon, so nothing was stopping me from activating the generator. There was still a few gallons of gas in the room, so I filled up the generator and turned it on. "Let there be light," the Hunter said as the lights turned on, making everything visible to him, followed soon by the sounds of him gagging in disgust. "Worse than I'd imagine. Looks like nothing went to waste. Even the marrow was sucked out of the bones," he told me after he managed to calm down.

"Try to find something useful," I told him as I started drawing another Anasazi circle around the vents, best be careful in the lair of the beast. The only other rooms of any interest was a bathroom that saw very little use and a smoking room that was completely empty aside from ashes, drew warding circles in there too. My knife was starting to get dull from scratching the concrete.

"Think I got something," he called out as I made my way to him. He was sitting at the desk next to the busted radio, reading what looked to be a journal. "Says here that he was vacationing at Lake Ontario a few years back, and he fell into a cavern filled with these 'strange symbols' while hiking through the woods." That pretty much spelled out the rest for us. "Visions of this tall being of decaying flesh and bones with the horns of an elk and a man's skull filled with needlelike teeth. Driven to paranoia as a result, built this bunker to get off the grid and isolate himself from the 'dirty government,' began to distrust the supplies he got before holing himself up, captured a 'spy' one day, and you can tell the rest." A very unfruitful winter, trustworthy supplies run out, and the spy starts looking mighty tasty. "Last entry was three years ago."

"Around the same time people were disappearing," I returned, going through the guns for something useful. Not entirely sure why, unless this person had silver or incendiary rounds, this whole thing would be pointless. "How did this escape our notice for so long? We only got word that something was happening here recently, and I only heard of it being a werewolf."

"Take a look around you," he said, looking through the journal for anything else. "He believed in using every last bit of the stuff he gathered. The reason we heard about this at all was a single woman that managed to escape. Talked about the thing's growls, claws, watching them from the campsite before taking a friend of hers when she went to gather more wood. That was the beginning of the month. I can only assume I'm still alive because it only knocked me out, and living people stay fresh longer than dead ones." My eyes followed a trail of blood that went into another room with a shut door. I didn't want to open it.

"This is why these things need to die," I groaned, grabbing a Remington hunting shotgun. I was about to put it aside when I saw the best thing I could've hoped for: a box of dragon's breath shells. "And this guy was prepared," I said, examining the shells. Filled with magnesium shards and burns hot but short, it's definitely what I needed to cripple that wendigo. I just need to get a clean shot on it, and the rest should be easy.

"Hey, got the cameras on," he said, bringing my attention back to him. The feed showed night-vision and several places throughout the woods, though many were blank. The reason for that made itself clear when one camera started shaking, then was replaced with static. "And there goes that plan. Probably found out you turned on the generator." I quickly disassembled the shotgun and got about cleaning it.

"That's fine. It was never going to be easy," I told him as I continued my work. After a few minutes, the shotgun seemed to be in full working order again. The room was silent with the other Hunter gathering up all the human remains and moving them to a separate room. That healing magic he cast on himself must've really helped heal him from those days of hanging and malnutrition. I loaded a single shell when he interrupted me.

"I'll test it for you." I looked at him. He had a gas can in one hand and was standing next to the door I suspected the bodies were stored in. I got up and handed him the gun, turning on the safety to avoid a misfire. He tossed the gas can inside, took the gun, turned off the safety, and took aim. "May your spirits find rest, for your fight is now over," he said before shooting, the muzzle belching out a gout of bright flames. We shut the door and held it as the gas in the room exploded, burning away the bodies and bones. "I think that'll do it," he said, handing me the gun.

"Right." I took it and ejected the spent shell. I emptied the box into my pocket and loaded six shells and cocked it, ready for the final fight. I climbed out of the bunker and into the cold forest, shotgun in my left hand and my pistol in my right but held in such a way that it was still concealed. I kept a look out for the wendigo, but it wasn't making any noticeable movements or actions. I think it understood this was the end. One of us was going to die here. Either I did, and it would then need to be on the run, though whether it knew all that was questionable, or it dies, and that's the end of it.

It knows I can hurt it, likely even kill it, but I think it hates me enough to want to make sure it kills me—out of spite and vengeance if nothing else. I heard a slight hiss before I was tackled to the ground from behind. The shotgun fell from my hands in front of me, but I kept hold of my pistol. I whipped my right arm over my shoulder as I felt the monster's teeth dig into the nape of my neck. It froze when it felt the barrel of my gun on its head, unable to decide whether to try to flee or to kill me before I shot it in the neck. Once, twice, I unloaded an entire clip into its neck, even after I felt the body fall limp on top of me. I got up and managed to pry its fangs out of my neck, groaning in pain as I did so, before tossing it onto the ground. I pulled out my silver dagger and stabbed it right into the base of the monster's skull, severing the brain from the spine.

With the blade of silver in there, the healing should either be nullified or held off long enough for me to do what I needed to. I went over to the shotgun, picked it up, and checked it over. Once I was satisfied with its condition, I turned back to the wendigo, walked up to it, and fired straight at the monster's heart. The body arched and clenched as an unearthly screech echoed out for miles as it ignited and burned. Soon the entire body was wrapped in flames, now for the next step of this particularly gruesome work.

"*Burning fires of purification, cleanse this soul of corruption,*" I chanted in the native language of this monster's origin land, causing the flames to change from orange and red to white. The screams got louder as this fire burned at the very spirit of the wendigo, turning some of the body to ash. But it wasn't what I needed to stop it for good here. I reached into the fire and grabbed the hilt of my dagger, wincing as the flames from earlier still made it hot to the touch. The purifying fires didn't hurt me, I was an uncorrupted soul, as I strad-dled the monster's chest and plunged the blade into the creature's chest. I did this again and again, getting faster and faster with each stab, before carving a hole open and jamming my hand inside. I kept digging through the rotted flesh and bones until I found something hard and cold.

"Gotcha," I whispered, wrapping my hand around it before rip-ping out the withered and frozen heart of the beast. The body began to rapidly burn away into ash, losing what gave it the healing powers it once had. Before the body was consumed and the flames died, I stuck the heart into the fire and got it to burn. The screams of the monster continued until I took the silver dagger and plunged it into the heart. The withered organ shattered and burned away into noth-ingness, finally killing the wendigo monster for good. There was a single whisper, *Thank you,* telling me that I had freed the man's soul.

"This...sucked," I groaned, feeling more tired than ever, stuck between thinking that I'll never hunt without Nex by my side again and that I was weaker than I thought if this was difficult for me. I got up to return to the bunker and get my fellow Hunter when I saw it—a towering humanoid figure with piercing yellow eyes, great elk-like antlers and a maw of shining needle teeth, glaring at me with nothing less than pure hate. This was it, the spirit wendigo. I did not back down and returned my own glare at it. "Get back to your prison, monster," I ordered. It roared at me before charging, getting in front of me in a single second, trying to rend me with its claws. I did not move, standing firm and watched as it seemed to turn to dust and was sucked away back to its prison. With that settled, I returned to the bunker, jumping down the hatch.

"Requesting extraction," I heard him say as I wandered inside. In front of him was a glyph of a long dead language glowing crimson. I didn't need to look to know he was bleeding—that glyph was blood magic stolen from demons for one purpose. Emergency communication. Every Hunter learns this spell before any other and works at mastering it until we nearly die from blood loss. "Repeat, stranded in the Appalachian Mountains of Northern West Virginia and requesting extraction. Target was a wendigo, not a werewolf, and successfully slain by the Phantom. The target was a wendigo and is now dead," he said after noticing me. The symbol flashed a few times, leading the man to sigh. "Understood command," he said as the glowing dimmed away and the blood evaporated before him. "They're sending someone, but you're to 'return to your post, the way will appear.' Whatever that means."

"Don't worry, I know what it means," I said as my mask suddenly picked up a dimensional magic signature, the kind that led to the school. "Will you be fine here? Where your team died?" I asked as he shrugged and went over to the cot.

"All I can do now is stay here and wait," he said, lying down on the animal skins. "Wouldn't be the first time I've seen people die. Won't be the last either. That's the burden of soldiers everywhere." Trained to kill, expect to die, rinse, and repeat. "Besides, I've learned not to get attached, not after losing my wife and kid to an ogre. I've only one reason left in life, service to the Order." He pulled out a pendant from underneath his coat. "It's all that drives me now." He gripped the jewelry in his hand and rolled onto his side, telling me this conversation was over.

It was a classic story in the Hunters' Order. If you weren't born into it, then you came across some creature in the worst way possible and lost someone important to you as a result. The rarity was someone that joined because they wanted to, whether it was some kind of glory seeker or serial killers that was put to work for us. That last one…is rather complicated to talk about. I climbed my way back

JOSEPH LANKFORD

out of the hatch and followed the dimensional shift's signature until
I came across a cave, then it suddenly hit me.

Every time I finished with a hunt or mission, I was near a portal.
Either a natural one like with Saya after the vampire incident, or they
seemed to be made like with that Tengu and just now. This portal
was not here before, but when I was told to return, it just showed up.
There was no way this was a coincidence, even the Hunters would
need time to make these dimensional portals so readily deployed.
Not the span of the months I was there but decades at least. I was
tempted to contact my mentor, Wizard, but at the same time, I felt
like I needed to figure this out for myself. So far, the only thing I
really got out of this hunt was that most monsters absolutely *need* to
be put down. Maybe not all of them, but there is a pretty big difference between the useful and the destructive.

CHAPTER 16

NO LONGER ALONE

I WAS PREPARED to be all stealthy and sneak back into the school, but the guard at the Gateway was gone. All the security measures were gone, the only thing there was a sign that said, "Leave at your own risk." I'll give it this much—that is a foreboding note, not that it would actually do much. Why was it even up? I just gave up figuring that out and kept walking until I made it back to the dorms. I needed a hot shower and to just pass out. But that hunt didn't go the way I wanted it to, short and easy, why should the rest of the day be any different?

I had made it to my room when I found a box, seemed to be from a bakery, with a small card next to it. I smelled a moist and sweet aroma that seemed to tell me that Kashi's cake trip was a success, though why would he bring it here is beyond me...or why he and Lance were sleeping on the couch. I found a card next to it that said, "Open in one minute," and then it changed like a timer counting away the seconds. I let my curiosity control me, and when the final second chimed away, I opened the box. I was not expecting the bright flash of light or the sounds of thudding and oomphs as people fell. When the light faded and my sight cleared, I saw that I was still in the same room, but now I was surrounded by everyone: Max, Saya, Lucrezia, Monica, Zoe, even Lance and Kashi woke up.

"It worked!" Monica cheered, recovering quickly while every-one else was slowly getting up. "The summoning charm worked!" She went over to the table and pulled a cake out of the box to show a spell seal written on the inside of the lid. "At the start of the month, I received a letter from my family saying that my ancestor had something crucial ready for someone who would be one of my best friends. That someone would change the course of the world, but that someone would need something to aid the struggle. So he had a weapon made and scattered the parts around the world, where my other friends would find and bring it together," she explained before patting down and groping everyone. "Ha ha! Success!" she cheered as she assembled the pieces.

"Is that a knife?" I asked, looking at the parts. It looked like three metal blades that seemed to be shaped to attach to each other to make a single blade, two blocks that looked like they were the grip, colored crystals with something that seemed like a revolver turner, and a leather sheath that looked like it would house an eight-inch blade.

"An enchanted bowie knife to be precise," she said proudly, set-ting the pieces on the table and sitting me down in front of it. "Now it was said that you had to be the one to put this together. No one else could do so," she said, uncharacteristically serious, before making sure everyone backed away and pulling something out of her pocket. "Now are you ready?" she asked, ready to read off the instructions.

"Is no one going to ask how that spell seal got on that box?" Kashi asked…probably the sanest question about all this.

"My ancestor's instructions were very thorough," Monica said, pretty much stating that she somehow set all this up.

Though this does question just how much she knew, I had to review how dangerous I considered the girl before I got to work. She explained how to assemble the blade while I took the chance to examine it. The three blades were silver and iron, the two silvers formed the body while the single iron was the core and the tang, all of which had so many enchantments carved into the metals that it may be nearly unbreakable and unbending. The moment I fitted the pieces together, they glowed with a bright light and seemed to fuse into a single blade, the etchings glowing with magic before fading. Silver is the most effective against most monsters, but iron is more for the spirits and magical creatures. Pure cold iron tends to absorb and cancel the magical energy that those kinds of beings need to live.

"These are terrible metals for making any kind of blade," I said aloud after fusing the metals.

"Only in a world where magic doesn't exist," Monica agreed while everyone else began eating the cake. "It's a good thing magic does exist."

Next was the guard, which had the wheel and crystals as an attachment. The crystals fitted into each chamber of the wheel, meant to channel a different element through the blade: wind, fire, water, earth, and a small switch for what looked to runes that said "sanctify" and "corrupt." The guard itself seemed unimpressive aside from the "elemental wheel" as Monica called it. Supposedly, it's meant for anything that needs more than silver or iron to die...like the wendigo I was fighting earlier.

I really hope this knife works now, I thought to myself, but I also needed to wonder who her ancestor might have been and how this blade was supposed to help me "change the world." I moved on to the hilt, and my hands started shaking. It was an ancient dragon horn, pure white ivory with an incomplete magic formula carved into the body. This could amplify any spell on the blade and make it so much more dangerous to anything I'd use it against. But there seemed to be a piece of the assembly missing as well as another spell I was having trouble reading. I put the two pieces together on the tang, and I got my answer as the whole thing began to glow with heat.

"Dante!" everyone called out as I cried out in pain, the hilt turning searing hot in my hands, but I was unable to let go. I felt the spell seal get branded onto my hand until it finally began to cool and fall from my fingers and embed itself on the floor. They all came around me, concern in their eyes while Monica examined my hand.

"What the hell was that?" Kashi asked, everyone backing away from the blade. "What is going on?"

"It says here, 'Now that the pieces have been assembled, the binding link shall sear itself into the hand of the one to wield the blade,'" Zoe said, reading from the instructions that Monica discarded as she used healing magic on my already healing hand. "It just started to appear on this."

"What else does it say?" I asked, calmer now that the burning subsided.

"It says, 'This last enchantment serves to bond this blade and its master. When he reaches for it, he will go to the blade. When he pulls, the blade will go to him.'"

Monica and I shared a look, nodding. I got up, and she moved everyone out of the way, leaving a clear path to the knife. I raised my hand, closed it like I was grabbing the knife, and pulled. Instantly, I felt the weight of the blade in my hand; I didn't even see it move. Next, I handed it to Monica, who jumped out the window and floated down to the ground. Once she touched down, she turned and held the blade out while presenting the hilt. I reached out and grabbed again, once again getting the knife in my hand as I suddenly appeared in front of Monica.

"Let me look at that hilt again," she ordered, prompting me to hold it out for her. "Figured as much. That spell seal that allows this teleporting reflects intent. You want to go to it, you appear where it is, and vice versa. Magic instructions can be confusing sometimes." This was the most serious I've seen her—it was odd. "Anyway, *party time!*" she cheered before grabbing me and getting us back to my dorm. Good to have her back to normal. "Thanks for engaging in this selfish wish of mine, but let's give Dante his first real Christmas!" she ordered, earning a unanimous cheer.

The rest of the night was a party despite my protests and just wanting to go to bed—stories, laughter, some odd cooking competition among the group with some ingredients Monica managed to conjure up, a moose showed up, the whole thing became a kind of mess. Point is that everyone made the best of the situation before the summoning spell ended, and everyone went back to their families, except for Kashi, Lance, and myself. We made moose jerky.

The life of a Hunter tends to be one of solitude, but for once in my memory, I didn't feel alone.

CHAPTER 17

MATTERS OF THE HEART

JANUARY CAME AND went with nothing much happening: we hung out, went to our classes, it was peaceful, and... I kind of liked it. It was a nice change of pace, and I found myself opening up a bit more to the others. Zoe, Monica, and I practiced with the enchantments on my knife, throwing it and teleporting, which was to get rid of the sense of vertigo I was getting every time I did that. The enchanted crystals were as predicted: red, fire; blue, water; green, wind; brown, earth; and the switch below that wheel made it holy, normal, or corrupted. Holy was for demonic and spirit-type creatures while corrupted provided an extra kick against other monsters. But to use that magic, I needed to use the dragon horn amplifier to activate the latent spell within the crystals: fire heats up the blade, earth can petrify things, water has limited control of other liquids, and wind has something similar. I could find a lot of uses for this blade.

My time with the guys was for more physical activities: wrestling, sparring, other group exercises to better stamina and endurance. Kashi, in particular, pushed himself and gained another tail while trying to roast Max and myself during a run. We like to push ourselves, and it's more interesting if you have fireballs flying at your head. Hey, I had nothing to do but work out, train, and study. I may have enjoyed the peace, but I did get bored from time to time.

Soon the days gave way to February and with that came Valentine's Day. The month and day of love was apparently a big deal at the school as a whole, and groups have been going on field trips to only one location, a very important place for the holiday—Italy, where Saint Valentine lived his life. Yeah, the idea was to study the history of Valentine's Day as it is a big holiday in several countries and to the Christian religion. I think some of them know that Saint Valentine was never a romantic and only gave a letter signed "Your Valentine" before his execution. But it's also an excuse to get out into the world and properly try to integrate.

It was the week of Valentine's Day itself, and it was my turn with the rest of the group. I think Monica went behind our backs to organize this because I didn't think being all together like this was a smart move nor that it happened by chance. But the more the merrier and the easier it is for me to study their interactions with human society. I think my problem with it being my friends stems from the unwanted possibility that I might have to erase them if they get revealed. It's a dangerous game that's being played, one that I refused to let us lose.

We were following around a tour guide, going into detail about the saint and how the day of his death became the day of courtly love. I wasn't really paying much attention to him—I was more watching Lucrezia who was holding onto my hand and watching everything and everyone rather tensely. Normally, she'd be more close and flirty, whispering sweet nothings while burying my arm in her chest, but now she seemed scared. If I had to guess, it was because we were in Rome and she's a member of the demon race. I could see a few controlling themselves, "deal with the devil" types are more common than one would think, but being in one of the religious capitals of the world might be more than a little terrifying for a demon. Soon the tour ended, and while everyone else went to the gift shop, Lucrezia and I went to the Trevi Fountain near our hotel.

"Wait here, I'll get us some refreshments," I told her, sitting her on a bench while I went to a quaint little gelato shop we had passed on the way. I went with simple chocolate and vanilla and made my way back, thinking that not much could have happened in that time frame. Shouldn't be unreasonable, the students of this school are supposed to be learning how to blend in and not become targets. I should've remembered that anything can happen in any amount of time given the right circumstances because when I got back, Lucrezia was facing death.

She was frozen, a look of someone facing utter horror but unable to do anything against it painted her features, her body trembling in the demand to move but too paralyzed to actually do so and eyes locked on a single person who was slowly making his way toward her. Dressed like a priest with oil black hair and his bangs covering his patched right eye, hanging from his neck was a cross that looked like a pair of silver daggers. No Hunter did not know this man, a legendary sword master among the Order that made a habit of going after demons specifically. One day, drunk off his own arrogance, he summoned a demon prince and fought him. The battle took an eye from both of them—the demon clawed his out while he took the demon's own for himself. He let the healers restore most of his face, but he replaced his missing eye with the demon's. A constant reminder of his foolishness, though no one expected the other side effects.

He constantly sees a fog of sin and darkness among people and can tell the repentant from the cruel, the pure from vile, and demons for what they really are. On top of that, he stopped aging, and any demon he looks at with his demonic eye is paralyzed and helpless before him. He retired from the Order shortly after that because he was just as feared among the Hunters as among demons, becoming the personal shadow bodyguard to the pope himself. And now he is here, walking to Lucrezia, who is a succubus—I needed to hurry.

"Nex, stop him," I quickly ordered as I began power walking to Lucrezia, still frozen and staring at her would-be executioner. Nex slithered among the shadows of all the tourists until he finally reached the priest, just as I reached Lucrezia. He broke eye contact with Lucrezia, and I needed to bring her out of the trance. If we play this right, we can pretend this didn't happen. I reached her and gave her the chocolate gelato. "*Boop*," I said, pressing the frozen treat against her nose at the same time Nex distracted his target, making her jump in surprise. "Everything all right?"

"Dante…what? What was?" she asked, looking between me and the now-disappeared priest. "What…the…" I leaned in and licked the gelato off her nose, silencing her while also making her blush.

"Sorry, can't waste good gelato," I said with a smile before handing her the chocolate cone. "Everything all right? You look like you've seen a ghost and not like the banshees that like to be our alarm clocks."

"I… I thought I saw…" She was still shaken but steadily calming down. I wrapped an arm around her and pulled her to me in a warm embrace.

"You've been tense ever since we got into the city," I interrupted, rubbing her shoulder in soothing circles. "Listen, how about we get Monica to cover for us and we get to someplace else in this beautiful country? How about you put on that nice sundress you got and we head for Venice?" I suggested, feeling her relax more and more. "Go get ready, I'll make the arrangements."

She nodded gratefully and began eating her frozen treat.

"All right. But you might not be able to keep your hands off me when you see it." She teased as she began to head for the hotel, stopping to turn back to me with concern in her eyes. "Be careful, Dante," she said, fear creeping back into her voice. I just cracked a smile and laughed.

"Babe, I have nothing to fear here in Roma," I said with confidence, making her smile as she made her way to the hotel.

"Well, you certainly didn't lie." I heard a heavy voice speak from behind me. I turned to see the priest from earlier standing right behind me. Nex returned to my shadow, and he gestured for me to join him in front of the fountain. "I was wondering what this whole thing was about. So many different beings coming to the city and leaving every few days. I didn't do anything because they were behaving themselves, but I felt that familiar itch when I saw that demon," he explained before muttering in Italian, almost so quietly I didn't hear him. "*So a succubus this time?*"

"They're just trying to survive, Father Francesco," I said, starting to explain to him about the school and its purpose when he stopped me.

"I already know about that little academy, Phantom. I may be retired, but I'm not completely out of the loop," he returned. "I've been around for five centuries. I know important information when I hear it." Probably should've mentioned how old his story was during all that exposition earlier. "You weren't the first Phantom I've met."

I would say this was my chance to learn more about the previous Phantoms. Every time I hear anything about them, it was always about how they were ruthless and unstoppable, but my cover was more important and my other friends were coming by.

"Thank you for the advice, Father," I said with a smile as Max and the others walked up to me. Francesco seemed to understand what was happening and played along.

"Think nothing of it, my son. The Lord always watches over us," he returned with a warm smile as he walked away. "I'll still be watching you and the girl," he whispered before walking into the crowd. Monica came up to me the moment I locked eyes with her.

"Hey, Monica, I was wondering—" I started.

"Don't worry. I've got you covered. Just hurry over to Venice," she said, surprising me before she leaned in. "Gondola rides in the late evening are magical." She stuck her tongue out mischievously, leaving me dumbfounded. "Yes, I spied on you and her. Where's my gelato?" she demanded with a pout. I merely sighed and handed her a few euros.

"Here, just do your thing," I said before heading for the hotel to change myself.

I changed out of the school uniform into a red T-shirt with a black hoodie jacket and black jogging pants and came back to the fountain, finding Lucrezia in a black sundress that reached her ankles with a swirling pattern of stars wrapping around her form. She was as stunning as could be expected from a demon of lust—absolutely.

"Well, shall we get going?" she asked, soaking in all the stares from all the people around her while I quickly made my way over and wrapped an arm around her.

The walk to the train station and subsequent ride was a peaceful one. No fights, no terrors. Francesco was watching us but only I knew that, and then we were in beautiful Venice. The salty sea air, along with some other scents, danced throughout the city, playing with my nose as the various people made and ate their meals in the evening hours. The setting sun lit the waters on fire as Lucrezia and I made our way to a little boat rental shop where we could take a gondola and tour the city. Lucky us, I was able to secure a private ride for the two of us and convinced the guy I could handle the boat on my own. I may have used a spell to do that.

"Told you I had it handled," I said after getting us out of the canals and out into the sea, a number of scuffs on the boat with Lucrezia glaring at me. "I wanted us to get the best view," I defended as I set the oar down and jumped into the cabin with her, spinning her into my arms so that we could both look out to the setting sun. The sea was set ablaze in the amber light, turning the waters into liquid flames as we rocked to the tide.

"You're lucky this is a gorgeous sight," she said, smiling before leaning into me. "This mostly makes up for the dozen boat collisions."

"It was only six," I returned, getting a giggle from her.

"But I have a good idea of how you can finish making it up to me," she turned and tried to kiss me, but before she could, I avoided and planted my own at the edge of her mouth. More on her cheek than her lips and dodging it yet again...for the hundredth time. I counted.

"Err...too slow?" I said, trying to play it off as a joke. A succubus kiss has always been dangerous, either enslaving men or draining their lives, and I would never allow that to happen. I guess it didn't work as I hoped because she wasn't laughing. She was shaking, but it was definitely not from laughter.

"Dante...what do you think I am?" she asked, her voice laced with sadness and anger. "When you look at me, what do you see?" she demanded, looking up to me with rage and tears in eyes. "I know *what* I am, but do you actually see me for *who* I am? Are you even trying to look beyond my race?" she screamed, looking for an answer.

I knew what I *should* have said anything other than the words that spilled out of my mouth—words that were the result of years of knowing the dangers of every creature and how to avoid it.

"You are a succubus," I hated saying that, that I couldn't stop the words from being spoken.

The look of heartbreak was one of the worst things I have ever seen. Piles of corpses of my allies, innocent people killed by some hungry or twisted being, people and animals being eaten alive, all that I've learned to stomach. This was something I've never wanted to see and would beg to have it erased from my memory and history. She didn't say anything, just sprouted her wings and flew off, leaving me alone on that boat as it rocked against the waves. I don't remember how long I stood there, watching as she shrank in the distance before disappearing from my sight altogether. The darkness of night fell over the world, the city lights fighting against the sunless sky before I finally decided to row back to the city. Just as he promised, Francesco was waiting on the walkway.

"Would you like some couple's counseling, my son?" he asked as he hopped into the cabin while I rowed.

"Bite me, Father," I returned as I kept rowing, aiming to return the boat back to the gondola rental.

My comment seemed to only amuse him as he let out a low chuckle, leaning back to enjoy the ride.

"Out of all your brothers, you are most certainly the odd one," he said, likely knowing that he was baiting me.

"How so?" I may not be in the mood to talk exactly, but I still wasn't one to give up on useful information, and I've been wanting a chance to get more of the history of the Phantoms and the Order itself.

"Well, you're the only one that seems afraid of his significant other, for starters," he said, replacing much of my irritation with surprise. "Not so much you hooking up with a succubus, which is the least interesting part, but that you seem to fear her." Now he had my full attention as we grew closer to the rental shop, where I can get rid of the boat. "None of the others ever seemed affected by their respective lovers. Every Phantom I've met never had a human lover. A Yuki-Onna, an Incruentatus, one time had an elf that was made into a vampire, and now a succubus. I guess it was only a matter of time for that one but never a human."

"And they never died as a result?" I asked, completely shocked since the first would freeze men solid while the others drained life away in one way or another. Francesco merely looked at me like I was crazy.

"No. They were never affected," he answered, talking like he wasn't sure he was even sure who he was talking to. "Your brothers were always immune to those effects." Why does he keep calling them my brothers? Predecessors make sense, they came before me, but brothers? He didn't even make it sound like they were just members of the Order but that they were my blood family. "Why don't you know this? What do you actually know?"

"I just know they were the best of the best."

He looked at me with disbelief, slowly building to a rage. Before he could continue, I felt my phone go off. I looked to the caller ID, reading Lucrezia's name, and decided to answer. I hoped I could make things better before I lost the chance forever because I did feel something for Lucrezia—something I wasn't sure I wanted to admit to. "Yeah, Lucrezia?" I started, hoping for good news. That didn't happen, and I wonder why I ever hoped for it.

"*Not her, but thanks for answering,*" a deeper, unmistakably masculine voice responded and putting me on edge. Not for me but for Lucrezia. "*We know what she is and what you are, demon,*" he said with a mild amount of scorn. So these are people that know a bit of what the Hunters are trying to hide but maybe not about the Hunters themselves. Wouldn't have been the first time some idiot got their hands on something magical and thought they were hot stuff for it. "*How about we make a deal? I know this is a bit underhanded on our part, but none of us here were willing to part with our souls simply for a hit.*" Classic demonic deals, a favor for a soul. Sometimes it's something else the demon contractor would want, like one's lover in this case.

"So what do you want me to do?" I asked, getting a text from Monica. The message said, "Sicily, Palermo." That witch is on the ball, and I am going to have to talk with her later. "*They must be causing you a lot of trouble if you're willing to go this far.*"

"Some in over their head fools that call themselves Hunters poking their noses where they don't belong." I can actually taste the irony. *"You take care of these guys, and we'll release this lovely succubus back to you. If you don't, I'm sure we'll make a fortune off her,"* he said, and I could feel him smiling, something I couldn't wait to undo.

"Just sit tight. This will be over soon, maybe a day or two," I answered before hanging up.

Standard protocol for normal humans learning the truth is to wipe their memories and remove any and all things that weren't meant for them. Protocol for them making enemies of the Hunters is much the same. Protocol for pissing me off is their death…but they were still humans. The Hunters make it our mission to protect mankind—am I going to turn my back on that for a succubus?

"Phantom!" Francesco called out. I turned to him, watching as words formed and failed as he seemed to want to tell me something but was unable to do so. "There is so much that you do not know, so much that I should be telling you, but I can't right now! What I can say is that Phantoms are immune to any poison, curse, or any other ailment that would slay any mortal. They are protectors of the innocent, and most importantly, wherever a Phantom goes, death follows. Go to your enemies, slay them, save the innocent, and remember who and what you are!" he said before running off, almost as if he were chasing something.

What he said was what I needed to hear. The Order was formed to protect people from the monsters in the shadows and the wild. But I would be foolish to ignore that there were humans as foul as any demon—history has shown plenty of them.

"Thank you, Father," I muttered as I ran to the road. I needed to do what I felt I needed to do—save an innocent. Save Lucrezia. Save my girlfriend.

CHAPTER 18

SAFETY TO SANCTUARY

I WANT TO say I got there very quickly, say that I showed up by the dawn of the next day and heroically saved the damsel. Look, I get that magic exists, and there are plenty of ways I could get there instantly, but this is reality and here's the issue with that. One, magic is like a scientific application, and it has rules, such as having been to a location first and using the right materials for the spell catalyst, which takes time to set up. Two, magic has never been my forte anyway. In the end, it took me fifteen hours to get to my destination. Ten and a half hours by three different trains, twenty minutes by ferry to the island, and the rest by a Vespa scooter—it was pink, and I don't do pink.

In other news, I noticed that, despite the fifteen-hour journey, I wasn't tired, thirsty, or hungry. It couldn't be adrenaline since that would've been drained from me a while ago, nor did I feel any adrenaline in my system. If I had to guess what it was, I'd have to say it was linked to whatever experiments were done to me. I already regenerate from most any injury, who's to say that they made sleep and nourishment a lesser issue as well. I'm gonna have to wait till later to fully research what changes were done and then decide if I wanted revenge or not. If it was more beneficial than mentally scarring, I'd probably thank the guy, but for now, it helped me focus on the task at hand.

I had my mask on to try to find any trace of Lucrezia or the kind of magical energy these wannabe spellcasters would leave hanging around. Lucky for me, magical residue hangs around for a while, especially when they are novices at hiding that kind of energy. I found the trail and followed it to the seedier parts of the city, right to a building that had certainly seen better days. I got a few stares on the trip, but nothing too unusual for a city—or was that only New York? Anyway, I reached a back alley that led to the building in question, a couple broken lights, and boarded windows with a single man standing guard.

Many thoughts were going through my head: how many inside, are there any innocent people in there, what are the odds against me, how was I going to do this? While I was thinking this, my body was moving on its own. I dismounted the Vespa, which Nex ate (literally ate, I heard the groans and creaks of the metal as it was torn apart), and made my way to the apartment building. I flexed and clenched my hand, feeling a familiar weight suddenly appear in it. I closed in to the building, and when the guy noticed me, no words were spoken as I threw my bowie knife at him. The hilt smacked against his head, and I was soon holding the blade again, teleporting to it. I took hold of my enchanted blade and spartan kicked him through the door, breaking it open and making my way inside.

Needless to say, I could and should have been quieter since that was a very loud smash. I also should have found another way inside since there were two guys in the hallway, staring right at me. I threw my knife again, passing between them while they reached for their guns and teleported behind them. All my training clicked as I subconsciously went to lethal measures, quickly stabbing the two while their backs were turned and cutting their necks to ensure they died. It was quick, and I moved in a flash—stab one, twist and stab the other, return to the first and slice at the neck, twist and stab in the throat of the other. It was terrifyingly easy to get to that mindset against other humans, but as Francesco said, "Where I go, death follows." Not that I wasn't going to reexamine this later, but for now, it was an asset.

I heard footsteps coming, descending from a staircase and heading my way. I found no easy hiding space, so I did the next best thing and grabbed one of the mobster's guns. A standard Glock, pretty well-maintained, I just needed to click the safety off, and five mobsters reached me around the same time. We took aim at each other and started shooting; I got off three shots, disabling two and killing one, while the others released a hail of bullets at me. The guys in front that I shot needed to be moved aside so the guys behind could have a clear aim at me, giving me precious few seconds to grab one of the downed guys from earlier and use him as a shield. With that, I charged forward while the corpse absorbed the bullets. I only got a couple grazes and a maybe one in my thigh.

I reached the people still shooting at me and got to work, slashing with my knife, pistol whipping and shooting until they were all dead, once again, giving me some time to prepare. I looked through the new set of dead bodies for anything useful, and lucky me, I did. Two guys had Spectre SMGs, one had a SPAS-12 shotgun, and the rest had pistols, so I was able to reload. Just then, four guys came in from where I entered and shot me in the back. I bit back the screams from the pain and braced myself to keep from falling while assessing the damage. Small arms fire, pierced my lungs and scratched my heart, but I could feel my body repairing the damage already. It feels like that needling and ants crawling under your skin feeling after your arms or legs fall asleep, except in my chest. I turned to glare at my attackers, two charging at me with knives while the other had a crowbar, and watched as Nex quickly decimated them before I could do much.

The moment they got within a few feet of me, spikes of bone and shadow erupted from the floor and impaled them all. From what I saw of the last guy, he was scared senseless and was about to run before he began to sink into the floor. His screams of terror and agony were quickly silenced as he was absorbed into the darkness, the monster in my shadow feasting on his meal of corpses. Times like this were a healthy reminder of how terrifying Nex was. I was done healing shortly after that, the bullets falling down my back as they were ejected from my being. I loaded up with my pilfered gear and proceeded deeper into the building. The traces of dark magics were oozing from the upper floors, resembling sealing spells signatures and demonic energy, which made me wonder what they were doing.

My run through the building was pretty much the same for the next the floor as it was the first one: I enter, get attacked, fight back, leave dead bodies in my wake, and proceed. Just very quick, very brief shoot-outs, a simple matter of firing first and firing fast, well, until I got to the last room, second floor of the apartment anyway. It was locked, sealed shut with an interesting array of sealing spells. Anything faster than ten feet per second would be repelled along with other spells, meaning I couldn't break it down, and the lock seems to need a very specific key to open it. Whatever is beyond this door was something valuable, and I couldn't get in. It would probably be ineffective, but some idiot part of me wanted to try anyway. I grabbed the door handle and pulled, pulled with all my strength, and got nowhere.

"Damn it!" I growled, again trying to pry the door open. Suddenly, my skull throbbed, and pain erupted throughout my entire body. I clenched my eyes in some vain attempt to squeeze out the pain that was afflicting me. But when I opened my eyes, something had changed. The door that was in my way was crumbling and falling apart to fine metal dust. I looked to my hand and saw a black color fading in my veins. *What was that?* I thought in confusion. That wasn't any sort of magic I was familiar with. I didn't even recognize it as *any* sort of spell or magic. I didn't know if I could repeat it. I don't even know what it is. But whatever it is, it would have to wait for later. I went into the room, and I hated what I saw.

There were five beautiful women in five beds, bound and gagged, eyes glazed over like they were in a trance with binding seals on the floor. I didn't need to think about it too much to understand what was going on here—the question is, Why? Not why do this, but why are they all succubae? I scanned them, and they were all succubae. The question is, Why trap them? Why make them prisoners? They feed off life energy through sex, so why do this? The only thing that was different out of any of them was one wearing a bracelet with a very prominent S. She also seemed the closest to snapping out of her trance. So I went over to her bed, pulled out my knife, and set its magic to "blessed water" and, with a single swipe, washed away the dark magic with moisture from the air.

"Huaaah!" she gasped as if a weight was removed from her chest. "Hunter! Please, help us!" she begged, surprising me. "We've been like this for a month. These warlock mafioso wannabes kidnapped us from Sanctuary." Sanctuary? This is the first I've ever heard of this. "I was trying to show my friends to it when they captured us. Please, save us!" she pleaded, once again forcing me to question what I knew…later. For now, things seem pretty clear—bad people doing bad things with innocents in trouble. Time to do what I do best. I cut her free and left the room, following the final trace of black magic energy. A room on the third floor with a completely unguarded door. I opened the door, found some guys in black robes, one holding a ragged leather-bound book and was sealed inside a circular barrier. I was starting to get annoyed by how often I walk into traps.

"You must be the guy I talked to on the phone," the guy I suspected to be the leader said in a forced suave tone, coming into the room in a black suit with a white dress shirt and red tie. This guy was so clichéd I felt sorry for Italians everywhere, and then he starting undoing his cufflink and took off his coat. "I do admit, this whole thing seemed really crazy when I found that book. But *wow* did it get results! All the drugs, guns, women, and money a guy could hope for with just a few well-placed enchantments. Then I found out what else was really there, and if half the rumors of those demons were true, I'd make a mint off that alone."

"Are you really doing this?" I asked, not wanting to be subject to this particular cliché. "I get it already. You got some power, got a little drunk on it, got cocky, and now you've gotten on the bad side of folks that know a *lot* more about the stuff than you." I released an ear-piercing whistle, and a wave of darkness crept from my feet to envelope the entire room. "And there's a lot more terrifying things than you could ever imagine." The entire room had this fanged grin, going from wall to wall, and in an instant, the people were gone. No magic teleporting, no screams, they were just gone—devoured by a being of pure darkness that knows nothing of mercy, bound to the one that bears the title of Phantom. As the darkness receded away, there was a lingering trace on the door that the guy from earlier walked out of.

Thinking that my goal was beyond that door, and with the magic dispelled because the caster was dead, I headed straight for it. Same security, but this time, I had the key...after Nex gave it to me. I unlocked the door, and there she was. Her black sundress was ripped in places, and her skin was covered in purifying burns. They look like nasty sunburns but are smoking, a natural reaction when demons are in contact with anything consecrated, and the term was coined when a Hunter quite literally tortured a man possessed by a demon to exorcise and get information about a few deals the demon made. It wasn't nice, but from what I heard, it was necessary—children were in trouble. The thought of Lucrezia being tortured in the same manner made me wish Nex took his time devouring that man.

"Lucrezia!" I called out, putting away my mask. "Lucrezia, wake up!" I was by her side in an instant, cutting her free and cradling her in my arms. She showed some reaction, slowly waking up but sounding very tired and in much pain.

"Dan...te?" she asked as her eyes slowly opened. "It hurts...," she groaned, wincing in pain as the burns seemed very recent. My mind raced to think of something when I remembered what Francesco had said. I was immune to most anything that would kill a normal man, time to put that to the test. I planted my lips on hers and waited. Within seconds, I felt something being drained from my body, and her tongue tangling itself around my own as she grabbed onto me. Slowly but surely, she was recovering from the torture she went through. When she finally released me from her lip-lock, she looked to me with tears in her eyes. "You came for me."

"I needed to apologize," I told her, picking her and carrying her away. I didn't think she was in any condition to walk around on her own, and frankly, I didn't want to let her out of my sight. Not again, not so soon. "Look, I know this doesn't really excuse my actions, but I've never before had any good experiences with demon-kind." I wasn't lying, but she wasn't supposed to know the truth. "I promised myself that I wouldn't let my former experiences decide my actions."

If I did, I would've killed everyone in that school. "Guess I did a bad job of that, didn't I?" She rested her head against my shoulder.

"You should have told me," she returned, struggling through how tired she was to try to offer me some comfort. "Promise me you'll be more open with me from now on, and I'll respect your privacy," she said before closing her eyes again, this time, I was inclined to let her sleep. That was until I saw people outside the building, people that were wearing the Hunter's emblem and talking with that succubus that asked me for help.

"Oh crap," I said, panicking at the situation. Hunters were here, dead humans were here, succubae were here, I didn't think I would be able to escape without Lucrezia surviving this. My mind raced for answers, any answer, so much so that I never noticed that someone was in the room.

"Are you done?" he asked, finally drawing my attention to him. "'Cause we really need to get rid of all the evidence here, and you should probably get out while you can." He had tan slacks, a white wife beater, a pink button-up shirt, and a neatly trimmed mustache and short black hair. He then gestured to me to follow him, and after looking out the window again, I only grew more confused. The succubae from earlier were receiving medical checkups and treatment, from Hunters? I needed to learn more, so I followed the Hunter.

"So...what's happening?" I asked, clearly showing how lost I was on all this.

To the guy's credit, it seemed like he expected this.

"You're not from around here, so I shouldn't be surprised," he said as I followed him out of the building, mostly in silence like he was trying to figure out exactly how to explain it. "See, some fifty odd years ago, one of the demon-kind was found by a nun in the Order that was gifted in healing magics. The demon himself was badly injured and the sister nursed him back to health despite knowing what he was. When he recovered, he demanded to know why. Her response? 'The teachings of the word is that of love, love of all the Lord's creations. If I hated you solely because you are a demon, I would fail my faith.' She healed his body, then she healed his soul, and he surrendered to the Order shortly after. But the sister refused to let him be executed and gambled on the chance to save others. Thus, the two of them created a project called 'Sanctuary,' a volunteer program where Hunters of the Order try to give demon-kind a second chance." My eyes widened in surprise, surprise that this actually existed and I never knew about it.

"So why do so few know about it?" Lucrezia asked, apparently waking up sometime during the explanation. "If something like that really exists, why doesn't everyone know about it?"

"Security," he answered as we got out of the building, the cleaners going in now, and the less you know about what they do, the better. "Not everyone really seeks redemption, nor do many think some deserve it. So word of Sanctuary is only spread by word of mouth and very rarely at that. The requirements for anyone to learn about it are very strict so as to avoid risks to the project." We reached a van that resembled an ambulance on the inside, only going inside when Lucrezia gave the okay. I think she wanted to know more about Sanctuary like I did. That, and it was very unlikely that we could find a way out of this situation. "That's why it took us so long to get around to 'taking care' of this particular matter. Needed to find any leaks and threats and remove them. For a nobody thug, he had a lot of contacts."

"So is it over?" I asked, letting Lucrezia sit in the van, though she refused treatment.

"Almost," he answered before signaling the driver. The driver began chanting in Latin before driving off, faster and faster, toward a wall. Instead of smashing against the brick and stone, we sank into it before appearing in front of a monastery. "Now it is," he said with a smile as everyone got out of the vehicles. Lucrezia and I were the last, and I was awestruck. From the looks of it, we were on a floating island in the clouds with its own farm and garden, completely free from the influence of the outside world.

"Good lord," I softly spoke, taking in the sight. The amount of magic needed to make this whole place possible was staggering, and that wasn't the only surprise. Dozens of different demons were wandering about, farming, gardening, interacting fearlessly with the Hunters. So many questions were going through my mind at the moment. Was I dreaming? How many people know about this? If the higher-ups knew about Sanctuary, then why am I bothering with the school? The guy was still talking, going on about the hope that Sanctuary represented and what it could mean to making peace when I started feeling ill.

"Ugh…my head…," Lucrezia groaned, turning my attention to her. She was turning transparent as if she were fading away. I looked to myself and saw much of the same.

"Forced summoning?" the guy said in surprise. "Who found this place?" Everything else was drowned out as a bright flash of light shone and we fell to the floor. When I opened my eyes, we were back at the dorms with everyone else crowding around us.

"Dante! Lucrezia! Are you okay?" Kashi asked as Lance and Max helped me up while Saya and Zoe did the same to Lucrezia. "Monica said that there was a kidnapping and you had to save her. What happened?"

I looked to him and said very calmly, "I'll tell you when I stop throwing up."

And then I started puking, a side effect of long-distance summoning like what Monica used. Instant rapid displacement plays hell with your body.

CHAPTER 19

HEAT IN THE AIR

I WAS IN pretty hot water, and my usual "kill them all" instincts would be the absolute worst thing to listen to in this situation. We're in the school, it's known that I hang out with these people, I'm supposed to be spying on this place, and I also...didn't want to kill them. I'm so used to either sealing away or killing any monster or danger that not wanting to do so was a new feeling. It confuses me, and I don't like that.

Anyway, back to the problem; now that the excitement of our reunion is over and everyone was safe, they wanted answers. Specifically, they wanted answers on what happened to Lucrezia, how I managed to save her, and how we seemed to disappear from Monica's scrying magic. It was going to be hard to keep my cover, but they have seen Nex in action, so I could use that to my advantage. The biggest risk at the moment was whether Lucrezia could keep the secret. I don't think anyone *but* Saya would believe that the Hunters helped us, and Lucrezia still seems to think it didn't actually happen.

"Well, here's what happened," I said, taking hold of her hand and praying that she'd let me do the talking and that Nex would listen. "Lucrezia and I had a fight, which resulted in her running off. Apparently, when she was tired and drained from flying away, she was captured by a bunch of warlock wannabes." She leaned in closer to me—I think seeking a sense of safety and security from my presence.

Now I wish I had those guys suffer even more than Nex eating them, unless he swallowed them whole, in which case, I feel sorry for them. "With Monica's knife and…my shadow familiar"—*Nex, help me out here*—"I infiltrated their hideout"—shadows converged around me, and I felt my body shift to a new location, appearing behind the group—"and managed to rescue Lucrezia." She immediately latched back onto me, cutely pouting at me for the transgression of disappearing so suddenly. I looked back to the group, and it looked like they were on the fence about my explanation, like they were trying to figure out if there were any other details that I may have been hiding.

"That does explain a lot actually," Monica suddenly said, gaining everyone's attention. "Traveling around by that shadow of his wouldn't be tracked by normal scrying magic. He must have gone pretty far from that building for me to lose him so easily." It was probably because Monica is the expert in spellcraft, but the others accepted her words and my explanation held. They left Lucrezia and myself alone after that, though I could've sworn I saw a smirk on Monica's face as she left the room.

"Dante? Why didn't you tell them about the Hunters or Sanctuary?" Lucrezia asked me in a hushed tone. "Saya could've backed you up as an Incruentatus. The Hunters might not be as bad as we thought," she argued, something I kind of wanted to give her, but I understand people, even if those people aren't necessarily humans.

"Because one case of rescuing their friends might not be enough to convince them!" I snapped, making her jump. "This is over two thousand years of fear and hate, all targeted at anything that threatened humanity. This is the group that forced them into hiding in the first place. No matter how much evidence to the contrary, they'll still see an army of oppressors and murderers." How much blood did I have on my hands, a question I never thought that I would ask myself. "And if the wrong people hear this information, who knows what might happen. There might end up being terrorist cells, specifically trying to create war, and all their efforts would be for nothing. We need to keep quiet, hope for the best. That's all we can do at the moment." I can't let my secret slip. I'm not sure I understand anything either. Before I can reveal myself as a Hunter, the Phantom, I need to understand what is happening in the Order.

We agreed to keep silent about the Hunters, but my position was getting more and more precarious. This has been the longest I've ever stayed in one particular location, the longest mission I've ever had, I still didn't get any change in orders other than "observe and report." I'm not used to being compromised or even being undercover, and I'm risking the success of this school and any project like Sanctuary the longer I stay here. Lucrezia stopped my train of thought on that by kissing me on the lips, and from there, it escalated. It was mostly the "we're safe, glad to be alive" high that led to a heavy make out session. Nothing beyond that, but she was fine with that. Compared to before, this was a huge amount of progress. We ended up sleeping together, *just sleeping*, much to Lucrezia's chagrin, tired and didn't want to leave each other after almost all of yesterday, and I needed a way back to my dorm room. Monica had me meet up with her on the roof with promises of getting to there without arousing suspicion.

"Ready, Dante?" she asked, drawing a magic circle on the ground.

"Yeah, thanks for doing this, Monica," I said, heading for the circle.

I needed some time alone to think—that's when she said this.

"No problem, Phantom."

It took me a couple of seconds to realize what she said, my eyes widening in shock, looking at her smirking face. Out of reflex, I threw my knife to her and teleported to it, holding the blade under her throat and grabbing her hair with my other hand. Never once did that smirk leave her face, a smirk that said that she wasn't afraid of anything. She's staring death in the face, and she's not budging.

"How long?" I growled, pressing the edge against her throat hard enough to cause bleeding, and she giggled.

"Since before you came here," she said, tapping me on the nose. "Everyone else told you I was doing divination, right? I already saw all this. Sure, I died in a couple hundred of those futures for telling you too early, but eventually, this would happen." She leaned her head forward, and I moved the blade back with her. "You don't want to kill me. Even though I know your secret and you know you should for security reasons, you won't because you don't want to kill your friend. Any of your friends." I can hear my brain yell at my body, ordering it to prove her wrong, but I couldn't. My hand refused to move.

"What are you after?" I finally asked, never moving my knife.

She continued to smile, showing her pearly whites. "I just want the most interesting outcome, Dante," she said, moving the knife away from her throat as she got closer to me. "And in this case, the most interesting happens to be the best outcome. An outcome that you are instrumental to making a reality. To that end, I am and will always be on your side, which is why I've set up a little something to make everyone forget about this little incident about Lucrezia's kidnapping."

"And what would that be?" I asked, sheathing my knife.

Immediately, Monica dropped any sense of seriousness and actually managed to glow with tiny lights appearing around her.

"Puppy love!" she cheered with a smile, apparently not giving up on making Max and Andrea a couple. I just waited for her to explain what scheme she had cooking in that brain of hers this time. "As you know, lycans have a mating season of their own. And it starts today!" she said with a smile.

"That's your plan?" I asked the psycho witch. "Monica, everyone knows there is a barrier seal around the entire area of the school, specifically to prevent that from happening with the beast-type monsters. It would take a master of spellcraft to undo it, not that anyone would be crazy enough to let a massive pack of hormone-driven lycans go on a mating spree since that would be a rather vicious riot," I said, Monica still smiling. "And you did precisely that, didn't you?" She nodded. "Helping me out was just a bonus and not your real intention, wasn't it?" She just smiled wider. My response was to punch her directly on the top of her head before running off. "We seriously need to talk about you controlling your impulses, you crazy witch!" I yelled, jumping off the side of the building.

Okay, how bad can this possibly be? I thought to myself, instantly regretting it as a pair of furry bodies crashed through a window in the second story. All I could see was gray-and-brown fur as the two wrestled, snarling and clawing and biting at each other in a battle for dominance. "Why did I ask that?" I asked myself as I quickly questioned and debated whether or not I should get involved in this fight. That was answered for me when the gray one bit onto the throat of the brown one, and my body just reacted by my tackling the pair.

The force of the hit pushed them onto their side, and I began to pry them apart, punching the gray one in the neck to separate them and slip in between to push them away from each other. They didn't like someone getting in the middle of their fight, and the brown one slashed at me with her claws. By the way, I just found out they were female lycans. Fur-covered boobs are still boobs; that's a very distinct feel, and I think I know who the gray one is. After the brown one tore a few gashes in my side, and I fought through the pain, I took my knife and jammed it into her forearm. The silver and getting impaled had the effect on her I wanted as she fled from me as fast as she could.

There's that done, I thought as the gray one kept trying to get around me to her now-fleeing opponent. "Now for you!" I growled, grabbing her and throwing her over my shoulder before punching her face. "Andrea, if that's you, either turn back, or I'll beat the sense back into you!" I roared, and she caught my fist before morphing back to human, naked. Guess her tube top was not as elastic as I thought. "Monica deactivated the seal that keeps you guys from going into heat, so what is going on?"

She didn't stop glaring at me, but she did answer. "We're still wolves, Dante," she explained. "Say what you want about us being more human than wolf, instinct doesn't just go away. We all want the strongest and most fit mate, so we need to establish dominance."

"And that one was eyeing your man?" I asked, looking back to where the brown lycan retreated.

"She can't. There's no alpha male or female among us," she answered, and that explained the fighting.

The school's lycans are becoming a pack, and they have no alphas, and only the alphas pair up for mating. Monica would know this—meaning, she believes that Max and Andrea are the future alphas.

"Don't you and Max fight all the time?" I asked, and she just smiled while licking her lips.

"He'll never back down, and that turns me on," she said, and I needed to get away from her.

No other reason than I felt the need to just *get away*.

"Okay! Leaving!" I said, letting go and walking away as she turned back to her lycan form. "Just promise you won't kill anyone." She let out a howl of challenge and charged off. "Why did I get involved?" I asked as a dozen other howls and growls and snarls and crashes sounded off as all the lycans in the student body began fighting for dominance. "Oh yeah...that's why." Needed to stop anyone from getting killed over this.

I ran around the school grounds, stopping fights that were clearly over, as the wolves fought each other for supremacy. I wasn't the only one as I saw various members of the school safety committee attempting much the same. I almost forgot those guys existed. "Attempting" was probably a bit too generous since they were apparently disorganized and only carting off the losers to the infirmary. Speaking of public safety, the statue sentries haven't appeared either.

"All right, what's the damage?" I demanded, grabbing one of the committee members as she ran past me.

"Dante, if you must know, the golems have no magical energy powering them. *Every* lycan is in heat and fighting, and Volk, our chief, is gone," she said, trying to stress how serious this was.

"What the hell is he possibly doing!?"

"He's a lycan, so he's probably fighting to become the alpha," she returned—this was just a bad day, and I'm going to make sure Monica gets punished for it.

"Fine, I'll take charge," I told her. "It's not much, but keep doing what you guys are doing. I'll figure something out." She ran off to follow my order. "Now how the hell am I going to do this?" I asked myself 'cause I had no idea and just made a promise I was 85 percent sure I couldn't back up. What to do, what to do, asking myself that over and over and praying that I'll get an answer out of the ether. "Okay, Dante, think. They're seeking out fights to establish dominance. How to stop this is to establish an alpha. How to gather them together?" I wondered, hearing all the howls crying through the air. I'm an idiot. I ran into the forest, finding a pretty nice clearing. Perfect for a showdown.

"*Aroo!*" I howled myself, cupping my hands over my mouth. I howled again and again, trying to make it seem as aggressive, as challenging as I possibly could. Very soon, I heard the thunderous stampede of what had to be hundreds of lycans. "Let's give them something to listen to, Nex," I said, soon seeing the shadows rise from the corner of my eyes as the lycans came to me. The wolves came to the clearing and froze at the edge. Whatever form Nex took, it did the trick. "Now listen up, all of you!" I demanded, making many cower before me. "I'm not going to tolerate all of you fighting like rabid animals until two of you finally claim alpha status, so I'm doing this now. *Anyone too scared to get near me is disqualified!*" I shouted, a clawed hand slamming down next to me as an unearthly screech rang out from above. The result had many of them retreat by a few feet. Only three came forward, Andrea, Max, and...russet-colored one that I didn't recognize.

"Thank you for making this simple," he growled in a Russian accent, so it was Volk Gulski. Haven't seen that guy in so long. "But I will not back down. Keeping this school safe is among my duties, and as alpha, I will—"

He was backhanded and tackled by Max.

"This isn't a debate or a vote, Gulski," I said as the two got back to biting and clawing at each other. "This is survival of the fittest." And that's pretty much what happened—they clawed, bit, bashed at each other, Andrea waiting until the victor was decided. Volk was tossed aside, struggling to get back up, and Max ended it with a hard blow to his head. Volk stayed down, and the new Alpha howled loudly to declare his supremacy, followed soon by every other lycan in the field. Andrea then grabbed Max and bit down on his neck, him doing the same to her when she let go. Neither howled in pain, so I assumed they had "marked" each other before nuzzling affectionately. Ah, the beauty of na—

"Nex, stop them!" I quickly ordered when Andrea started releasing certain pheromones that every male lycan was reacting to. My familiar slammed a clawed hand down on both of them, knocking sense back into them, but *man*, did they look mad at me. "We're out in public and surrounded by other lycans that lost mating rights. Have some decency."

The pair began to turn back into human form, only to be smashed by Nex again.

"No changing. You're all still naked. Back to the dorms and get dressed," I ordered, hearing a bunch of whines as the pack retreated back to the school. "Why did I ever think my school life was easy?"

CHAPTER 20

AFTERMATH OF VALENTINE

SO YEAH, THAT was essentially how my February went this year. Started completely average with a school trip to Italy, went farther with my girlfriend than I ever thought I would, learned that the Order and Phantoms have been trying more things than just killing and sealing away monsters, let the lycans pair up and tamed pretty much all of them, and found out that Monica knows more than she ever let on. The results are my continuing confusion with my own faction, upgrading my relationship to making out with my succubus girlfriend, the safety committee hounding me to join them after the "Lycan Alpha Riot," and the need to demand answers from Monica. Well, it was time to start a new day, and I will be confronting Monica with Saya there to help out. I just needed to deal with this latest nuisance of my mornings.

"Ugh, why does the morning always seem to suck?" I asked upon opening my eyes, my body feeling like it had a weight pressing down on the whole of my being. As time ticked away and I woke up more, I tossed my covers off and crawled out of bed. My eyes drifted to my dorm mate—mates now, actually. Because they became a mated pair, they've been sticking close together and even got permission to stay together in the same dorm room. Since this was a first for the school, they weren't exactly prepared for the situation. And since I was also technically the true "alpha" of the lycans, I kept them from crossing a certain line. To say Andrea was upset with me is an understatement.

"Wake up!" I called out, kicking the mattress hard enough to shake it and waking up the pair. The nude pair—I hate lycan sleeping habits. Andrea growled at me, like she's done for the past five days. The damage done to the school, and the bureaucracy of school administration, kept the pair from getting their own room for quite some time. So I had to deal with the two of them together—the only solace here is that Max was on my side since they don't want me to bring out Nex again. "Growl all you want! No hanky-panky until you get your own room. And even then, I want it to be safe."

"I'm not going to stop being mad," she warned.

I just waved it off and went to the kitchen to chug a protein shake. After getting my breakfast and getting dressed, it was time for the next part of my day. Every day, I was asked to join by a different member of the safety committee, always at the entrance to the dorm, like clockwork. I reached the door, and there was a member with dark skin and bleach blond hair. Just another grunt and they all started to look and sound alike because I just stopped caring to listen.

"Dante, we'd like to—" he started.

"No," I very quickly said while letting Nex suck me into his shadow.

It got me away from those nuisances. I'm starting to think I should exclusively travel this way while at school, and soon I was spat back out in the same forest clearing where Max and Andrea became a couple, where Saya and Monica were waiting.

"SSC?" Saya asked, using the acronym of the group to save us all time. I nodded, and she let out an exasperated sigh. "I'm starting to think you should join them, and they'll finally shut up."

"But he won't," Monica sang while…dancing for some odd reason, "because he wants to keep his precious little secret, knowing the kind of damage that will happen if it leaks." She just kept swaying and twirling to an unheard melody, as if hearing the song of nature. "He's just going to keep on with his secret until he finds the answer."

"And do you know the answer I'm looking for?" I asked, partially hoping that the magical little mischief maker had it.

"That would be spoiling," she admonished with a smile. "So I didn't look for that. I simply saw the end result." She started waving her hands as if conducting a symphony. "You can know the beginning and you can know the ending. But in the end, the most fun is in getting there." Lights started appearing in front of her, dancing about with her unheard orchestra before she rejoined the dance. "What comes from knowing how it ends if you don't know how you got there? What's the point in the conclusion without the lessons along the way?" She smiled as she danced, slipping her hands into mine at some point and pulling me into the flow of the dance. I could even hear the music she was dancing to.

Is she an eccentric person, or is just that *in touch with magic?* I wondered as she began humming along to the music, to what I think was the song of magic.

"You will learn, you will love, you will lead, you will fight, you will protect, and when you've done all you were meant to do, you will sleep," she sang, pulling me along with her dance before letting go, and the music slowly faded. "But what will you do along the way, Dante? With the Cold Moon in your hand?" My hand instantly went to my bowie knife, pulling it out and examining the blade, as if I knew she was talking about it. "My ancestor said it'll gain its name after the 'twilight of guiding lights,' but I decided to look ahead for that one."

"Certainly better than calling it 'knife,'" I conceded, putting it back into its sheath. "I assume you already know the next question I'm going to ask?"

She actually pretended to think.

"Do I? Or is this one of the times that I'd like to be surprised?" she said, never losing that smile, just before saying exactly what I was about to ask. "Whose side am I on? What is my end goal? Didn't I already say it, Dante?" She hopped in front of me and leaned in close. "I am, and always will be, on your side. Because what you do will bring about the most interesting outcome for the future. I'm just along for the ride," she said before skipping away, humming to herself.

"I maintain that she has a few screws loose in that head of hers," Saya said, walking next to me. "Do you think you can trust her?"

That was a good question, but then again, I'm not sure *who* I trust anymore at this point. Did the Order always know about this school? Why did Phantoms fall in love with demi human creatures? How much about the Phantoms, about the Order, about myself did I really know?

"I don't think it's a good idea to trust anyone that says that they can see the future," I finally answered. "You never know if they're telling the truth or just manipulating you to their own benefit. Until I know more, let's keep watching her."

After that, we returned to the school. I rejected the SSC offer again, I went to Lucrezia, and we just watched a movie, a cheesy romance picture—some sense of normalcy to end a day and get my mind off, not knowing what's what anymore. It was a very nice feeling.

So obviously, it didn't last long. And what came next was the hardest challenge of my life.

CHAPTER 21

MESSAGE FROM A VISION

THE DAYS WERE passing by relatively peacefully: going days and weeks with no calls from the Order, no crisis that needed dealing with, and I didn't even spend much time thinking about what I didn't know about the Order and myself. I was just being what I thought was a regular high school teenager—studying, hanging out with my friends, dating my girlfriend. I even noticed that I had now started calling them my friends. I wasn't even upset, I was... I didn't even know. I wasn't used to any of this. I don't know how to handle it. I'm content, I'm anxious, I feel the need to do something, I lack the desire to do anything, and I don't know what I want or what I need to do. It was maddening, but I wasn't at all mad. But that all ended when I got another headache.

"I don't make the rules, Andrea," I told the alpha female for the hundredth time. "But I'm in agreement with the school board on this. We may have a bigger dorm, but you two are still not allowed." She growled before attempting to pounce on me, only to be caught and carried away by Max while she ranted about how she needed "relief." "Isn't mating season done?" I asked after he stuck her in the bathroom, where she continued to yell. "Shouldn't she be calmed down by now?"

"Still teenagers, Dante," he answered, sounding just as agitated. "Besides, we never got around to doing it since a certain someone was now our chaperone," he said, glaring at me with the same irritated look Andrea did. "The pressure can only build so much, Dante." That was something else that changed; Max, Andrea, and myself got a two-bedroom dorm, and I was *still* expected to keep them from mating and having all the results of doing so. Doesn't help that they still didn't finish fixing the "heat suppression" seal around the school, needing to modify it so Monica doesn't break it again. Speaking of, she was given three consecutive days of "in school suspension" where she was locked in a room and forced to listen to the same terrible pop song on repeat the entire time. I heard she cracked in the first five minutes and tried to claw her ears out—that was not a pretty sight.

"That sounds like a 'you' problem," I dismissed as I got ready for the day of whatever schoolwork and social dilemmas I'd get involved with today.

"I'm sure she'd consent to using protection if you'd let us! She's willing to challenge you for alpha status again!" he pleaded.

"Then just rub one out! Both of you!" I returned, slamming the door. "Dealing with this crap is giving me a headache," I groaned, rubbing my head as I got a mild throb.

I made my way out of the dorm building and just slapping the safety committee guy in the face before he could ask me to join again. You'd think they'd stop asking me at some point, but they've been annoyingly persistent. I was hoping the time away from the others would relieve me of my headache, but it stuck with me throughout the entire day. It was there through math, history, science, lunch—it did not stop throbbing. I was able to ignore it for the most part. That ended when I was heading back to the dorms.

What the hell is this? I wondered as I felt like my brain was about to split apart. I screamed in agony before dropping to the ground, cradling my head and wishing the pain would stop. I only felt this kind of pain once before, when I had my mission in Japan. Only this time, it was a *thousand* times worse. It ended after I had a dream about Onigashima, which turned out to be a mission. If I had to guess, and this was actually a desperate wish that I was right, it would end after I got some sleep and had another possible prophetic dream. I wondered if I were a "seer" or something, someone that constantly saw the ever-changing future, and I needed to sleep if I wanted to see, or something along those lines.

"That's idiotic," Monica bluntly said after I suggested it. We met up in the infirmary after I collapsed, the staff on hand giving me painkillers and telling me to rest. "Most seers and oracles from the ancient days were mainly drug addicts with only a few actually getting legitimate future sight without magical spells," she explained while I was still trying to cope with my skull-splitting headache. "Someone is sending you these visions, but that's not why you're experiencing these migraines. Something is blocking them, actively preventing you from seeing want you're being sent."

"I guess that makes sense," I groaned out, still grasping at my head. Of course, the last time this happened, the Orochi was almost resurrected and I'd rather not risk a third time to confirm these actually tell me where I need to be and what is going on. Instead, I'm going to take a different kind of risk. One that's debatable as to whether or not it's more dangerous than risking the world—at least to my personal health. Then again, I do want these migraines to stop. "Think you can undo whatever is blocking it?" I asked Monica, getting her to look at me like I just asked her to cut open my head, which I was.

"Dante, you know what you're asking me to do, right?" she asked, making sure I was in the right state of mind. "Normal spell seals is like engineering, software coding, and defusing a bomb. Spell seals on the body is like performing surgery and the spell that's keeping you from getting whatever visions those are is in your head. You're asking me to perform neurosurgery. Do you even trust me enough to do that?"

"Of course not," I answered. "I'm fairly certain you're insane and would spend half an hour poking at my brain just because it would be squishy. I'm not asking you to do this because I trust you. I'm asking you because I don't have another choice." She pouted at me but nodded that I was right. "Besides"—I took out the bowie knife and cut my hand off—"I think I'll be fine," I said as the parts reattached themselves. She merely put on a massive grin.

"Give me an hour," she said as she ran off to do whatever it was she needed and/or wanted to do to get ready.

I was returned to my new dorm room with everyone storming in to try to help me not be in pain. The only effective treatment was Lucrezia using her own demonic magic to put me into a trance and then invade my mind. It was that lucid dream state, not the deep subconscious, so I didn't have to worry about her learning something I'd rather keep hidden. Instead, she had me rest my head in her lap while she stroked my hair—it was relaxing, and I soon lost track of time. Then she disappeared, and I was in a world of chaos.

Snow and ice had covered everything, giant pyres lit the landscape since the sky was lacking any light, giant wolves and a massive snake were destroying everything, lightning flashed and thunder rang out, it was the picture of only one thing: Ragnarok, the Nordic apocalypse. I think it's been established by now, but yes, even the pagan gods exist as do many of their myths. The good news is that this won't actually destroy the world—there's definitely going to be some major fallout, an entire pantheon almost dying out, and if the Order extends the Sanctuary project, then it's going to get pretty full. The question I had was, Why was I seeing a vision about Ragnarok?

The image shifted to me fighting a man that was shining with a brilliant radiance until I broke his neck. From there, it changed to me riding on the back of Nex in the form of a beast of darkness and bone as he devoured all that he came across. I was fighting the giant serpent Jormungand and Thor before settling on me, cradling a dying Odin in my arms. The next scene showed me at the base of a massive tree, trying to tear off a seal that was causing my arms to break apart until I freed something even bigger than any of the monsters fighting the Aesir gods. I then saw myself, my friends, and the few would-be survivors of Ragnarok, watching as the entirety of the nine realms of Yggdrasil disappear in a flash of light. The last image I was shown was me standing on the docks of a small town surrounded by lush fields of green and mountains with a ghostly silhouette of a massive man-o'-war vessel. For some reason, I have no idea why, but I knew that was Northern Norway and the ship was the *Flying Dutchman* itself.

"What the he—!" I shouted, wondering how or why a nautical mythical vessel of the dead was in any way associated with Nordic myths when I shot forward and slammed my head against something.

"My head!" Monica cried out in pain.

"Dante, that was mean! She was just helping you!" another Monica said.

"You should apologize!" a third Monica said, and I just noticed that there were three different Monica, each one dressed in surgery scrubs and were little kids.

Kashi must have noticed I was looking confused because he explained what happened.

"She said she needed some extra pairs of hands to properly work on you, so she split herself into three." We all looked to the witch as the three little girls merged back into one whole Monica. "Apparently, she meant more of her hands because we weren't allowed to help."

"And I didn't spend an hour poking the 'squishy part,'" Monica said, rubbing her forehead.

"She stopped after I smacked her for doing it at all," Zoe informed me, causing me to glare at the witch.

"So is everything all right?" Lance asked, making me think back to the vision I saw.

I don't know why my friends were there with me, but I wasn't going to let them get involved with Ragnarok.

"It's fine. Nothing you need to worry about," I quickly said, maybe a little too quickly judging by the looks I was getting. "I...just need to make a little trip again. That's all," I told them.

Monica nodded and helped out.

"Yeah, if you say it's okay, then I believe you," she said with a smile. "Though I have the feeling this is going to be a long trip. *Friends, we must prepare him a backpack!*" she suddenly declared, grabbing everyone and running about the dorm and packing a bag for a long trip. I personally had no idea how long I'd be gone, but the thought was nice.

CHAPTER 22

JOURNEY TO THE HALL OF THE DEAD

GETTING OUT OF the school this time was harder, mainly because it turned out that Volk had the place staked out and under guard. Guess I could leave with impunity for only so long before they found a way to stop me, especially since they made a barrier of light to stop Nex, and forcing my way through would only have negative results for when and if I got back. So in the end and long story short, Volk cut me a deal in which I join the safety committee and help with virtually every small problem, but I could leave once a month with no need to explain anything. Otherwise, he'd have to detain me and investigate my various activities. Yes, it was blackmail, but there might be an apocalypse on the horizon, so I didn't really have a choice. I'm now their grunt, and Volk promised to keep me very busy.

That's how I got out this time, showing up in this nowhere port in the northern reaches of Norway if the signs were anything to go by. It was the middle of the night, cold and damp, with a backpack my friends packed with survival gear, my knife, and I was waiting for a ghost ship that had nothing to do with Nordic lore—*what the hell am I doing?* This didn't make any sense! What did the *Flying Dutchman* have to do with Ragnarok? Why was Ragnarok even happening now? What would the damage be? What the hell is happening! These thoughts raced in my head as a heavy fog appeared suddenly and enveloped the land.

"She's here," I said, knowing that the ship had come. I couldn't see it through the fog, but I could feel the presence of the cursed dead. I was at the edge of the dock, listening and waiting, soon rewarded with the sounds of a rowing vessel and creaking metal as a pale light shone. A few more seconds and a rowboat with two pale ghostly figures in loose cotton shirts and pants, wearing bandanas, appeared, a lantern with a pale green flame giving light. I didn't say anything, I just jumped in, and they began rowing out again. It felt right; for some reason, I knew that I had to do this.

"Heading to Valhalla, right, Phantom?" one of them asked. I know I didn't introduce myself, but I had the feeling they already knew. The more I thought about my vision, the more I believed it was more like instructions. I was being ordered to come here, these spirits were ordered to take me there, I had a mission but no idea who called the shots, and I just obeyed. "Shall we head off the proper way?" he asked, grabbing the lantern and smashing it on the bottom of the ship, setting the entire vessel aflame with the pale fire. I jumped, almost freaked out…before realizing that I wasn't burning. "Ha! You should've seen the look on your face!"

"The moment we board, I'm going to see if I can't hurt you," I promised, palming my knife.

The rest of the trip was silent as they rowed us to the massive, weathered ship of those who died at sea. I boarded the vessel, facing an entire crew of ghostly specters with various sets of seafaring uniforms. From the era of pirates to modern navy, from soldiers to fishermen and everything in between, the crew of near a hundred spirits manned the massive vessel. Also, true to my word, I stabbed the two ghosts that gave me the ride here. Pure iron does hurt spirits, and their pained screams make me feel better.

"Oi! That's enough, you bilge rats! Back to work!" a hoarse and grizzled voice growled out. There he was, the captain of the ship of the damned: Hendrick Van der Decken, the only one among the crew that looked like he was still alive yet more ancient than any of the spirits. A wide brimmed hat and a ragged red sash on his waist set him apart from the other seventeenth-century spirits. "Been a while since I had to escort one of you lot. Death should have sent you earlier, so I wouldn't have to be bothered with this," he growled, stepping up to and analyzing me before turning away with disgust. "You're too green to be a Phantom," he growled before marching away, barking out orders.

"Who the hell are you to decide that?" I demanded, storming after him. "If you know something, you're going to answer my questions." I grabbed him by the shoulder, pulling him back to face me.

He punched me in the face, hard enough that I felt something in my cheek crack, so I returned with one of my own under his chin. He wasn't even fazed, and I think I broke my knuckles.

"Pathetic. I doubt you've even felt your father's cold touch," he growled, storming off to the wheel and setting us off. "Get moving, lads! We're heading to frozen waters!"

I followed after him while my body healed. Francesco talked about me having brothers, and this guy talks about my father. I never once even remembered having family beyond the Order, but others seemed to know more about my probable family. I'm getting some damn answers before I get to Valhalla, and this guy is going to give me them one way or another.

"Hey! You think you can just walk away after saying something like that?" I yelled out. "I want some answers!"

"Yes, I was there when the *Titanic* sank," he said suddenly. "That was a long night. I'm taking you to Valhalla because something is messing with the magic of Yggdrasil and closed off the realms, and it isn't the giants, which is a little odd since other pantheons don't meddle in each other's affairs. Last time that happened was with that Serapis fellow, but the Greeks were already killed by your brother and reborn as the Roman pantheon. And yes, this is the last year of Fimbulwinter in the Nordic realms, so Ragnarok is nigh upon them, during which you'll free one of the final fragments of the dragon, just like your brothers did before you." He turned and looked like he had just explained everything to a child. "Did that answer everything?"

"Just the Ragnarok ones," I returned. "Wasn't going to ask about the *Titanic*, which I assume comes up a lot, but it was that bit about my family that got my attention." That actually surprised him. I guess my family must be famous or something—hold on. Did he just say that my brother already killed the entire Greek pantheon by the time people began worshiping Serapis? Serapis came into existence as a mixed origin deity during the Ptolemaic dynasty, predating the Order by a few centuries. Considering that, I'm starting to question my own humanity now. "I just thought they were killed in the line of duty of the Hunters. I've never known anything about them."

He just started laughing. "Oh, you're serious," he said after laughing for a few more seconds. "That's not right. Every Phantom knows about their brothers and father."

"So does this mean I'm not actually human?" I asked, feeling a chill go down my spine. How much of my life could be a lie? What was being hidden from me? "Please, tell me abou—*holy crap, it's cold*!" I yelled out, suddenly freezing in icy cold winds and snowfall. "What just happened?"

"Fimbulwinter," Decken answered, glaring straight ahead. "We're coming upon Valhalla here shortly." Crossing planes of existence did *not* take as long as some people would think. "Focus, you can feel it in the air, can't you?"

I did my best to block out the stinging chill and the howling winds and felt a dark magic in the air—powerful and corrupting, the kind of thing that comes from selling a soul.

"What kind of force is interfering here?" I asked, going through the names of so many different and powerful devils in my mind. This definitely wasn't the work of giants or anything else in the Nordic pantheon, but this was much older and darker. "What happened?"

"That's for you to find out," the captain returned before the *Flying Dutchman* slammed into something, throwing me forward and off-balance.

I managed to stay on my feet and saw the shimmering light of a barrier construct that we just rammed into, though the vessel itself slowly passed through it, like something sinking into gel. The odd colors of the barrier soon engulfed the ship as it continued through to whatever was beyond it, Van der Decken laughing loudly. "Nothing can stop the reapers! Our path will never be barred by any means!" he cried out as the ship lurched forward, free of the barrier and sailing toward a rainbow—the Bifrost Bridge.

"Remind me, where was Valhalla located?" I asked the ship captain.

Valhalla was a tricky place since most refer to it as a great hall for the honorable dead. Maybe it was located in the mortal plane or somewhere in Asgard since Odin is the chief of the Nordic pantheon and rules over Valhalla as well.

"We'll be coming upon it soon, boy, but did you notice something odd?" he returned, scanning the area. "Something that's just not right?"

After he mentioned it, I did notice a change in the air. I could still feel the oppressive maliciousness, but there was still the hearty laughter and drunken merriment that would come from your typical einherjar—the honorable dead that make up Odin's army. I also couldn't feel the cold of Fimbulwinter, like we went into another, separate dimension since the long winter is supposed to affect Asgard as well. As I tried to focus on this question, we came to a gateway with a relief of two Valkyrie bearing shields and spears on the doors. "This is your stop. Through there will be one entrance to Valhalla."

"And maybe some answers," I said as I jumped over the edge, landing on the bridge of light. It felt weird standing on light like this, like I was walking on a lane of shifting sands. I faced the doors and prepared to steel myself to enter the Nordic realm, but then I remembered a question that was bugging me for a while. "Hey! Van der Decken! Why were you the one to lead me here?" I yelled as the *Flying Dutchman* began to sail away.

"My crew and I can sail any sea or ocean! My blessing and curse in exchange for the eternity of sailing the endless waters!" he yelled back, cackling loudly. "And I still wouldn't trade anything for it! As for the 'why,' the Valkyrie are missing lad! No one has seen them for years!"

"That's not concerning in the least," I muttered, adjusting the shoulder straps on my backpack. But what happened and why, if

Ragnarok is looming, am I now acting? Why just me and not any of the other Hunters in the Order? Is this fate, fate that I have to deal with this alone? Because if so, then I officially hate that psychopathic chick, or trio, or whichever fate is represented as. I took my first steps toward the doors to Valhalla and promptly fell back as my backpack suddenly felt like it gained five hundred pounds.

"I'm pretty sure that I'm going to be very pissed with Monica."

"No, you won't," I heard her muffled voice coming out of the backpack. I took it off and unzipped the first pocket, and like a jack-in-the-box, Monica popped out. "Hi, Dante!" she cheered happily, looking excited for adventure.

My response was to push her back in, zip it shut, and throw it back on the deck of the *Dutchman*, which was already gone. Defeated, I unzipped the pocket and pulled out Monica, who had a catlike expression on her face.

"You timed this so I couldn't leave you behind, didn't you?" I accused as, to my great and nonexistent surprise, the rest of my friends came out of the backpack. "That was a one-way gate, wasn't it?" Monica nodded excitedly. "I'm stuck with you now, aren't I?" She nodded again. "*Why!*" I demanded.

"Aren't we supposed to be friends?" Max returned, helping Andrea out of the bag. "The last time we left you alone, Lucrezia got kidnapped and you didn't trust us enough to help." You guys don't need to see how I handle things. "The time before that, you and Saya disappeared without a word to anyone and were gone all day. The two of you still haven't told us what happened."

"Family business, I said that," Saya told them as we shared a glance, wondering just how bad the current situation is.

"Dante, the point of friends is that you trust us to help you when you need it," Max said as Kashi, Lance, Zoe, and Andrea stood together. Lucrezia latched onto my arm while Monica just smiled since she knew she already won. Saya and I just sighed.

"Fine, I had a vision of Ragnarok and the sense that I was going to be involved in some way," I flat-out told them, shocking most of the group. "I didn't want to drag you into this mess because I don't know what will happen." Now they looked like they wanted to back out, like I was crazy—well, except for Max. Max pushed past us to the gates.

"Well, let's do this," he said with steely determination, pushing the gates open, only to get no results in doing so.

"Lame!" Zoe yelled out, causing a few chuckles among the group. I marched toward the gates and placed my hand on it. The Valkyries glowed with a heavenly light as they parted, and Valhalla was revealed to us. A bunch of rambunctious, drunk, violent people laughing and occasionally killing each other while the scent of mead and roasted boar hung heavy in the air. Yep, this was Valhalla, an incredibly spacious hall with runic and ornate carvings of dragons and wolves in the pillars, tables, and walls. A massive boar on a spit over an open flame and many rows of mile-long tables of einherjar celebrating like it was their last day in life. At the other end of the hall was a group of more ornately armored figures, and I had a feeling I knew who they were. Of the group, one was missing a hand, one had fiery red hair and a hammer, one was glowing, and I'll admit was incredibly handsome, and the one in the center had a heavily scarred eye, but both eyes seemed to be fully functional.

"What the hell?" I whispered, looking directly at whom I assumed to be Odin.

He's supposed to be lacking an eye since his sacrifice of it for knowledge. The others made sense, except for the shining one—that could only be Baldur, and he's supposed to be dead. Something was very, *very* wrong, and I tried to feel out the air to see if I couldn't sense what. Before I could, we were noticed.

"Welcome, great warriors!"

CHAPTER 23

EVE OF THE TWILIGHT

"WELCOME, GREAT WARRIORS!" the fiery-haired man yelled out, holding his tankard high and red-faced with intoxication. "It's always good to have new guests! Though…this seems to be the first time in three years—*bah*! Who cares? The end's never gonna come anyway!" he shouted before laughing and downing his tankard. "Another!"

"I must apologize for my fellow Aesir," the one with the missing hand said as he rose from his seat. "Thor has been drinking non-stop since the Norns declared that Ragnarok is no longer a concern." The Nordic Fates, the ones that foretold the events of Ragnarok in the first place, just decided that it would no longer happen. I don't believe that, not for one second. Before any of us could say anything, we were suddenly mobbed by other people, either by regular einherjar, Vanir, or Aesir, my friends and I were separated—something I didn't think would end well.

"Never mind all that!" the scarred-eye man called out. "Eat! Drink! And make merry!"

Soon, each member of our group was pulled into various festivities around the hall. Some played games; some were drinking competitively. I think Saya and Lucrezia were talking with Freya, and Max just got into a brawl because some people were apparently angry drunks. Such was the life in Valhalla, which was why the Vikings loved it. Though I had this odd feeling that Baldur, the person that was shining, seemed to be glaring at me. Those thoughts disappeared as I was dragged away to someplace out of the party.

"I doubt I have to tell you about this, Phantom, but things are very wrong here in Asgard," the handless Aesir from earlier, had to be Tyr since he's the only one with a missing hand, said as he pulled me along. We left the hall of Valhalla and entered the fortress city of Asgard, a majestic kingdom of the Aesir that was completely silent and dead the further away from the hall we got. "The obvious is that Baldur is alive and Odin has both of his eyes. He gave that up for knowledge a long time ago and kept it that way to remind him the price to pay for power," he said with urgency as he led me through the city. "And this is the worst of it. Here at the Bifrost." Everything looked entirely normal—unless you knew Norse mythology and know who stands watch at this bridge constantly while remembering a massive barrier surrounding the realm.

"Tyr, where's Heimdall?" I asked, now terribly uncomfortable as to what might happen. "What is going on? Who is doing this?"

"I have no idea, Phantom," the deity said as he gazed out into the distance. "One day, three years ago, Odin set off for one of the springs he visits, and when he returned, he had Baldur back with him, alive and well. He then said that, 'So long as Baldur lived, Ragnarok will never come,' which led Frigg to once again get the vows of all things to never harm him and kept him in the hall of Valhalla ever since, which soon got this barrier that the All-father said was now connected to Baldur's life."

"Well, that's all good and everything. Mama wants to keep her precious baby safe, but there is only one problem with that," I said while walking to the edge of the bridge. "The winter has already come! This is the eve of Ragnarok itself, and they are in no condition to fight. Whoever told Odin that Ragnarok has been stopped for good was lying to him."

"You think I don't know that?" he snapped at me before growling in frustration. "If I had to guess, Odin's fear finally got the best of him, and he was doing whatever it took to prevent Ragnarok. Just like always, his attempts to prevent Ragnarok only fails us in the end. Except this time might destroy us completely."

"Ragnarok is supposed to be such a fierce war that all the realms and the world are affected by it, but how is it that it ends with *just* the Nordic realms' destruction?" That part always bugged me—apocalypse happens, but the world itself has a few major disasters at best but nothing world ending. Ragnarok is one of the fiercest conflicts, how is it supposed to be contained?

"We Aesir are the sacrifice to keep it contained," Tyr answered, looking out to the distance and rubbing the stump where his hand once was. "We fight this war while you break the seal of the dragon Nidhogg and erase everything." Did he seriously just say that I have to essentially nuke the entirety of the Nine Realms? To say I was puzzled and shocked was like saying fire is hot. "Don't look at me like that, boy. This is our destiny. The old guard did its duty in guiding and protecting our charge. The Hunters can handle the rest."

More confusion and I was getting tired of that. "This is the first I've heard of any pantheon accepting death like this so easily. What have I been missing?" I asked, which apparently confused him, which led to him sniffing me and looking more confused.

"Something is very wrong with you. This does not bode well for anyone," I heard him mutter. "This is our purpose, Phantom," he said aloud, "guiding humanity. The silly creatures always seem to refer to something beyond their power and comprehension as god-like or such, but none of us were that. Egyptian, Nordic, Shinto, Greek, and Roman, none of us were gods until humans called us such. We were guides and protectors, meant to nurture humanity until it no longer needed us. Even now, some of the others continue to watch over and guide them in their respective regions. But for us, the animosity has grown too great between we Aesir and the giants we call our enemies. Some will survive, but the warriors need to bury the grudge. Unfortunately, peace cannot be our way, especially with what both sides have done to wage this war."

"So what the hell am I supposed to do?" I asked the Aesir. "That barrier looks too strong and complicated to dispel by normal means, and so long as it stands, then the other Aesir won't do a thing."

Tyr sighed in resignation, looking back inside the fortress. "There are two beings we need to find," he finally said, apparently

"I couldn't tell you when she died," Loki sighed with regret. "Even after everything, she stayed a dutiful wife, caring for her husband, and where did it get her? An eternity in a prison with me." It sounded like genuine regret was in his voice, but I took that with a grain of salt. Loki was a trickster and known liar/manipulator. "Ever since I felt that change in Asgard, I've been concentrating my powers for when I'm finally free. Course, by then, Sigyn was gone and kept moving because of a spell to continue to protect me. I understand punishing me for the things I did, but why did my children have to suffer?"

"You were just that hated," I answered, feeling sorry for those that were associated with Loki but not with the giant himself, "and the others were just that feared. Fenrir is a massive and powerful wolf while Jormungand encircles the whole of Midgard. Why did you have Baldur killed anyway?"

"To serve as a reminder," Loki scoffed; apparently, this was a sore spot for him. "Tyr already told you about the role of the so-called 'gods' and that even we are subject to the whims of fate. They tried to make him invulnerable to avoid that fate in defiance of fate and the Creator that made all of us. I don't regret my actions, even after all my torture, but Baldur was seriously overrated. All that talk of how 'generous' or 'pure' or 'gracious' yet the mortal scholars are hesitant to accept anything that said he was just as vicious as any of the other Aesir. As for his wisdom? Kvasir actually used his wisdom to *help* all the realms. Baldur didn't do much beyond getting spoiled in comparison. Yet they tried to resurrect Baldur while no such efforts were made for someone that was *actually* helpful."

"So this was one part spite, one doing what you thought was a healthy reminder?" I asked, somewhat confused by the display of loyalty to a higher force.

"And just because I'm an ass, I will admit to that," he said before pointing at his chains. "So are you going to actually free me or just ask questions?"

I rolled my eyes because, of course, I wanted to kick-start an apocalypse, who doesn't want to do that and put their friends in danger. But the longer I wait, the better chance that Tyr and Frigg were upholding their end of the bargain in getting my friends to safety—also, the better chance that that course of action would fail, and this ends even worse for my side. I hated gambling.

"How am I supposed to do that?" I asked the bound giant. "I don't remember hearing anything about how you get out of this stinking hole other than you eventually break out."

You'd think any legend would include some information like that.

"Do you have any enchanted swords of legendary sharpness?" I reached for my knife, but it was enchanted to be unbreakable and lethal to anything, not enchanted sharpness. I looked back up to Nex, who moved back to my side and began to shift through the massive armory he had within himself...for five minutes before admitting that it didn't have what I needed.

"What about Juuchi Yosamu?" I asked, remembering the blood-thirsty katana. "That's a legendary sharp blade."

"Enchanted," Loki said, reminding me about the chains that bind him, "and you might want to hurry, Phantom. Time flows differently in here." That shocked me, and if he said to hurry, then it means that time moves faster outside this prison.

"What's been happening?" I demanded, all sorts of terrible thoughts going through my head of the possibilities of what might be happening. Loki, smug as ever, smirked in some twisted sense of victory.

"That thing wearing Baldur's meat suit said he had a vision of you and your friends unleashing Ragnarok, almost immediately after Tyr found Heimdall and before they said that the wolf and the serpent are freed." My blood turned to ice. "They reacted about as well as you'd think. Odin had them imprisoned and interrogated to find you." He began chuckling as I ground my teeth in frustration. "That succubus has some real fire in her, though. Baldur offered her freedom for a price, and she spat in his face. They're now gearing up for the war while Frigg managed to convince the rest that Baldur should remain in Valhalla since he can't die. Ready to prove that wrong?" he asked just before I roared and tackled the stone from which I entered, trying to break out.

"Open! Open, damn you!" I yelled out, forgetting the plan in favor of trying to break out and save my friends.

Loki just laughed, pissing me off even more.

"That's not going to work, Phantom!" he finally said between laughs. "You must free me first. Now how are you—"

He didn't even finished as I rushed up his body and kicked him across the face, just to shut him up. "Listen to me!" I roared out, grabbing onto his face. "I don't care about you, almost no one does! I know you only care about yourself and your damned vengeance for this torture you've gone through for however long you've been in here!" Suddenly, my arms began to burn in pain as if they were trying to tear themselves apart, but I ignored it and powered on. I didn't even notice the giant wincing in pain. "I'm only freeing you because you are crucial to this war. Otherwise, I'd kill you here and now so that we can be done with it all. Now *shut up* and *let me do my thing*!" he screamed out in agony as I finally noticed the flesh of his cheeks breaking apart, melting, and evaporating, all at once. I looked at my arms and found my fingertips turning a pitch-black that seemed to grow and recede, like my healing was fighting a rotting necrosis. Curious, I held on to my feelings of anger and desperation and touched one of the rocks Loki was bound to, watching as it immediately began to break apart from where I touched it. *Act now, think later*, I promised myself as I quickly moved to the chains at his feet and grabbed on, pulling on them in an effort to tear the giant free. After a few seconds, the chain snapped, and Loki gasped in relief at the sense of freedom. I repeated the process twice more, and Loki was freed.

"Yes. *Yes!*" he roared in triumph, turning to me. "Now time to uphold my end." He waved his hand, and the stone melted away, giving me a way out. "But before I go." He turned and poked me really hard in the chest with a glowing finger. For another five seconds, my arms felt like they were about to explode before they went numb and my fingers were all black. "There appears to be a magic seal in you that's holding back your true abilities. What I did should last until Ragnarok is over, but you should really find someone to fix that. Your brother Xanth should make short work of it." He then disappeared, off to get to his army and ship of nails, leaving me to yet again wonder about what secrets were connected to me. That was before slapping myself and remembering I had to save my friends.

"Nex, let's go!" I shouted as Nex enveloped me in the darkness and, after a few seconds, shot me back out in front of Valhalla's gates. *That was disorienting*, I thought as a sense of dizziness from the rapid displacement hit me like a freight train. When that passed, I pushed the doors open and found my opponent. Shining bright like a beacon was Baldur, sitting on Odin's throne with a smile that said anything but pure and gracious.

"We both know how this is going to go, pal. Answer my questions, and I promise you a quick death," I said before marching toward him.

"Seriously?" he asked before snickering. "That's your offer? A simple mortal offering the unkillable a quick death. In case you forgot, Mother made sure to cover all the bases this time. Not even mistletoe will harm me."

"And if you were a god of anything intimidating, I'd be worried," I returned, grabbing a tankard and throwing it at his head. As expected, it bounced off with no reaction beyond smiling in amusement. "But that invulnerability is the only thing you have going for you, and we both know it. Loki is free, Fenrir and Jormungand are rampaging, and I'm certain that Surtr is coming with that blazing sword of his. The only thing preventing Ragnarok is that barrier that I hear is connected to your life, and you're supposed to stay dead until after it's over. Besides, shouldn't you of all beings know that nothing good comes from defying fate and destiny? Or are you really Baldur?"

He pushed himself off the throne and began to walk toward me. "It is Baldur's body and his mind, but not the soul," he admitted, keeping that smug expression on his face. "The emotional are so easy to manipulate. Odin should've known how futile it was to stop Ragnarok from ever happening, but he was afraid of it and latched on to the idea I gave him. 'I can stop the giants from reaching Asgard and bring life to your son in exchange for your obedience.' He jumped at the chance without even thinking about it, and he even sacrificed an

the face and sending him flying like he did me. I looked to my hands, seeing black electricity dance around my fingers before looking back to Baldur, who had healed from the damage I did and was looking at me with fear. "Guessing mommy dearest missed one yet again, huh?"

"Your family would never make the kind of promise she wanted, Death kin," he growled, his face turning back to rage once more. "But I refuse to be beaten by the likes of you!" He charged at me, so I grabbed a plate and threw it at him, only to shatter on contact with his face. That pretty much confirmed that *my* physical contact was what was necessary to beating him, now to actually do it. While he cleared the debris from his face, I met his charge with my own and hit him with a lariat. He went down, and I made the mistake of slowing down while he was still awake.

"Aw crap!" I said as I felt him grab my ankle and throw me across the hall, smashing through a support pillar and into the wall. "Ungh!" I grunted out as I slammed against the magical reinforced wall of Valhalla before dropping to the ground. "Ouch!" I said as I got back up, just in time for Baldur to close the distance and start pummeling me. After a few punches to my face and gut, I started blocking and throwing a few of my own. I eventually slammed a fist into his gut, hard enough to make him double over, hooked his head into the crux of my elbow, turned and ran up the wall, flipping over and slamming him into the stone ground. While still lying on the ground, he pounded the back of my head before rolling to his feet, yanking me to my feet and hitting me with an uppercut that sent me flying. I have hard times with the "nigh invulnerable," don't I?

"Is this truly a Phantom?" he asked as I got back to my feet. "The feared warriors of Death itself? You're a joke!"

He lifted a table and swung it at me. On reflex, I held up my hands to block it, and the moment my hand touched it, the table broke into splinters. I have so many questions and no time to get any answers, not even sure how much of his words I can trust even if he *did* start telling me. I charged at him, while he kept swinging the table at me, leaping over and dodging the massive piece of furniture until I got close enough to throw a kick into his gut. The moment I made contact, I was blasted back and fell on my back. Confused, I looked at my feet and saw a shoe that was ruined—much like everything else that hit Baldur.

"Seriously!" I shouted in frustration, reaching down to my other shoe while the Aesir charged at me. My foot's clothing turned to mulch in my hand, just as Baldur got within kicking distance. I tucked in my legs and shot them forward, slamming them into his gut and making him double over. Balancing on my hands, I moved my feet around him and slammed my heels into the back of his head. I jumped back to my feet and stomped on his head before he could get back up, again and again, burying his face into the ground. When he stopped moving, I grabbed him by his hair and threw him onto another table. Apparently, all the punishment had done its job, and he wasn't healing as quickly, just slow enough for me to wrap my hands around his neck and choke him. He struggled, but I only tightened my grip and watched as the flesh on his neck burned away under my hands.

"Wait!" He managed to gasp out, gagging as he fought against my grip. "I can tell you anything you want to know! The truth about the Phantoms and the Hunters!" he promised, but I didn't care.

"The only thing I want now is you dead," I growled as I squeezed even harder, and his neck was gone, leaving a severed head to roll away from the body. Baldur's reanimated body was now dead, meaning the barrier should be falling. Soon enough, I heard an anguished and furious cry of "no" coming from quite a distance away, a loud haunting howl, waves crashing, thunder ringing, a horn's call, and an earthquake of thousands of massive feet slamming. Before getting out of Valhalla, I went to one of the brazier lanterns and knocked it against the wooden walls, setting the entire hall on fire. I felt Nex absorb Baldur's body, just before I passed through the doors. The barrier around Asgard continued to fade, and I saw a massive army of giants coming, some were on fire, some deathly cold blue, and a ship with Loki at the helm. A bright flash of light caught my attention as one fire giant began destroying the realm of Asgard with a sword that shined like the sun. Surtr, king of the flame giants, was here, and he truly lived up to the name "giant."

"I think I'll take my chances with the Aesir," I said as I started running away.

CHAPTER 24

THUNDER'S RAGE

So now Asgard was going up in flames, I had just murdered a Nordic deity that was the living shield around the realm, and now I was heading for the battlefield where the worst of the fighting was supposed to take place. I doubt I'm ever going to cause as much devastation as what I'm doing here, and I'm not even done yet. That should cause some concerns, and I still need to get some answers, but there's only one person left that could give me answers, and I doubt that he's in a talking mood. Not that I had much choice if I wanted to get anything before the nine realms are destroyed, but I just hope I can get to him before he gets eaten.

Since the war was now starting, that meant that I had to get to the battlefield of Vigrid. I was also running out of time because it suddenly went dark, and during Ragnarok, that meant one thing. I donned my mask and scanned the sky, seeing the twin wolves, Skoll and Hati, devour the sun and moon. Not the *real* sun and moon, but…you know, physics and magic get really strange in my life. Cut me some slack, okay? The main point is that the worst of Ragnarok was coming, and I wasn't anywhere near Vigrid yet.

"Nex, we need to get moving!" I told my familiar before it sucked me into the darkness. Considering the sun and moon of the nine realms was just eaten, it wasn't too much different—just a lack of sound, scent, and I felt like I was floating in an endless oblivion.

I haven't spent enough time in here to really register just how creepy it was. Eventually, I felt the wind rushing past me, and my vision returned, and it was like my premonition. Hundreds of massive pyres burned, giving light to the sun and moonless world, the giants were marching across the field toward the Aesir and their army, and a massive serpent was spewing poisonous gas while snapping at a figure that was flashed with lightning...right above me. *Well, we're here but not close enough to where I need to*—I was thinking before several bolts of electricity slammed into me and separated me from Nex.

"You! You caused all this!" I heard Thor roar as more lightning struck the hammer in his hands, a short-handled block of enchanted steel with magic runes carved into it on all sides. "You will pay!" Then he was whipped across his chest by the serpent's tail before the head followed to snap at the Aesir, only to get knocked aside before it could. All this was a grim reminder of a detail I wish had not been in my vision, that I was going to get into this fight between Thor and the world serpent—why is this my life? Before I could do anything else, I got struck by that tail, right in my chest, and for some reason, I decided to hold on.

"Damn it!" I cursed as I was thrown upward and fell onto the back of Jormungand, didn't even have the chance to catch my breath before the serpent began writhing again. I tried to hold on, grasping at any handhold that I could get until I felt my fingers sink into the scales beneath them. "I swear, when this is over, I'm letting Monica vivisect me so we can figure out what the hell this is," I promised while holding tight, bracing for the next massive movement from the snake. From what I could see, he was rearing up for his next strike when another massive creature slammed into him. The new one looked like a moray eel with clawlike pincers in its mouth biting at the snake. "Nex?" I wondered, seeing shadowy blackness and bone white plates, the familiar calling cards. Before I could continue, I felt something slam down next to me, revealing Thor who was glaring daggers at me.

"You bastard!" he growled, lightning cracking around his hammer. "I will crush you like so many giants before thee!"

Thor, there is a reason he's the most famous of the Nordic pantheon. He brought rain for the farmers and was also the guardian of mankind in those days, fighting off giants from attacking the world while most of the others sat at different posts or just on their butts. But despite his reputation as such, Thor was also a pigheaded sore loser, and that is *not* an exaggeration. His rivalry with Jormungand, whom he absolutely hates, is all because he failed to lift the serpent while trapped in an illusion. Instead of learning to think before he acts, he swore vengeance and once tried to kick-start Ragnarok by fishing for the giant snake.

"You should've known this would happen, Thor!" I returned, drawing my knife. "This was fated to happen. You shouldn't have tried to defy it." He thrust the hammerhead at me and shot dozens of lightning bolts, which I managed to block with a shield of wind. Instinct alone made that possible because I would've been zapped if I were any later in adjusting and activating the magic in my knife. "You have your chance to fight him. Just take it!"

"Not until I grind you into paste for this, Phantom!" Like I said, sore loser. He roared in fury as he charged at me, lightning sparking off his hammer as he closed in. As he swung his Mjolnir at me, I bent backward under it and swung my knife opposite and parallel to Thor's own swing, which the wind managed to cancel any electric charge that could've zapped me. Before I lost my balance, I grabbed onto Thor's belt and pulled myself up, letting me slam my forehead into his face. His hard head didn't extend to his nose, which I think I broke from how bent it looked. "I am the mightiest of the Aesir!" he roared out, letting his fiery rage take over.

"Aw crap!" I muttered as he swung his hammer overhead, bursting with electricity. I jumped to the side in an effort to dodge the electrical discharge, which put me too far over the side of Jormungand, and I had nothing to grab onto. I'm roughly a thousand feet in the air, and I don't know if I can recover from becoming a stain on the ground. However, for some reason, I forgot we were fighting on a giant snake that might react to a few billion volts of electrical energy coursing through its body. The entire body of the beast writhed and bumped into me, which I reflexively grabbed on to. The weird energy in my hands did its work and gave me a handhold after tearing a long gash in the snake's scales. The body continued to shake and tremble, and I saw the head of the beast still wrestling with Nex…who seemed to have grown in size.

Think I understand what I need to do, I thought as I began to climb back up the side of the snake, just as it swung at Thor again with its tail. He went over my head and was falling to the ground himself now. "I hate today," I groaned before throwing my knife skyward, the blade shooting up like a bullet, as I jumped off the snake and toward Thor. He was…less than thrilled about the sudden contact and tried to swing at me. I narrowly dodged the blow to the head and punched him in the chin, dazing him and giving me the time I needed to do what I had planned. I held onto him and reached for my blade, teleporting me and my passenger to it, almost to Jormungand's head, which was still wrestling with Nex. Thor came to and shoved me off, then threw himself to the snake's body. Before he got out of range, I threw my knife into his shoulder, and when he landed, I appeared right behind him before ripping my blade out of him.

"Just die already, you bastard!" he roared, swinging his hammer again but much slower with his now injured shoulder. I dodged and closed in again, stabbing him in the bicep and activated the water magic, using it to essentially paralyze his arm and body. Didn't even think that would work, I was just guessing.

"Listen to me!" I roared in his face. "This is your destiny! You are the only one that can stop Jormungand! Why are you focusing on me when you know that won't do any good?"

"Why is this our reward?" he yelled right back at me. "So many years we've spent protecting those humans, serving our Creator dutifully, yet we merely did all of that to simply die in the end? What was the point? Why all the struggle? Why!" he demanded, his voice cracking in the end. "Everything we did, and our reward is that we die?"

I wasn't sure what to say. It made sense that he'd crack like this.

"Yes. You die," I admitted. "You die, just like everything else eventually does. Death is unavoidable because it's the only thing that comes to all things equally." I didn't know why I was saying this,

157

the words just spilled from my mouth. "But with that comes liberation, your freedom. The last great journey of any life, going to the afterlife." I pulled out my blade and stood up, offering him a hand. "You've still one job left to do. I'll help. Let's go." He just lay there, glaring at me, before grasping my hand and letting me pull him up. Once he was on his feet, Jormungand began shaking again, along with more thunderous marching. The army of giants had arrived.

"The ultimate war of my people, and I die in the beginning." Thor sighed out as he pulled out a pair of iron gauntlets and handed them to me. "Here, if we're fighting this leviathan, then you'll need these."

"Is that Jarngreipr?" I asked, taking the enchanted iron gloves while he nodded. "Don't you need these to actually wield that hammer of yours?"

He just chuckled and hefted the brutal weapon. "I've had many centuries to master my Mjolnir," he answered as lightning sparked off the hammer. "Those gloves were for your brother anyway, the only man I'll admit was stronger than me." I only slipped on one glove, concerned that it might fall apart at the worst possible moment. Besides, always have a spare on hand. I looked back to the coming giants and finally noticed the massive wolf among them.

"Fenrir. Damn it!" I cursed, turning back to Thor. "We need to hurry this up. I need to get to Odin before that wolf eats him." Nex seemed to sense my intentions and disappeared, confusing Jormungand greatly. "So how did fate say you kill this thing?"

"Same way I killed all my enemies," he responded. "I hit it with my hammer."

I sighed in annoyance as Jormungand slowly seemed to remember us.

"I got an idea, but you'll have to distract him," I said before making my way toward the head. "Strike when I tell you to!" Thor shot himself skyward, slamming into the serpent's chin and snapping it skyward. He hovered in the air, channeling lightning from the sky through him and Mjolnir and at the snake. Jormungand released a furious hiss and sprayed poison from his mouth before snapping at the Aesir. Stubborn, the both of them. "Let's do this!" I growled as I started running down the length of the serpent's body, throwing my knife when most useful to skip past entire segments of the beast's coiled form. All the while, Thor was blasting him with lightning and the occasional whack with Mjolnir as Jormungand continued to spray poison and try to eat the god. If we didn't kill this thing soon, a toxic fog would cover all Vigrid, and that would put the Aesir side of the war at a terrible disadvantage.

Faster, faster, faster, faster! I urged myself as I ran harder and harder until I reached the final stretch, the wildly whipping around head and neck. "How the hell am I gonna get up there?" I asked, watching the head snap about. I looked to my knife, getting an idea that I didn't think was possible, but I also don't have too much time to second-guess myself. I set the elemental earth gem and stabbed it into the snake's scales and thanked my luck that this knife was enchanted because I couldn't pierce the scale at all and would've broken my blade. When that failed, I jammed it underneath and between the scales, actually succeeding in both finding purchase and the magic doing as I wanted, slowly petrifying the scales and giving me a secure handhold. I was almost thrown off as the serpent thrashed violently, chasing Thor as the Aesir dashed around the battlefield. Less steep than earlier, but I'm still glad I now have this bit of knowledge.

"Let us end this, you overgrown reptile!" Thor roared out, slamming his hammer into Jormungand's chin, just as I reached the base of the skull. Before the head could slam into me and send me flying off, I stabbed my knife into the top of his head, and it stayed. I flashed back to it and amplified the magic, speeding up the petrification. The results were shown as Jormungand slowly found it harder and harder to keep his head up. With our victory in sight, I slammed my palm onto the stoned flesh and began to channel whatever that power in my hand was. Instead of it turning the stone to dust, it broke and cracked into a chunky gravel, and once again, I'm happy I didn't eat earlier.

"Thor! Do it!" I called out to the Aesir, sensing now was the perfect chance for him to kill the serpent. With a mighty roar, Thor charge Mjolnir with lightning and threw it at the center of Jormungand's head. The blow exploded with such force that I was sent flying. There was a massive crater in the snake's head, and despite how much pain he must have been feeling, he snapped up Thor in his jaws. The cry of pain told me that this must've been the fatal blow Thor would suffer in this fight. Instead of mourning his loss, I decided to make sure this snake died. I reached for my knife, teleporting back to Jormungand's head and found Mjolnir sparking and almost touching his brain, which was already burned and perforated with thousands of bone and rock shards.

"Time to finish this," I whispered, ripping out my knife and sliding down the crater toward the hammer, making sure I had Thor's glove on before I reached it. Once I did, I grasped the handle, ripped it out, and with a roar of my own, slammed it back into Jormungand's head. Once it made contact, a thick bolt of lightning shot down into the tip of the handle. I lifted it and repeated the process, getting another bolt, and another and another. I stopped after five when I finally noticed that the serpent wasn't moving anymore. Jormungand, the world serpent, was dead, and Thor wasn't much further behind. After some climbing, I managed to get out of the crater in the snake's head and kept a hold of Mjolnir the whole time. Before any of you say anything, the hammer was never too heavy or enchanted so that "only the worthy can wield it"—it's just awkward as hell to properly use because of its short handle. Still pretty heavy, though, my arms would be burning if I could feel them. Anyway, after finally getting off Jormungand, I landed next to Thor, who was trapped in the snake's mouth and impaled on one of the fangs.

"And here I thought the poison cloud was what would do me in." He managed to joke before coughing up mouthfuls of blood. "Ugh, oh, this hurts. Not bad…but I think it's because I'm losing all feeling in my body." I got up to him and placed Mjolnir in his hand before placing my own on Jormungand's fang, breaking it apart into dust. "Thank you for my hammer, but do you mind helping me with these last nine steps?" That's how many Thor was supposed to take before he dies—it was the least I could do. I helped him up and supported him as he held onto his hammer, taking our time with the last steps of the Aesir. One. "You were right, we shouldn't have tried to defy our fate. The Greeks tried that, and the first Phantom destroyed them. Death's enforcer, the Creator's executioner. The mercy that we'd change our ways before he kills us." Five. "Phantom... Dante. Could you do one last thing? My hammer is supposed to go to my sons, Magni and Modi. Make sure...they...get..." He didn't finish, dying as soon as he took his ninth step. I lowered the Aesir down and gave him what last rites I could before taking Mjolnir away from his corpse. Nex soon returned to my feet.

"How long is that wolf delayed?" I asked the shadow, only receiving a sense of urgency as my answer. "Then let's go. Odin has a lot to answer for," I said before dropping Mjolnir into Nex's abyss, the familiar sucking me back in waist deep and gliding over the battlefield. Toward Odin...just as I saw something flash and fly toward me—aw crap!

CHAPTER 25

OATHBREAKER'S REGRET

"Nex!" I shouted, leaning back and sinking into the shadows before a spear could run me through. Odin's Gungnir, to be precise, which is an enchanted weapon that will always strike a killing blow on its intended target. I'm pretty sure that I'm the intended target and that it's not going to stop until I'm pierced by it…though considering I haven't been skewered yet, I think being inside Nex helps avoid the impending impalement. Now I just needed to figure out how I was going to prevent dying because of that spear *and* get to Odin so I can get my questions answered. All this, this whole Ragnarok mess, has been *really* irritating.

Okay, a homing and instant kill spear is tracking me. Fenrir is closing in on Odin and will eat him. I'm not sure what questions I'm going to ask, considering they just keep piling up the more I think about them, and time is running out, I thought to myself, trying to make a plan of action for any measure of success. I didn't want to fight Odin, I just needed answers, but would he give them? Why did he choose to betray his role? Was it really fear as Tyr said? Odin did a lot of terrible things in his attempts to hold off Ragnarok, it's one of the reasons why he was titled Oathbreaker. Guess that probably answers one question, but I still have plenty of others that I need answered. While struggling with my thoughts, I noticed a celestial-like gleam coming from my side. Light, in an endless abyss of shadow, certainly would get my attention. I looked and found a spear tip in the darkness, and it was pointed at me.

"Aннн!" I screamed and tried to swim away, for about ten seconds, before I noticed that I wasn't moving but neither was the spear. Considering I was inside the shadow monster that was my familiar, I am only realizing that I have no idea what he was capable of doing or even how he worked most of the time. But all this did give me an idea on the future conflict. I am capable of healing, not sure how severe, but I have cut off parts that reattached themselves, and I have regenerated from getting impaled before. If Nex is now in some control of Gungnir, then I can use this to my advantage. I'd have to make it quick though, even now I can sense the magical energy in the spear fighting against Nex's control. I braced myself and got ready for the next trial ahead, which was fortunate for me because less than a minute later, I was shot back out and was facing the armored and angry Aesir. "Odin All-father! I am the Phantom! And your time has come," I said with my mask materializing on my face.

"I should've recognized you the moment you walked into my hall," he growled. "I never thought I'd ever actually drink enough spirits to lose my guard like that." He was a giant of a man, thick and muscular with many scars and weathered skin underneath shining armor and a gray fur cape, long gray hair and beard, with a winged helm on his head. He didn't look like he even needed a weapon to either crush a skull or tear someone apart, probably since he was the patron of berserker warriors as well. On his broad shoulders were two black ravens, and standing at his sides were two wolves of gray and black color. The ravens told him everything he learned while the wolves were his loyal dogs that ate all his meals while he only drank liquor—that potential hangover scares the crap out of me. He would be leading his army of honorable dead, but they were already preoccupied with their own battles, so it's just me and Odin with his pets.

"We both know that you've had a rather questionable history," I said as I circled the ancient warrior, "but all of it was to delay Ragnarok. What finally made you neglect your station and allow this war to come to your doorstep?" I was looking for an opening. He was letting me look for an opening. I was unable to find one as wolves guarded his would-be blind spots. No matter how I attacked, I would be kept preoccupied until the other two joined in the attack. No blind spot, outnumbered, there was no way I could attack him in a manner that would give me an advantage, and Nex was still struggling with that damned spear. That's when I got an idea, a terrible one, and I should punch myself really hard for coming up with it in the first place, but it was the best I had. "Please, tell me, *mighty Odin*, and do speak up. It's hard to hear you over the sounds of war and death," I taunted while getting in front and closer to the Aesir.

"Then you need to improve your hearing, *boy*," he returned while putting a calming hand on his wolves as they growled at me, ready to tear my throat out. "Everything I've done was to delay Ragnarok, the twilight of the gods, not the destruction of the world," he said as I inched closer, keeping his focus on me. "Ragnarok would only start when Asgard and Valhalla fell, that's what I aimed to prevent. I heard a voice offering me a chance to protect my people, and I took it. That was always my duty, Phantom. The Hunters kept the world safe from every other threat, the army of giants and undead shouldn't have been too much for them to handle, especially since they are the hidden army of mortal kind, or have the Hunters been lacking as of late? There certainly wasn't a Phantom when I made my deal three years ago," he said, stunning me.

I was fifteen, been in the Order my whole life, and I know I've made a name for myself.

"I may not have reached the same acclaim as my fellow Phantoms, but I've been around for longer than that Odin," I returned, getting closer than arm's length with the Aesir, but the god shook his head.

"No, the birth of a new Phantom is something I would've noticed," he said before grabbing me by the throat. "Something is wrong about—" He began to lift me when Nex released Gungnir. By some miracle, it was able to alter the trajectory of the spear from my shadow so that it missed my heart, lungs, and the other organs that world immediately kill me if they were ran through. Instead, I felt my spine shatter, stomach sliced open, diaphragm cut, I would go on but then the pain registered, and *sweet, merciful Creator* was this a bad idea! But it worked in my favor since the spear tip was in Odin's chest. Ignoring the burning pain from my impalement, I grasped the shaft of Gungnir and broke it off, falling to the ground as Odin reached to his chest. If I had to judge from how deep that spear seemed to sink into his chest, it probably nicked his heart. I don't know how I should feel about that, but now's not the time. I can't move my legs, and two ravenous wolves are coming at me.

"Crap!" I growled as the wolves immediately bit onto my arms and start tearing them up. Powering through, because if I didn't I would definitely die, I positioned the remains of the spear I was still holding on to in my left hand and repeatedly stabbed it into the side of the wolf on my left arm. It yelped loudly as the Gungnir's blade sank into it again and again. Once it let go, I threw my arm and rest of my body into the wolf on my right side, stabbing it in the neck. It gagged and gasped before falling over dead. Not slowing down, I rolled back onto my back and got ready to throw Gungnir at Odin, only to witness something odd.

"Get...OUT!" he growled while clutching his chest. I could feel my lower body burning, so that probably meant that I was able to walk again as I struggled to make my way to Odin. While doing that, I watched his scarred eye flash brightly before his hand went to it and grasped at it in pain, his body glowing brightly like he was overheating, and then he exploded. Not the chunky and messy kind, just a massive shock wave of pressure and light. When it was visible again, Odin was on the floor while his ravens and wolves dissolved into nothingness. "Ah! Damned dealmakers!" he cursed as I slowly stood up, though I did feel like my legs were going to give out from under me at any second. "So this is how I end? That's disappointing," he groaned out as I reached his side.

"You made it sound like you were possessed," I said, trying to understand what just happened. I thought he just neglected his and the rest of the Nordic pantheon's post. This...wouldn't change anything, but I'd feel a little bit more guilty for doing what I've done so far. The war was already here, and fate is playing out as foretold. Nothing is stopping it. "Odin, what happened?" I still wanted answers, how and why this happened would be an important factor. If I can prevent this from happening again, then their deaths would have greater meaning than simply holding off the chaos of this final war they have.

"I was," he admitted, "because I was weak. The endless years of service, the endless conflict, everything I did, all of it to delay what was inevitable, I was simply tired of it all." I could actually feel his life force fading, he sounded weak and tired. Hard to believe from one of the mightiest of the old pantheons. "I was heading back to Mimir's Well, ready to make another sacrifice to gain greater insight and wisdom as to what to do since we haven't heard from the Creator since our own inception. That's when I heard it, a voice that sounded as ageless as that of the Creator that my desperation made me believe. Should've known better, but I was weak. Convinced me that 'as long as Asgard stands strong, Ragnarok will never come' and offered to bring back Baldur, and through him, a barrier that would keep the realm safe." He coughed a bit, Gungnir's lethal magic playing its part. I think I only survived because of how careful Nex and I were with positioning the spear; otherwise, I'd be dying. Even now, I still felt the heavy tax on my being from regenerating and the intense burning from organs, bones, and muscles piecing and sewing themselves back to perfect condition.

"And I ruined that when I killed Baldur," I said, seeing how most of this came about, then made true another part of my vision, taking the dying Aesir into my arms.

"They said nothing of my pantheon could harm him if I had allowed them to stand watch with me," he continued, coughing a bit more. "Never said that I could only watch before it possessed my body. Nor that my soul and power would become its own." He moved his hand away from his bleeding chest to his scarred eye, which was now milky white. "I tore this out when I first went to the Well of Insight. They brought it back and used it to possess me. All I could do was watch as they stopped my people from doing their respective jobs and spiked our mead to keep us all in a delusional state. They are powerful, Phantom, and older than any of the old guard," he said before tearing out his eye again—that was disturbing to watch. "Take this. It still has the power of Insight from the Well. Use it when you need wisdom," he said as the eye turned into a blue tiger's eye gemstone, clean and pristine as if he had not ripped it out of his face a few seconds prior. I took the gem and felt the ground shaking.

"Is that...?" I started before he grabbed me by the chest and pulled me down.

"Feed me to the wolf! Quickly while my soul is still mine! It's the only way!" he roared as a *massive* black wolf tore through the ranks of soldiers and came bearing down on us.

"Nex!" I yelled again, prompting the shadow to wrap its dark tendrils around the wolf and buy me precious time. I grabbed Odin, I was still holding onto Gungnir for some reason, and I was glad I was, as I ran into the gaping maw of the wolf. I made sure Odin was on the teeth of the beast as they slammed shut with a loud crunch. Odin was now dead, I was missing an arm, and Fenrir was swallowing me and the god. *This was not my best plan*, I thought before stabbing Gungnir's head into the throat of the wolf before I slide too far down. Just then, the mouth of the beast was pried open, and my arm reformed from a red mist—I think it was from my bitten off arm, but I'd need to do more research.

"Come on, Phantom! Let's end this!" a voice yelled out as I saw the figure of a bare-chested man holding the wolf's maw open. "Move!" he yelled out before taking his sword and slashing at Fenrir's mouth, making him howl, yelp, and thrash in pain. With my restored arm, I summoned my knife and threw it toward him, allowing me to teleport to his side. Once there, he continued to slash at the insides of the wolf's mouth, and I threw Gungnir at where the brain of the canine would be. The remains of the spear still had its lethal enchantments and pierced through Fenrir's head. The beast stilled, and the two of us ran out of the mouth, just as the mighty wolf collapsed onto its side. Vengeance for the All-father was...mostly served, still have to find the ones responsible for this mess, and since I do know my lore, I knew who my timely ally was.

"That's done. What's next, Vidar?" I asked the Nordic god of vengeance. With Thor dead, he was now the strongest of the Nordic gods and someone that was supposed to survive this war.

"We end this," he answered, pointing at an eight-legged horse, Sleipnir. "I'll gather the survivors and your friends, Phantom, and we'll escape while you destroy everything." As he said this, the horse made its way to me. "Sleipnir is the fastest steed we have and can travel anywhere in the realms. Your destination is at the roots of Yggdrasil in Niflheim. The steed knows where to go. You must release the Malice Striker."

"Nidhogg? I'm really supposed to release a dragon with the power to destroy all creation?" This was like gathering the force of a supernova to stop a world at war—it would wipe out everything!

"I only know that you're supposed to do it. Not why or what will come of it," he returned, looking at the battlefield, where a giant figure of fire was destroying everything with a sword shining like the sun. I could feel the heat from where I was. "Go! We're running out of time! I'll do my part. You do yours!" he roared before throwing me onto Sleipnir's back and smacking its hind, causing the horse to bolt with the speed of light. I held on for dear life as he carried me to the furthest reaches of the Nordic realms, a land of ice and death, Niflheim.

CHAPTER 26

PHANTOM'S DUTY

I HAVE NO idea how I managed to stay on that horse, no idea how my skin didn't peel off from the sheer force of the rushing wind, and no idea how I even had vision to see. Sleipnir's speed was not exaggerated as we flew past everything, and I still don't get how I saw it as clearly as I did. The moment we left Vidar behind, Sleipnir flowed through the raging battlefield of Vigrid like water with the grace of the winds. Curved around battles, ran past attacks, all the way until we reached what remained of the World Tree, which the eight-legged steed proceeded to run down to the realm of our destination. It wasn't even like I was riding a horse, more like a very small jet with legs, especially since the horse was running on the freaking air.

After clearing the battlefield, the ride was…uneventful but visually impressive during the few times I actually managed to get a good look. Granted all I saw was a few fertile fields, shining light, bleak darkness, and the fiery hellscape of the realm of fire—on second thought, it wasn't that impressive. I was probably just happy to see something not getting destroyed and knowing I was partly to blame—this hasn't been a good day for me or anyone involved. Moving on, Sleipnir soon got us to a land of icy fog, meaning we reached Niflheim.

Great…now to find Nidhogg, I thought as the horse continued to run, not noticing that it was slowing down little by little. *Where can I find an ancient force of malevolence that is destruction incarnant?* I wondered, listening to the sounds of gnawing, tearing, and snapping all around me. Nidhogg, continuously gnawing on the roots of the world tree that keeps it imprisoned, the loud sounds keeping me lost in the endless realm of cold mist. Suddenly a mighty gust of wind struck us, but not from in front. It was more like something was sucking in air with the force of an F5 tornado. Sleipnir twisted and ran, fighting against the wind as best as he could. But unfortunately for me, that "destructive aura," or whatever this power of mine is, destroyed Sleipnir's saddle and reins, which removed my hold on the mighty steed and let me get blown away by the vacuuming air.

"Damn it!" I cursed as I flew through the air, completely at the mercy of the rushing air for about a minute when it finally stopped. I slammed against some thick branches and roots, felt my ribs fracture and mend after it happened, and then rolled to a stop when I was in front a wall of interwoven roots, each one as thick as the Empire State building. I stood up, completely in awe of the wall, not because of its sheer size but because of the power it radiated. This was more than just the world tree—this was the strongest magical prison I had ever seen.

Finally. I heard something speak, sounding so ancient and powerful my whole being trembled in fear and awe. *My master's child has come.* That was when something pierced through the wall and tore its way down, a single talon that was the size of an aircraft carrier had ripped open the wall of roots, which were patching up just as quickly. After that, a gigantic beam of light shot through the barrier, and before the damage could be undone, a massive eye appeared and somehow ceased the magical repairs. *I've been waiting for so long.*

"Nidhogg!" I yelled out, unsure if the massive beast could hear me. Suddenly I was wracked with pain, like my everything was trying to rip itself apart. I felt cuts appearing on my arms, and blood welling up in my head before leaking out of any hole it could. While I was grunting in pain, trying to hold back any screams of agony, I saw the most complex spell seal I had ever seen. If I understood what I saw correctly, then it means the spell drew on the power of Yggdrasil itself to regenerate constantly, and so long as the nine realms exist together with the tree, then that would be indefinite.

You were meddled with, Nidhogg growled, making everything tremble with the dragon's rage. *Humans and their arrogance, why bother with protecting them?* Nidhogg is talking like he knows quite a bit about me, saying that I'm his master's son just like Baldur called me kin to Death and others talking about my brothers spread throughout history. What am I?

"Nidhogg! What are you talking about? What am I!" I roared before coughing out mouthfuls of blood, my flesh continuing to tear and crack, and my feet shuffling slowly toward the seal that kept Nidhogg locked away.

If you do not know yourself, then the matter is worse than I thought, he continued as I got closer to the seal. *Humans and their disgusting arrogance. Whenever they have all they could want, they destroy it by craving more and mistaking their place in the world by forgetting their own powerlessness.* I felt my leg snap, bones sticking out of my thighs, I would probably be screaming in agony if it wasn't for my puking up blood now. Either being in the presence of Nidhogg is destroying me or something else, and from what the dragon is saying, it's something else. *Trying to command their protector is* beyond *forgiving! Not that it'll last for much longer. All but the most stubborn spells on you are already fading.*

"Answer my question, dragon!" I managed to roar out, reaching out for the seal on the wall of roots. Even now, my bones continue to shatter, my skin peel, and my flesh tearing. I was in such agony, but I continued on without any sense of control, like my body was on autopilot. I didn't know how long I wasn't in control, what was really happening, or why this was happening, but at the same time, I felt a sense of calm despite everything happening.

The Phantoms are the sons of Death, peace and free will sacrificed for the power and ability to protect those unable to keep their own peace and safety, he said as I reached the seal, my arms still struggling with their destruction and my regeneration. *They do what is necessary because they have no life to lose.* I finally touched the seal, my hand exploding in the process, and I had just an instant to see the seal fade and the wall rot before it all exploded.

* * *

I had no idea how much time had passed, but I know I blacked out from the explosion. I was still regenerating, so it either couldn't have been too long or I had *a lot* of wooden shrapnel; honestly, I'm amazed I didn't die. That last line I heard from Nidhogg probably has the answer, but I was brought out of my musing by the hurried and concerned nuzzling from Sleipnir. He let out an urgent neigh as I slowly got up, my body literally still rebuilding itself as I rose to my feet. The horse was adamant about me getting back on him, and looking up gave me all the reason I needed. There was an absolutely *gigantic* crater, so big and vast that it likely went to the core of Niflheim and all around me was a windstorm so powerful the ground was getting torn apart, but that wasn't the scary part. The scary part was the shrouded multiwinged, planet-sized, and yes, that's what I said, dragon that seemed like it was beyond the realms and flying in the Ginnungagap. That means there's a planet-sized dragon flying in the endless chaotic abyss that destroyed everything else that touched it—I'm officially terrified.

"Ride, Sleipnir!" I yelled out, throwing myself onto the horse's back as he neighed and charged on. Somehow he was running faster than when we were fleeing the battlefield to get to Niflheim, though I can't say I blame him. I kept watching Nidhogg as light gathered in what seemed to be his head, just before he shot a beam of light that completely covered the entirety of the realm of Niflheim. The beam held for a fraction of an instant, the visibility slowly died, but when it returned, I was in awe of the damage. Niflheim was gone, a realm completely destroyed. It wasn't going to be the last as Nidhogg readied another blast.

"Move, move, MOVE!" I yelled with urgency, spurring Sleipnir as much as I could. During the run back to Vigrid, three other realms were destroyed by Nidhogg's power. Helheim, Muspelheim, Vanaheim, all realms that would likely be empty by now with the war going on, almost as if that were the goal. The ultimate indicator of that was the fact that he left the Midgard door alone, and so long as that remains, then there is a way out of this collapsing mess. Sleipnir soon got us back to Vigrid, and I would've mistook it for Muspelheim if it wasn't for the apocalypse level storm of wind and rain. The flames are fed by furious winds to the point that, despite being low, blazed hotter than magma; the landscape filled with hundreds of massive towers of swirling winds that tore apart anything caught in their wrath, sending out bolts of lightning almost every second; the seas churning and splashing against the land, flooding the battlefield and washing away all the bodies and blood not sucked into the air; and the earth split and cracked with more flames erupting from every gash in the ground.

Come on, where are you? I thought to myself as I scanned the area, looking for any sign of the would-be survivors. I personally didn't care for the "gods" that were meant to survive, but I was more concerned for my friends. It was a weird sensation, being worried for them like this. Usually, I'd be trying to kill their kind, but now I couldn't imagine leaving here without them. I needed to recover my friends before even thinking about escaping. My answer came in a bright flash of light, one that wasn't followed by immediate death. I spurred Sleipnir toward that spot and found them, my friends and the surviving Nordic pantheon, all on a shining, single-masted Viking ship. Skidbladnir, the greatest of Nordic vessels, able to sail anywhere—I wonder how they got it from Frey.

"Dante!" I heard Vidar call out to me as I came within earshot. "Catch!" he roared, throwing a ribbon at me, bracing himself against the ship as I caught the cloth. "That's Gleipnir! Head for Midgard!" he ordered, keeping a firm grip on the leash that once restrained Fenrir. Deciding to trust the people that actually had the time to *make* the plan, I directed Sleipnir to head back to the world tree and just prayed that Midgard was still untouched. In a way, I knew that it would still be there, but I still prayed for the best-case scenario. Lucky for us, that's what happened. The other realms were destroyed, Asgard and the field of Vigrid being the last, but instead of just outright annihilation of Midgard, the portal back to the human world began to shrink. I scanned the area for Nidhogg, but he was gone. Yggdrasil faded away, leaving the portal back to earth and my group as the last physical beings in the Ginnungagap. We soon passed through the portal and were now sailing across the sky.

"Well…that happened," Max said once I was inside Skidbladnir with Vidar tending to a tired Sleipnir. "Does this happen often, Dante?"

"Well…not as big," I admitted, looking away and praying my cover wasn't somehow blown. "I go someplace, fight some things, make a giant mess, run away, it's like that."

That…wasn't much of an exaggeration, was it? Thinking back, it's hard to remember the last time I didn't cause a complete mess fighting something. Even the school had its own share of messes since I showed up, though Monica was responsible for the biggest one. Speaking of, the events of…however long this was because time works differently across realms, finally caught up to me, and I collapsed. I was still conscious, but my body could no longer hold itself up, and I face planted on the deck. That was not a pleasant feeling.

"Dante!" my friends called out in worry as Monica and Lucrezia came to my side, my succubus girlfriend resting my head on her lap while Monica worked her magic. Apparently, my own regeneration stopped a while back, and I still had several broken bones and torn muscles, which I didn't feel too much because adrenaline and sheer determination are the best painkillers ever.

"You realize, Dante, this will certainly cause some major backlash to the world," Monica warned as she slowly healed me, taking time to properly mend my body. "I get that you had the vision of causing Ragnarok, but did you really have to do it?"

"Are you guys safe?" I asked, earning slow nods and various yeses. "Worth it," I said before falling asleep.

I had to admit, it was nice to have something to want to fight for personally instead of a mission I was told I had to do. I may not be fully human, not even entirely sure what I am to this day beyond the few things I was told. Son of Death, protectors of mankind, I'm not even sure the title of Phantom is really just a title, but for now, I didn't have it in me to care. My friends were safe, the world continues to turn, and everything seems all right for now…till the next mess.

In your typical story, there would be one more chapter that usually said, "Everything is fine, they'll get through this as a team, what could possible top this?" but no. This isn't the end of my journey, this was only the beginning, and I had to leave everyone behind for this trip because monsters, spirits, demons, and gods I could fight. Against a *true* Phantom, I was nothing.

CHAPTER 27

MY VACATION FROM HUNTING

I WASN'T SURE how much time had passed since I fell asleep, but I can safely say that I didn't get enough rest. It was like my eyelids had scabbed over, and I could hear the muscles in my eyelids protesting their movement. But judging from the yelling and arguing, I wasn't likely to go back to sleep anytime soon. Eventually, I opened my eyes to see two buff men with rune tattoos fighting over Mjorlnir. How they managed to get that hammer out of Nex, I had no idea. However, everyone on the ship seemed like they were ready to beat the two unconscious themselves.

"It's mine! I'm the stronger one of us!" the larger of the two said, bearing sandy blond hair and was currently winning the tugging match between the two. Guess that was Magni, Thor's son with a giantess. Famous for tossing a giant's carcass off his father after Thor killed said giant. Got the giant's horse as a reward if I recalled.

"You already have that horse! Let me have this!" Modi returned, the smaller of the brothers and born of Thor's actual wife. He had a more reddish blond tone to his hair and was a head shorter than his brother. Modi's only claim to fame is that he's Thor's son, and I feel kind of bad for him. However, that sympathy fell out the window because they woke me up. I looked around to the other gods and goddesses, but it seemed like no one wanted to get involved. Probably since this was a matter between brothers, and they should

176

treat it like such. I'm going to disagree with that since this is partially Thor's fault because he wanted to give *one* thing to his *two* sons. The thunder god did not understand math.

"All right. This should do it," I heard Monica say. I looked over to the witch, finding her reading six different books on magic enchantments, dwarven craft, and rune magic, all at the same time. She then took a stone tablet the size of a domino block and carved the Othala rune on it, a square standing on a corner with extended lines that resemble legs. That rune symbolized family inheritance and made me curious as to how she planned to use it. She got up and marched over to the arguing brothers, prompting me to go over because I just saved her and my other friends, and I was not about to let her get attacked by two oversized brats. "Give me th—AAHH!" she shouted, ripping the hammer out of their hands and then falling over because of how heavy Mjorlnir is.

"Forgot how heavy that is, didn't ya?" I quipped as Monica pouted at me from the deck floor. She held out a hand, and I helped her up, her expression didn't change, but now it was aimed at the hammer on the floor. "What are you planning?"

"Legacy of one, inheritance of two," she started, dozens of magic seals and circles appearing around her as she channeled a massive amount of power, "split the power that you knew. Given strength to see them through, to have the power to protect their few." She finished before throwing the glowing rune at the hammer, which made a rather larger explosion that tossed the four of us on the ground and covered the deck in smoke. "If that worked, you officially have to shut up," Monica announced, sounding utterly drained.

"What did you do?" I asked, not exactly hurt but also not too agitated.

I guess it's hard to top releasing a dragon that destroyed much of the nine realms, which was my fault. She didn't answer as the smoke was quickly cleared, most likely because this was an open-air deck, and we were traveling rather quickly through the air, and we saw what she had done. Mjorlnir was gone, and there were two different hammers in its place, one with a bigger head and one that was slimmer.

"What happened to my hammer?" Magni and Modi both cried, glaring at each other when they realized what they said. Before they could restart that fight, I punched them both on the side of their chins, causing them to stumble before collapsing to the ground.

"Not dealing with that crap again," I muttered before turning to Monica, who was standing back up despite looking utterly exhausted. "So what did you do, Monica?" I asked as she got behind me, wrapped her arms around my neck, and just collapsed, which nearly threw me off-balance.

"If I did that right, then I divided the power of Mjorlnir between them," she answered, yawning from exhaustion. "I'd say we should test it, but now is not the time for that?" She yawned again. "Nighty night, bro." She then fell asleep, and I guess I was her new teddy bear. This witch confused me very often.

"Well. Does anyone have any idea what we should do next?" I asked since at this point, we were just wandering about in the sky. No one spoke up, no one had any idea, and I felt like an ass since I was trying to force a bunch of refugees to put their grieving on hold to make sure they had a future. My friends were also asleep, probably just as tired from everything that happened. For now, everyone was safe, and Aesir and Vanir could use the time to let their emotions out. Just then, Nex started to balloon up suddenly and then spat out a body. Baldur's body with his head reattached. Then the god gasped for air.

"Baldur!" the Nordic gods cried out, rushing to their favored god's side. Some had relief, others looked terrified, and I guess I couldn't blame them. Last time they saw the guy, he was possessed by some unknown force that almost ruined everything—odd how the destruction of their home was the preferable alternative.

"I'm fine! I'm fine," he announced, looking at me before kneeling down. "Thank you, for doing what was necessary, good sir. I am Baldur, god of light and the one to give hope to my fellow gods." I looked among the gods to see their reactions, and they were all looking at a woman in a dress that I swore was made of clouds with dark brown hair and a large blue flower brooch necklace. When she nodded, everyone breathed a sigh of relief. I guess that woman was

COMMENCEMENT

Frigg, Odin's wife and queen of the Norse pantheon. Guess she's also their official leader now.

"As for you, Phantom, I do have an idea of what we should be doing," she said, turning to me. It made sense that she would know. She was said to have the ability to see the future but was always helpless to change it. She tried with Baldur and failed. "I saw an island in the sky. Hunters and demons, fairies and angels, gods and mortals, all living peacefully with each other. A single word hung above it all, Sanctuary."

"That sounds like Project Sanctuary," I admitted, taking a look around to make sure my friends were unconscious. Lucrezia already knew, Saya and Monica probably knew, but not everyone else, and I was sworn to secrecy. "Project Sanctuary was started up by a nun and a demon she saved under the protection and guidance of the Order and is supposed to be a top-class secret. I myself only learned about it this year. But"—I let my head drop as I recalled what little details I had from the experience back in February—"I'm afraid that's all I can tell you. I can't remember the spell used to transport there, and I don't know its present location."

"We have a flying ship, Dante," Frigg remarked, baring a kind and gentle smile. "Skidbladnir can sail us anywhere."

Hopefully, this solved their refugee issue, and they can move on with their lives—I don't think they could handle any more stress. Now we just needed to figure out how to get the gang and me back to the school. I didn't even want to think about how much we missed, but I knew it was going to bite us hard. Just then, Monica woke up, jumped off my back, and ran to the side and began sniffing. Yes, she was sniffing.

"DESCEND!" she yelled out, waking everyone up. "Descend immediately! We're above a dimensional hotspot!" Trusting the girl, the gods began to furl the sails and drop us back down to earth. It took us about five minutes, and we...docked, I guess, in the middle of a clearing in a forest. "Finally! We've found our way back!" she cheered, going to a spot in the clearing and casting a spell, opening a portal back to the school. "I'm amazing!" she said, throwing up a

179

peace sign and smiling. "But before we go"—she turned to Magni and Modi—"time to test out those hammers, boys!"

The brothers smirked to each other and got ready to spar until Monica said this, "Dante, you do it."

"What?" they yelled as Monica snapped her fingers, and the two hammers were suddenly in my hands.

"If I leave it to you two idiots, you might hurt someone," she answered. "Thus, we're leaving it to a trained professional." She then adopted a devilish smirk. "Or you can try to take them from him."

"Monica!" I yelled out, just as the brothers started charging at me. "Monica, I'm going to get you for this!" I braced myself for battle, and the hammers responded to my will, electricity bursting from the heads of both. It was an odd sense, but it was almost as if the electricity in the hammers flowed differently. The larger hammer seemed to have a charge that stopped and was maintained while the slimmer hammer felt like it just charged to bursting. On a hunch, I thrust forward with the slimmer hammer, and it shot out bolts of electricity that slammed into the brothers. It stunned them for a second, but they kept on charging at me, Magni closing the distance much faster than Modi.

When the bigger of the two meatheads got within arm's length, I swung the bigger of the two hammers and slammed it into his chest. There was a thunderous boom the instant the hammer connected, and Magni was sent flying back. Modi watched his brother crash into the ground before turning back to me, where he took a hammer blow to his face and was likewise sent flying. That said, they both got back up and didn't seem any worse for wear. I lifted the slimmer hammer again and thrust toward them, shooting out bolts of lightning at the pair. I think they were surviving the electrical blasts because they were the sons of the god of thunder and lightning.

"I think that's enough, you guys!" I called out, ending the lightning stream as they got close to me and returning their new weapons. "The larger hammer would be for single combat while the other is for range and possible splash attacks." The two looked at me in confusion. "Multiple targets in one attack." They understood that. "They're good weapons, and you should continue to practice with them. In *safe* environments," I emphasized as I walked back to my friends.

"Awesome!" Monica cheered, going to the ship. "And as for my payment, I'll be taking Skidbladnir." All the gods gasped with looked of horror and outrage, except for Frigg, but I suspect she knows I'm going to tell Monica no.

"Monica, they have greater need of that vessel than we do. What are we going to even do with it anyway?" I said, walking over to her.

"It's a ship that can sail anywhere, Dante," she returned. "I'm pretty sure we can find some use for it. Besides, it doesn't even take up that much space." She then grabbed and proceeded to fold it up like a handkerchief, part of the enchantment on the ship itself. "See? Not even an issue."

"The answer is still no. They need it more than us," I said, staying firm. She probably thought I would call some member of the Hunters to take care of them, or she was going to cast a high level spell to do something, but I had neither time or patience to do so. We were leaving, and they were keeping their magic ship. Monica pouted and looked like she was about to throw a tantrum, so I karate chopped her directly on the center of her forehead, and she dropped unconscious. Her eyes went googly, and I caught her before she hit the ground. "The day that a swift blow to the head *doesn't* solve my problems is a day I *never* want to see." I sighed while putting her on my shoulder. "Let's go, everyone!" I called out as we went through the portal...and were immediately arrested by Volk and the safety committee for being gone for a month.

I won't bore you with all the details, but we were all subjected to two weeks of intense twelve hours of schoolwork and studying followed by ten pages of comprehensive tests, including ten-page essays for certain subjects, and class projects. The teachers even admitted that it was more punishment for skipping so much class and less needing to make up our schoolwork since we were going to do a month of summer school anyway, except for Monica, who somehow aced every test and project. She gets off scot-free, which annoys me. I also still had my new duties as member of the safety committee, and

Volk seemed to be making an effort to keep me busy. It was awful, but Zoe came to my rescue—surprisingly enough.

"Just let him come to you," she said as a full-grown black Clydesdale took slow, tentative steps toward me. "The idea is to let him get comfortable around you." The horse was called Hippo, and he was in the care of Zoe and her family ever since he had been born. I asked why they suddenly sent him over, but she just deflected the question and had me help her with him. In the two weeks of schoolwork, I'll admit I actually enjoyed my time helping her with Hippo—he was a fine horse. He wasn't the only new addition as Zoe's family also sent a raven named Griff, who took to me almost immediately for some reason.

"Come on, big guy. Come for the juicy carrot," I said, holding out the vegetable for Hippo. She said I had to earn the horse's trust before anything else could be done with him, and in two weeks, we only got to feeding him by hand. Then again, building trust takes time. Hippo got within reach and started nibbling the carrot before chomping down on it. As he devoured the veggie, I held out my hand to his muzzle and waited. My patience was rewarded with him pressing against my hand, allowing me to pet him. "I can't help but feel like this is going faster than it normally would," I said, slightly frowning as I rubbed the big guy's big head.

"Hippo just seems to like you, I guess," Zoe said, coming to the horse's side with some brushes and began grooming the large beast. "Who knows? Maybe in another few months, he'll let you ride him."

"I think that'll only happen if we spent half as much time together as Griff does with me," I said, thinking about how that raven always seemed to hang around me, often perching on my shoulder before I let him on my forearm when I'm going around the school doing my safety committee duties. "Speaking of, where is that guy?" I looked around for the bird before Hippo started nudging me with his snout, prompting me to pull out an apple and continue pet him.

"I'm sure he's around," she said with a smile. "Probably found something to occupy his attention for the moment."

We spent a few hours like that, feeding Hippo by hand, Zoe teaching me how to groom him, and generally going around the field. We raced—I lost. Hippo won sugar cubes I got from the teacher's lounge, and when it got dark, we had to lock him up.

"Night, big guy," I said, rubbing his muzzle as we finished and were about to leave. "See you later." He walked away, heading into the stables Zoe had installed behind the dorms, made with Monica and magic when the guys and I were busy. As we got to the front of the building, Griff suddenly flew to my shoulder. "Hey there, buddy," I said, leaning my head to the side to give him some extra room before extending my arm. He quickly shifted to there as I pulled out some grain from my pocket, and only now do I wonder why I started to keep food in my pockets. He quickly started pecking at the grain.

"He really likes you," Zoe said with a smile as I started to pet him.

"I think he likes that I feed him more than just me," I joked as the black bird leaned into my hand. "By the way, what has Monica been up to that required Lance, Kashi, Saya, and Lucrezia?" I asked, realizing I hadn't seen the witch or those four for more than a minute in the last few days. Suddenly, Griff cawed and pointed up as Monica came flying in on a broom. He then flew off my arm.

"DANTE!" she screamed, holding up something—looked like a widening...burlap...sack. I'm about to get kidnapped again, aren't I? "Come with me!" she said a second later as I got wrapped up in the sack. We flew for a minute or two, going fast enough that if I had eaten anything bigger than a few protein bars, I'd be puking my guts out. I got no breaks other than four hours of sleep.

"So where are we going?" I tried to ask, getting used to the crazy girl's crazy antics. That, and I'm going to give her another crack to the head for this. She needs to learn to stop kidnapping people.

"Just a little longer!" I heard her call out. I felt myself slow down and descend as we continued to move. Another minute later, I was thrown into hot water—literally. The sudden surprise gave me a bit of a shock, but I managed to avoid inhaling water and kept myself calm long enough to pull myself free of the sack. "Welcome, Dante, to our new—!" I punched her on the head and put her in a daze. "Owie!"

"Welcome, darling, to our new clubhouse." I heard Lucrezia say, turning to my side to see her…in a hot red bikini. I have questions.

"Lucrezia, what's going…on?" I started to look around. I found that we were in a cave with a huge open space with the hot springs I was currently in, an array of shining gems on the ceiling to provide the light, cushions and couches all around so there was always a place to sit, and a magma pool. "What's with the pool of magma?" I asked, as if that was the weirdest thing.

"For cool points," Monica said, coming out of her daze and with a cartoonish lump on her head from where I had hit her. "Don't worry, the heat's contained."

"Hey, Monica, where did you want this?" Max called out, carrying a fridge.

"Over there!" she said, pointing next to the entrance. I was about to ask how she planned to keep it cold and powered, but she looked at me and said, "You don't want to know." She even said it in a deep and serious warning tone. Some things are best left as mysteries.

Oh, and as for the matters of Ragnarok's aftermath, here's what I heard during my hectic weeks of schooling and work. After the completion of Ragnarok, there were several freak storms and surprise blackouts, but before minor earthquakes, electrical, and wind storms could turn into full-blown disasters, everything calmed down. Basically, for five minutes, the world was facing a series of natural disasters before stopping completely, and a week or two later, it was like nothing had even happened. That was the Order at work, making sure the supernatural stayed a fantasy for the rest of the world. While they were dealing with all that, I was excused from my duties as a Hunter and Phantom.

That all brings us to now, starting another day in what has become routine after a peaceful month or two. I'm dressed for duty, heading to class with my group in tow. Lucrezia walking with my hand in hers, Max and Andrea doing the same, Zoe with Griff on her shoulder, Kashi and Monica cracking jokes with Saya and laughing, Lance being silent and walking along, and I couldn't stop myself. I felt a smile force its way on my lips. I was happy, everything seemed at peace, I was okay with it.

"Later tonight, we can figure out which couch is the comfiest," Lucrezia whispered in my ear, though Monica somehow heard and butted in.

"No!" she shouted, throwing a hand up. "I got my hands on a big wide-screen TV for the club cave. We're having a marathon!"

"Movies or television shows?" Lance asked.

"Yes!" Monica smiled, not surprising anyone.

"I'd hate to interrupt, but I'm going to need to borrow, Dante." A new voice came out directly behind me, freezing me in my tracks. I didn't know what it was, but I felt completely paralyzed.

"Aww, can't it wait, Lance?" Monica whined.

"That wasn't me," he answered, making everyone else stop. Almost as one, we all turned to face a man in a black cloak. He was unhealthily pale with pitch-black hair and purple eyes, a silver-colored staff in his right hand that he was leaning on. He stared at me with those eyes, pinning me on the spot, and I felt like an ant compared to him.

"Sorry, but the last time he went off with some stranger, it ended up causing a giant mess of things," Max said, getting in between us and standing defensively. "If you want him, we're coming too."

Everyone else got into place at that declaration, standing around me as if to protect me. I wanted to shout at them to run, but my throat froze.

"I wasn't asking," the figure said, raising his left hand and flicking it. The result was that Max, Lance, Zoe, and Saya were thrown aside by an unknown force. He repeated the action, tossing away Monica, Andrea, Lucrezia, and Kashi. "Now come along." He reached out as if to grab me, and I felt a grip around my entire body. He handled us so quickly, and I still feel paralyzed. *Who is this guy?*

Nex! I could use some help here! I called out to my shadow familiar, my most reliable ally. I was shocked when nothing happened. Nex even disappeared from my shadow. *When...what's happening?* I continued to wonder as I was helplessly pulled toward the cloaked mage. It didn't take a genius to recognize magic, and he was using some pretty powerful spell work without spell seals or incantations. That's rare and obscenely difficult.

"This is insulting," he said, looking at me with disdain. "How dare they—"

Just then, the automaton defenses came. Close to a hundred of the school's stone golems appearing all at once, and I could hear even more making their way here. The mage merely grunted and tapped his staff against the ground, making a large ring of earth spikes erupt from the ground and smashing into the golems. The statues were smashed to pieces by the sudden attack with the mage sighing with contempt. Like he thought, the things he was doing were a waste of his time. As he did, the broken pieces of the stone golems were coming back to together, refitting and reforming into new and bigger forms. "Still no better," the mage said as he brought his hand up, grabbed at the air, and ripped it back down. As he did so, all the golems were instantly sucked into the earth…and they didn't come back up.

"Who are you?" I managed to finally say, still frozen in the air. "Someone like you doesn't just pop up from out of nowhere!" He returned his gaze to me, and it felt like my heart seized. More than that, my stomach started to churn, I felt dizzy, and my body felt like it going back to when I was facing Nidhogg. If that meant anything, this guy might be on par with the dragon that wiped out eight of the nine realms. Before anything else happened, the school's lycans and members of the safety committee released a battle cry as they charged at the mage. "No! STAY BACK!" I cried out, only to be tossed aside by the mage.

"How boring," he said before pointing his staff at the charging horde, electricity soon erupting from the tip. The bolts branched out, slamming into the chests of the *entire* first wave. The number from a first glance was well over a hundred, and the lightning chained from the ones in the front to the ones in the back. All of them were blasted back with painful ease, the smell of burned fur and flesh following soon after that, and the mage didn't even move a single step.

"Bastard!" Kashi roared out, bringing out all his tails and shooting fireballs at the mage. Unfortunately, before the fire could even touch him, it wove around him and condensed into a ball in his hand.

"Child's play," he said before lifting it to the sky, where it grew and grew until the area around us started baking in hundred plus degree heat. The guy made something like a miniature sun right above our heads, and he called it "child's play"?

"Endless bounty of the water heed my call." I heard Monica chant out, making me turn to her. She was surrounded by blue seals and glyphs with three of her grimoires in front of her, the ground started shaking, the sky around the star darkened, and I could swear she was trying to open a portal in front of herself.

"MONICA!" I cried out. "JUST RUN! EVERYONE! GET OUT!" I yelled out in desperation, but those words fell on deaf ears as they got back up. The mage waved his staff and, from the looks of it, erased Monica's spells. Then he reached out and grabbed at the air, resulting in Saya getting choked by the same power he used to grab onto me. In her hand was the bleeding heart gem, meaning she was trying to use the higher powers of her royal bloodline. And it didn't matter a bit. "Damn it!" I grabbed for my knife and charged, Max and Andrea in lycan form, Lance as a large gorilla, Kashi in his fox form, and Lucrezia was trying to get everyone to safety.

"This is no better," the mage said as he straightened out and seamlessly changed his grip on his staff, which set off alarms in my head about his skill level.

But I still threw my knife at him. Kashi was the first to reach him, a fiery yellow five-tailed fox with electricity and fire coming off his tails, and was instantly floored by the mage. It happened so quickly that I could barely follow it, an upward blow to the jaw, sweeping the legs out from underneath, and finishing with a strike at the base of Kashi's skull. His eyes lost focus, and he was out. Max and Andrea were next, stabbing Max in the solar plexus with pinpoint accuracy and stunning him before he twisted his staff around to Andrea on the top of her head. After that, the mage swung his staff with enough force at Andrea's neck that she flew into Max and was sent tumbling away. Lance was behind him, ready to slam both of his giant ape arms down on him. The mage didn't even turn as he stabbed his staff back into Lance's gut and lifted him on the end, bouncing Lance and letting his full weight drop onto that point before grabbing him by the head and tossing him aside like a rag doll, all of them smoking from the proximity of the fireball above.

You will pay! I growled in my mind, furious at what was happening to my friends. My left arm throbbed, my fingers turning as black as they were during Ragnarok, and my thrown knife closing in on impaling itself into the mage's neck. I reached out and teleported to it and felt my hand wrap around his as he caught my blade. A part of me felt like I knew that was going to happen, so I was immediately making my next move despite the setback.

"Too slow," he said, just as I grabbed onto his wrist with my other hand. It had the desire effect as his wrist broke apart in my hand, and I followed through with stabbing him in the throat, driving the entire blade in and poking through the muscles and pipes. Everyone waited with anticipation, some calming down since who survives getting stabbed through the throat and vertebrae? Well, this guy did because he grabbed my hand with his restored one and ripped the knife out of his neck the hard way, staring me right in the face as he did so. "That almost tickled," he said, letting go of his staff and punching me in the gut. I lost all the air in my lungs and was sent flying from the force, losing my knife in the process. "Huh, looks like my descendants finally did something right," he said, looking over the blade, not even reacting when a bunch of vines appeared and took his staff away.

"That's my ancestor's work!" Monica roared, apparently controlling the vines and pulling it to her. "And I don't think he'd ever do anything like this." Monica did the smart thing, taking his staff away. No magic user could ever really harness and direct the flow of magic without a proper conduit, and the spells he was using needed a very powerful conduit to manage that kind of power. "Now I'll break you with your own—AAHHH!" she screamed the second she touched the staff, dropping it as if it burned. "This isn't the conduit." I heard her mumble. "This is pure iron—DANTE! THE STAFF IS PURE IRON!"

"WHAT?" I was shocked because this shouldn't be possible. Even without a wand or a staff or a grimoire, there is always a conduit for magic to flow through. Even when I was melting that frozen bottle of water, I was using the ice and water as a conduit. Iron *can't* be a conduit because it absorbs too much magical energy to be properly used...unless he was using his own body as the main conduit. It was a horrifying realization as the air began to shift and distort around him, the earth beginning to shake, and the world around him seeming to bend to his being. That much raw magical energy is akin to being at the center of a nuclear blast for the amount of strain it'd have on a person for even an instant depending on the spell. Now I wouldn't be surprised if he created a star in his bare hands since that kind of power might be flowing through him.

"If you all understand your place, maybe you can end this little resistance," he said, holding up his hand toward the fireball and making it shrink. "I'm here for Dante. It's just a simple chat. No one else is invited. He'll still be alive by the end of it. I promise. Now sit," he told us, just as the fireball disappeared into nothingness. It was then that he swung his hand down and gravity increased tenfold, instantly flooring everyone. I kept glaring at the mage, furious with how easily he beat not just me but everyone. Before I could plead for their lives, we were suddenly in a new location. "The gravity is back to normal. I healed everyone. Now let's have that talk."

"Who are you!" I finally yelled out, glaring at him with my knife still in his hand. He came out of nowhere, beat the crap out of me and my friends, demonstrated godlike levels of magical control, he *couldn't* be some random nobody. There's no way I didn't hear of someone like this, but who the hell is he? He just smiled at me like I was a foolish child.

"My dear little brother, have you truly been so broken?" he asked, making my eyes widened. He smiled as his face melted away, replaced with a blank mask of shifting rainbow mist with purple seeming to be the predominant color. "I am Xanth, the Phantom Magus, and he who is one with magic itself."

CHAPTER 28

FAMILY REUNION

"Now IF I have your attention," my "brother" said while waving his hand and growing a tree in the shape of a chair that he sat in, "let's talk, my dear brother." He held out a hand, and another chair appeared, this time from dirt and rock. I glared at the Phantom, but without a face, I couldn't gauge his expression. He just stayed relaxed and seemingly patient, and considering how badly he beat me and my friends, he has good reason to be relaxed. Deciding it would be better to go along instead of trying to overpower him, which has ended poorly for me, I sat down in the other chair.

"Okay, 'brother,'" I said, taking the offered seat while his face returned. "Let's talk. First up, a question of mine, how are we related?"

The question made him close his eyes and take a deep breath like he was trying to calm down.

"This irritates me," he whispered as he opened them and waved his hand, creating a light display of nine figures. I saw Xanth and myself among the nine and slowly recognized the others from what little I remembered of them. "Yes, Dante, these are the Phantoms. Our brothers." A time line graph appeared beneath them, showing their "active" years. "Throughout history, there has always been a Phantom doing something major." He pointed at different places in the time line. "Founding the Hunter's Order, creating a treaty with the Incruentatus, sealing Loki, hiding away the nonhuman races,

Ragnarok, creating this school you attend." That last one...wasn't really as surprising, not when you expected it to be the case after a while. "That said, you should probably keep it a secret. From what I heard, this was supposed to be a controlled environment to see if hidden coexistence is possible."

"Meaning, I'm the new variable." I guessed, somewhat irritated at being used, but I could sympathize with the aims if it was successful. "I used to think the aim was to destroy anything that's a threat to mankind."

"Many think that the Order is strictly an organization to hunt and destroy anything inhuman, and most recruits are people of that mindset," he admitted, something I was already aware of. "However, that's not what the Order's mission is. It's about preserving balance." He pointed to that point in the line when he said "hide the nonhumans." "This one was and is the third major mission in my life, when I made the belief and common knowledge of all things supernatural and turned it to myths and legends, then personally separated many different dimensions so that the peaceful kind can hide away, not the guiding deities though. Many saw fit to hide among humanity and continued their mission." Another godly feat, and he doesn't seem like it's worth boasting about.

Wait...guiding deities? I thought, remembering something important. "Cold Moon," I whispered, thinking back to Monica's final message. "Twilight of guiding lights," Ragnarok is also known as the "twilight of the gods," my knife is supposed to be named at some point, and he claimed the knife's completion as his descendants' work.

"Yes, as the one that made this...or will make, I can't keep track, I should give this blade its proper name and final enchantment." He held my knife up, opened his other hand with dozens of condensed spell seals appearing all at once. "Pain in the neck, keeping track of things when you're traveling through time," he said in one voice while I heard five others whispering the enchantment into the blade. "I'm the only one that does it, used a spell to ensure that too. Anyone throughout time that would have the knowledge and ability to manage time travel, never will. The thought will never occur to them, and

191

that's not as risky as you'd think. People think too hard and forget simple solutions or obvious answers."

"So why do you do it?" No one should have that kind of power all to themselves, even a Phantom.

"Because my main tasks are at two different points in that time line," he answered, grabbing onto the blade and pulling it along his hand. "Long before my birth and long after I'm dead." As the blade left his hand, it changed. No longer in the shape of a bowie knife, but it was becoming a broadsword. "The amplification from the horn may use the spell, but the blood of a Phantom awakens the full power of that setting," he said before returning the blade to me. "Now... where was I?"

"Mission of the Hunters," I answered, taking a few practice swings and watching fire flow from the blade. "And that you hid away the nonhumans."

"Right. It all started with the first Phantom."

"The founder of the Order."

"Wrong! That's misinformation because some idiot historian failed to differentiate our two oldest brothers," Xanth returned, shocking me. "Our oldest brother was the original hunter and Phantom, but it was the Phantom that succeeded him that created the Order in the first's name. The first always did everything himself because training anyone to be able to help him was 'too annoying.' Big brother was lazy like that."

"But not lazy enough to be the original protector," I was saying.

"Balance keeper, Dante," he interrupted. "The Phantoms' ultimate duty is to keep the balance of order and chaos. Those two never got along, unlike Mother and Father who got along too well." I was about to ask, which he suspected. "Life and Death, Dante, our parents are the literal forces of Life and Death. We live with no life to lose, and we only gain our real power when we die." He then placed his hand on my hand, and I felt him scan through my memories. "Which you should've done a few times over by now, but something is interfering. This will hurt."

"What are you—" I was about to ask as he raised his hand and plunged it into my chest. "Аннннннннннн!" Remember when I felt like my body was falling apart back at the roots of Yggdrasil? This pain is better described as pulling hot and rough sandpaper across the most sensitive and raw nerves on my body. And he kept on going as he felt around whatever he was touching while I was paralyzed and helpless.

"Oh, now this is brutal and bad craftsmanship," Xanth calmly said as he continued his inspection. "If whoever did this was a bit more careful and refined, he probably wouldn't have needed to sacrifice so many lives just to make this work." I almost missed his sudden mischievous smirk as the pain suddenly intensified. "Edit this line, move this one around, and done," he said before removing his hand from my chest, letting me collapse to the ground.

"Wha...what did...you...do?" I growled out, gasping from the pain and trying to get up, but my arms kept failing me.

"Oh, just a little editing." He made the seats dissolve back into the earth as he got up and walked a bit away from me, summoning Cold Moon to his hand. "Yeah, whoever did that to you made it so you'd never fully die and fully attain your birthright abilities. What you've been able to use was just the bare minimum of what you could really do. Also, when you started looking, you stopped being able to hear Nex, and you didn't even notice."

"What?" I asked, thinking back and realizing he was right. I couldn't even remember what Nex's eerie voice sounded like.

"He only ever has us to talk to, and now he's been shut out." Nex started rising from Xanth's feet, looking like a sad and angry serpent while my brother stroked the shadow's head. "Yes, he will, Nex. But for now, he's doing my challenge." Nex sank back into the darkness as Xanth smiled at me, one that made me quite uncomfortable. "Now for the changes I made to your curse."

"Couldn't you have just removed it entirely?" I asked, finally getting to my feet.

"Easily. Or have you forgotten that I'm the Phantom Magus? Magic is my bread and butter. I could remove your curse, but what kind of older brother would I be if I just gave you everything?" He drew a circle in the air with his finger and then snapped them. "Earn your keep, baby bro, and prove your capability. You'll only regenerate from anything that doesn't instantly kill you, and when regenerating from such damage, you'll be able to use your power of destruction. But instead of explaining, why not find out for yourself!" As he was talking, a portal appeared and grew from where he drew his circle. "Without your Cold Moon, without Nex, all on your own, kill this beast!" From the portal came a long gray serpentine body with a thick leathery hide. The body was bigger than the biggest elephant with two clawed feet that were like trees and then there was the head. A snake's head with massive curved tusks jutting from its lower jaw with a tongue like a forked trunk that had two pincer jaws.

"A grootslang," I muttered in horror as it released a deafening roar, glaring directly at me.

CHAPTER 29

DESTRUCTION'S HANDS

THIS WAS BAD—VERY, very bad. I'm unarmed, facing a giant elephant-snake beast, and I have to kill it with a power I barely understand. A power that only activates if I'm regenerating from severe damage if Xanth is to be believed, not like I had any reason to, other than giving me a near impossible task. But impossible and near impossible are two different things in that one has a greater chance of success, which should be obvious. People tend to miss the obvious, though. The grootslang swung one of its thick forked tongue trunk things at me, and I barely managed to dodge underneath it, my brother laughing at my struggle.

"Come on, little bro!" he yelled out to me, probably aware that he got the beast's attention. "Any Phantom can kill this thing!" That clearly made the behemoth angry as it raised one of its clawed feet to smash Xanth. Probably to prove his point, he raised a single finger up to the foot coming down at him, and the grootslang froze. Not with ice but in the way that no movement was possible. He then floated up to the beast's head and snapped his fingers, which made a large gemstone appear. "Kill that guy, and I'll make you this beautiful rock."

"Oh, you suck!" I groaned under my breath as the grootslang turned its attention on me while Xanth kept floating high above us. I turned and started running, reviewing all that I knew about this particular monster in my head. The lore states that they're a creation of South African deities that were gifted with great strength, intelligence, and cunning with a cruelty matched only by their love of gems. When those gods regretted the decision to make them, they split most of the grootslang into elephants and snakes, except they missed one, and that grootslang propagated a massive brood in a vast underground cave network, where they remained, feeding on whatever came too close to their cave. They don't have a stated weakness, but they aren't any kind of magical or cursed being, just a normal chimera between two animals. One that's bigger than an elephant and about sixty feet long but still vulnerable to conventional means. And I'm still unarmed, so there's that problem.

That was too close! I thought as I flipped over another swing of its trunk before running as it tried to stomp me into paste. *How am I supposed to do this? Xanth said that whatever power was locked away inside me would only activate when I'm regenerating.* I looked at my left hand and gulped, grabbing onto my thumb with my right hand and broke it. "GAH!" I yelled out, stopping my run as the grootslang stomped its massive foot in front of me. I turned and ran toward the main body, and trying to stay out of its vision, swerving to the side and grabbing onto its thick leathery hide. To my dismay, my thumb had already healed.

That didn't work, I mentally groaned as I attempted to climb up the loose skin of the beast. I didn't question the lack of scales, but I was just grateful I had something I could climb. The grootslang seemed to notice me and rolled toward the side I was on. *Round two*, I thought as I braced myself to be crushed under the weight of the beast. I forgot about the beast's intelligence and cruel nature as I noticed it slowing its roll just as my feet were caught under it. I screamed out in pain as my legs were slowly crushed under its bulk like a steamroller, flattening me out. I put my hands against it, trying to push myself free but also hoping that this was enough to activate whatever power my brother thought I had.

Come on! Work! I focused on the feelings I had during Ragnarok when I was freeing Loki and when I fought Baldur, feeling some measure of elation when my fingers started turning that familiar black. The hide of the grootslang was slowly cracking and peeling, which was progress, but apparently, a pair of crushed tibia wasn't enough damage to make this power strong enough to do any effective damage on the beast. The grootslang rolled off me, and before I could crawl to my feet, I felt one of its tongue pincer jaws latch onto my neck and yank me up to its eye level. Broken legs weren't severe enough either it seemed since they were already healing at a rapid rate. I was now looking the grootslang dead in the eye, and I could swear I saw what it was thinking as its other tongue pincer grabbed my head and slowly started to pull and twist.

I struggled hard, grabbing onto the hard pincers and trying to use my strange power to either break them or pry myself free, kicking wildly, desperately trying to avoid death. I was told I'd heal if I didn't instantly die, but broken neck was really pushing it. But I think it was because I was afraid. I went into hunts without any fear plenty of times before, what made this so different? My lack of weapons? It wouldn't have been the first time I was in a life-or-death situation completely naked of arms. Was it because Nex wasn't with me? I fought that wendigo without him, and I never felt fear. What the hell was so different about now?

Dante! I heard someone call out to me, happy and inviting, followed by seven different voices. *Dante. Dante! Dante! Hey, man! Dante! Morning! What's up?* It took me a second, but I eventually recognized them as the voices of my friends, the ones that stuck with me throughout the year. That's what was different. I had something to come back to, something to survive for. Suddenly, there was a loud snap, and my body went limp, the result of my neck breaking and my spinal cord severing. I couldn't move, I couldn't breathe, I couldn't even feel, everything was muted, but I could still see...for however long that lasted.

The grootslang held me up, presenting my body to my brother, as if demanding the jewel it was promised. Xanth smiled, said something I couldn't hear clearly, and held up his hands. Slowly, a ball of light was growing between them that was then trapped in a bubble barrier. I guess he's going to literally going to make a gemstone from scratch. Did I...did I fail?

How long are you going to hang there, little brother? I heard him speak in my mind, my entire body tingling as the sensation of touch returned. I grabbed onto the beast's pincer, and it shattered like a dry sand clump. With my neck free, I immediately grabbed onto the pincer around my head and onto the tongue of the beast. I felt my neck pop into place and my bones stitch themselves together as the grootslang thrashed its tongue about violently. I was free from its grip, and my fingers dug into the flesh of its trunk tongue, subconsciously waiting for the proper moment to act again. When I saw my chance, I made the part of the tongue I was holding on to blow up in a visceral way, flinging me toward the serpentine head of the monster.

It burns. It hurts, I thought as I reached out and caught onto the nose of the beast, twisting my body the second I slowed down slightly to brace my feet on its head to slow down while tearing away the skin I touched. *But I feel...alive.* I thought before sinking my hands deeper into the grootslang until I was elbow deep in its skull. It released an unearthly screech of pain and terror as its entire body began to break apart. Its legs snapped under its weight, the serpent tail came off, the flesh cracked and melted. Almost a minute later, the remaining flesh popped like a balloon and bones turned to dust. I landed in a rather gross puddle, seeing the blackness on my body fade away as the burning went away. Probably meant I was fully healed.

"That's doing it like a proper Phantom," Xanth said, floated down to me with that orb of light still between his hands. "Now I believe I made a deal." He held up the orb, and all the ash and goop from the grootslang was absorbed into the orb. Less than a second later, the orb popped, and a beautiful clear diamond the size of a baseball was in his hands. "I did say I'd make him a beautiful rock." That phrase made me more fearful of my brother than him actually doing it. "Congratulations, little brother, you've learned how to make your curse work."

I glared at him.

"Elaborate on 'instant kill,'" I demanded since I now can't trust anything he says.

"Instant destruction of the brain or body," he answered, his smile never wavering. "You can't fully gain your powers unless you truly die, but until you somehow fix that curse on you, you will never become a true Phantom."

"You probably won't answer, but how—"

"Find the angel Lo," he interrupted, knowing I was going to ask for help on how to start this new journey of lifting my curse, "as in 'And Lo, an angel of the Lord came upon them.' He's been in obscurity ever since. Served as a founding member of the Order and has guided Phantoms in our lost times. Find him, and he'll show you what you need to do and where you'll need to go. I'll see you sometime in the future, I don't know when, but before I go"—he snapped his fingers, and I felt every blood vessel in my body from the neck down pop, making me scream in agony as I fell to the ground—"I'll be taking some of this." He pulled out another gem while I was on the ground regenerating and bleeding from everywhere. A black mist seeped from my body and flowed into the gem, turning pitch-black itself when the process ended. "Goodbye, my dear brother. Make us proud," he said with a smile before blinking out of existence and Nex returning to my shadow with my knife Cold Moon going to my hand. My brother's affection was a cold comfort when he made my blood vessels explode. I'm scared to see what a proper family reunion would be like.

CHAPTER 30

DROPPING TO MY LOWEST POINT

TIME PASSED AFTER that, and… I was being distant, to put it mildly. I had a lot on my mind, a lot to figure out: I wasn't human, someone or a group wanted to make me think I was, the Order might be corrupted to an unknown degree, I need to find out the truth about myself, and other less than intelligent thoughts. After I came back from my "talk" with my brother without a scratch, I was taken in by Gulski for interrogation, but I kept silent about everything that had transpired between me and Xanth. Since I refused talk, I was put into solitary without rations for some time before someone came in and examined me for any magic that was forcing my silence. They couldn't even find the curse afflicting me, and I was stuck in a blank room for even longer before Monica came in, volunteering to examine me. She told them she was able to find traces of magical energy but more akin to a memory and silence charm that were very well hidden, telling me through Morse code that we needed to talk.

"I can't even begin to tell you what that was," she said as we were leaving the detention hall. "That wasn't any kind of magic I know, and I studied magic a lot. What's afflicting you is…wrong. Just plain wrong. I don't even know how I missed it the first time!"

"'He' probably made it easier to find," I said, hopefully making the implication clear. I didn't talk to her after that. I barely talked to anyone after that. Gulski had me discharged from the safety committee and kept me on probation, always having someone keep an eye on me everywhere I went. That didn't go on forever as Nex dragged me away from the dorms one night once I figured out the schedule of the watch. I needed to get out of that building and away from my friends. I didn't and couldn't talk to them about this stuff. I didn't even want to talk to Monica and Saya about this, and *they know* my secret!

"Okay, Nex, any progress?" I asked my familiar once he freed me from his void. I've tried talking to Nex during this whole time I was being watched, but I still couldn't hear its voice. At best, it was like communicating with a dog with more expressive eyes…and that didn't make it any easier. Eventually, I had the bright idea to have him write what he's saying, but apparently, in all the thousands of years of his existence, writing any language was not a skill Nex picked up. However, he did figure out an answer and began showing me images that I could glean answers from.

Xanth told him not to tell me anything about my own past—thanks a lot, bro—but he could tell me about my brothers. The first Phantom was the original protector of Creation and fought alongside every other pantheon until mankind had the potential to fight for themselves but then just disappeared around the birth of Jesus Christ. The second Phantom appeared in that time and was protecting the small family of Jesus during the exodus to Egypt when a group of still existing Medjay joined him in creating the Hunters Order. Phantom after Phantom shaping history and legend until Xanth's turn and made all knowledge of the Hunters disappear from the public mind all over the world and turned the very idea of magic and mystical beings into myths and fairy tales, then it was just the Hunters' history they shaped. Nine different figures of impossible strength, speed, skill, and ability, all leading to me. No wonder Xanth was disappointed if *that* was the legacy I had to live up to.

"What is my life?" I asked myself, pulling out the phone I had for communicating with the Order. Dozens of missed calls, demands for updates, I stopped answering after meeting my brother. I've stopped so much from what I've usually been doing. I've stopped hanging out with my friends or spending time with Lucrezia, I barely eat, and I can't tell if I had even slept much. I pocketed my phone and started walking with no set destination but just the hope that it might clear my head. Another vain attempt as I've been trying to do that this whole time and have gotten no closer to succeeding than when I started.

Is everything all right? Dante? Dude, talk to us. I kept hearing the voices of my friends echoing in my mind, saying the same things from the brief moments I was around them long enough for them to talk. Part of me screams to talk to them, tell them everything, ask for help, but it was always pushed back by this odd need. I think it was the desire to prove myself to my brother and to the rest of my family, or it was just pride, and I'm being a stubborn jackass. Equally possible. At some point, I found the motorcycle I came here on, still hidden among the foliage I first hid it in with some plants wrapping around it and months of neglect showing its effects.

"Nex…consume it," I told the shadow as the darkness slowly swam toward the vehicle. I was doubting so much of my life now. Was I compelled to take this particular bike? Was someone trying to track it? Why did I take the motorcycle in the first place? I stopped, asking myself all these questions when I felt my pocket vibrate and pulled out the phone from the Order, seeing they were calling again. I didn't answer and instead felt my grip tighten around the device, making it crack and splinter in my hand. The sharp plastic and glass began to cut and stab into me, activating my regeneration and whatever my latent ability is, and reduced the phone to bits. "Who can I actually trust now?" I finally asked myself out loud. Just then, my other phone buzzed, the one I got from my friends.

"Dante? Where are you?" I heard Lucrezia ask when I answered. "I thought I'd come into your dream, and…Dante, please, just talk to me!" She begged…and just like that, I felt my wall crack just a bit.

"That guy that almost killed you guys? He claims he was my brother," I finally told her, her shock evident as I heard her gasp. "Then he said some things that…that really got to me. I never knew anything about my family…and I'm still trying to process everything. I know I've been distant, babe, but…this is just how I've been doing things my whole life. I'm sorry."

"Remember what I told you back in Italy? Promise to be more open and I'll respect your privacy?"

"I remember. It's…it's just hard. I was actually thinking about…"—*about leaving*—"never mind. Nothing good will come from that thought."

"I'm here for you. Never forget that. Summer break is coming soon, and the school staff decided to hold an open mic karaoke party to end the year on a high note. The girls and I have been practicing, and I even wrote a song. Can you come? Please?"

I smiled, probably for the first genuine smile in months.

"Okay…I'll be sure to listen."

We bid each other good night and hung up. I kept walking until I reached a clearing and just fell onto my back, looking up at the stars. I just lay there stargazing and felt some nagging voices in the back of my mind, one was saying to enjoy this for a while longer and the other was screaming at me to get a move on and start my journey. I had to leave, but I didn't want to. I need to learn the truth behind my history, but I'm scared about what I'll learn. I should probably tell them the truth about me, but I absolutely couldn't do that. I don't know how long I lay there, but I did suddenly get an epiphany. I'll say that person was my brother, and he needs me to learn the truth behind our family, that I have to do this, and it has to be me. "I'm going to have to leave without telling them." They'd try to come with me, and I can't allow that.

After I finally made up my mind about what to do, I spent the rest of the time I had doing what I should have been doing. Classes, hanging out with my friends, spending time with my girlfriend, listening in on her practicing on occasion, but at the same time, I never fully committed to it. I just enjoyed the time we all spent together, but I still had to be ready for when we had to say goodbye. Though something I did notice was Monica showing signs of mental fatigue, but every time I tried talking to her about it, she just dodged the question. Soon the final week before summer break was upon us and the karaoke party was going on. I was on the roof of the school building and away from the crowd with the only other being that I stayed close to these past few months, the raven Griff.

"Is it too much to ask for a little more variety? At least the acoustics are good," I said as the acts continued, stroking the raven perched on my forearm. So far, every act was either a siren or a mermaid, a banshee came up and screamed a few death metal songs, but I was waiting for the one act I cared about. When was she going to take the stage? The party's almost over.

"She's looking for you," I heard Max say from behind me, turning to find the lycan glaring at me. "Lucrezia's looking for you for a good luck kiss before going on. Why are you up here? Didn't you say you'd support her?"

"I said I'd listen to her song, and I can hear just fine from up here. I don't do well with crowds."

"Scared your brother's going to show up again? Dante, we've been over this. Friends talk to each other."

"My brother pops up out of nowhere, kicks our collective asses, drags me away to have a private family talk, and then proceeded to demonstrate just how weak I am. What's there to talk about? If he shows up again, the only safe option is to do what he says and no. No I'm not scared of him showing up again. It's…something else."

"You're going to disappear on us again, aren't you?" he guessed, my silence answering his question. "You are such an ass! Do you realize that? What about all that talk about helping me with my brothers' deaths? About Kashi earning his place among his clan? About Lance and his cursed state? Saving Lucrezia back in Italy? That whole Ragnarok mess! You've helped us! Why can't you let us help you?"

"You guys were captured and held prisoner during Ragnarok," I reminded him.

"Not the point, you know what I mean." As he said that, Lucrezia and the girls took the stage, with each displaying their skill with the instrument of their choice. Monica conjured up a row of piano keys, Saya pulled out a violin, Andrea had a lute, Zoe had a lyre guitar, and Lucrezia took the mic.

"This is something I put together for someone special to me." She started humming while Andrea's fingers danced on the strings of her lute and Zoe her lyre, Saya made her violin sing, and Monica joined the rhythm, and then Lucrezia sang. The words that came forth sang of hesitation between two lovers, how one fell in love while the other remained distant, how through hardship that distance closed but then the partner began to turn away again and more closed off than before. Now the pair almost never see each other, but one is still waiting, knowing that the other is still there, and no matter how long it takes, the one waiting will still love him. It didn't take a genius to figure out it was about us, the story of our relationship. I almost felt my eyes water, but no tears came. I don't think I'm able to cry.

"Are you seriously going to disappear on us? After that?" Max demanded from me as the final note faded away. "Dante, I'm begging you, man, don't do this."

"It's not that I want to, Max," I told him. "It's that I have to do this. I need to do this alone, and you'll just put yourselves in danger."

"That's not why I'm begging, Dante. I'm begging because I don't want to hurt you, but I will knock some sense into that thick skull of yours."

I scoffed as Griff flew off my arm.

"Do you honestly think—"

I didn't finish because he grabbed my shoulder, made me face him, and then he punched me in the face. Next, he kneed me in the stomach and slammed his elbow into my back, dropping me to the ground. He didn't do anything else while I got back up because Nex had restrained him.

"I know this thing isn't a part of you, Dante," he managed to growl. "But I didn't say anything because I thought it connected to what you really are. However, since it really isn't a part of you, you can't really claim alpha status anymore."

I glared at Max before snapping my fingers and having Nex release him.

"You really wanna try this?" I started stretching, knowing this was going to happen.

"No special weapons, no outside help, just whatever you are and me."

He began to slowly change as he said that, staying mostly humanoid. I pulled out Cold Moon and flipped it in my hand a few times before throwing it up and waited. The moment we heard a thunk, we charged at each other, Max becoming more wolf as the battle began. He swiped at me with his claws; I ducked under them, grabbed his arm, and threw him over my shoulder. The moment he slammed onto the ground, I swiftly moved to get him into an arm bar, trying to quickly dislocate or break his arm and have a quick end to this fight. I underestimated how determined Max was about this as he forcibly twisted his body to slam me face-first against the ground. I ended up letting go after getting dazed from the blow to my head, but I did hear the loud popping of his shoulder dislocating. We both got up, and I watched him pop his shoulder back into place with a loud groan.

"You're really committed to this, aren't you?" I asked as we got ready for round two, him turning full lycan and towering over me. "Round two it is."

We charged at each other again, and as he closed the gap, he pounced at me. I dropped to my back and kicked him in the gut while rolling back, throwing him over me and nearly off the roof. He caught onto the edge and pulled himself back on the roof, getting back to me before I could react. He grabbed me by my head and slammed me onto the ground and then proceeded to beat into me. I felt my skull crack and fracture under the force of his punches and stomps as I struggled to get back to my feet. Mixed with the pounding I was getting, I felt my body burn with a familiar sensation of my power activating. I didn't just spend the past couple of months trying to get my thoughts together.

Keep it light. Keep it shallow, I told myself as I felt the energy seep from my fingertips and into concrete of the roof. I got my desired result as the surface split and crack, turning to gravel on the right side. The sudden change and disruption of his footing caused him to slip and gave me a chance to move. I twisted and slammed my fist into his ankle, forcing him into sudden splits, then I forced my legs up and locked them around his neck and pushed with all my might. My face slammed against his as he fell, and I began pounding my fists into his fist as fast as I could.

This is what I learned about my abilities as a Phantom—an increase in strength, speed, and reflexes—but I figured this was normal for my kind and not what separated me from my brothers. My power was this strange energy that I can place into whatever I touch, causing whatever I touched to break depending on how much energy I used and how it spread. I felt my strength begin to wane as my bones finished healing from the blunt trauma from Max's fists, meaning I was slowing down as well. This is when Max dug his claws into my thighs and gouged some deep scratches into my legs. The sharp pain threw my concentration, which he used to bite onto my wrist and crush it in his jaws.

"Аннннн!" I yelled out and loosened my grip as a result, which freed Max enough to tear me off him and slam me into the breaking concrete. I think I made the break in the roof a little too deep as I felt something stab into me, pushing even further as Max punched me deeper into the ground. He then took his claws and tore them down my chest, that's when my mind left. I didn't necessarily black out, but I was in my nightmares, strapped down and being tortured.

Embrace your fate! I heard someone roar. *Hunt, Phantom! Kill them all! Anything that isn't human is the enemy! There is no other way! Kill them all! They cause you this pain!* I was stabbed into—scratched at—every kind of pain you could think of while screaming at me to kill anything that wasn't human. I snapped at that point, grabbing onto one of the arms coming at me and blew it off from where I grabbed it. I heard a scream of pain, but I didn't care, not when it was something that was hurting me. I didn't even see what it was when I ripped my body free and punched my foe in the head, grabbing their shoulder and slammed them onto the surface I was impaled on. I broke the figure's remaining arm with a hard punch to the elbow and dislocated the shoulder immediately after. I then reached for the head, intent on making it pop like a balloon, charged enough energy in my hand to do so.

"Dante!" I heard someone cry, and I froze. "Dante, what are you doing?"

I started blinking, and my vision kept changing every time I closed my eyes.

"Oh god! Max!"

"Monica!"

"Get off him!" I heard more voices call out as my sight finally focused on something that seemed like clear reality. Max was unconscious under me with several holes in his body and a missing arm. I froze, seeing my friend in such a state before getting thrown aside by Andrea in her lycan form who was growling while standing protectively over her mate. I finally felt like I had control of my own body, and all I could do was look at their horrified faces.

"Dante," Lucrezia stepped forward, letting me see her scared and concerned expression. "Dante, what happened?"

I couldn't answer, I couldn't even breathe, I just wanted to disappear. Nex answered that desire, and the world disappeared into blackness.

CHAPTER 31

MY JOURNEY OF SELF-DISCOVERY

You NEVER REALLY appreciate knowing the passage of time until you're without any sense of it. Seconds, minutes, I don't even know if it was weeks that I was there, floating in the dark abyss of Nex's body, curled in a ball and just wishing I would disappear. At least that way I couldn't hurt anyone I cared about ever again. It was the one thing I *never* wanted to do, and I almost killed one of my best friends. It was always the one concern I had had, ever since accepting the idea that I could have friends, that my life as a Hunter would either kill them, or something else I would never forgive myself for. Possibly the most self-destructive thing I've ever done. I learned to care. Now I was in an empty space of darkness, never getting hungry, thirsty, or sleepy, just wishing I'd fade from existence.

Nex, however, seemed to run out of patience as I was eventually shot out of his darkness and thrown against a wall. I barely felt hitting it, I just felt numb to everything, except for a sudden stabbing pain in my skull that got me to move. It wasn't like when I received one of those weird prophecy dreams—this was something else. Very similar to when Nex first spoke to me before I got used to it, possibly meaning Nex wanted to talk.

"What is it?" I finally growled out, getting a look at my surroundings. Nex brought me to a cave somewhere in the forest, and it was midnight under a bright full moon, which made seeing Nex easier in the darkness. He threw my mask to me, which I caught, and made an arrow that was pointing toward the Gate. "Let me guess, 'Enough moping, go do what your brother said,' or am I wrong?" The glowing red dots that served as his eyes glared at me, and I felt myself being moved by Nex. "What does it matter? What will I gain from doing this?" I asked, Nex rising before me with my mask being shoved into my face. "I know Xanth said I needed to learn about being a true Phantom, but what's the point? What will actually change other than knowing what my destiny is? My future doesn't seem to involve them." I didn't elaborate, Nex knew who I was talking about, and he didn't stop dragging me wherever he wanted, and I just let him do it. I didn't pay attention to anything until I heard someone whisper shout.

"Dante!" It sounded like Saya, making look up to see her, Monica, and Zoe sitting on a log with a sleeping Lucrezia on Monica's lap as the witch maintained a sleep spell. Saya was making her way toward me, angrily stomping, and then she punched me in the face. She has a vicious right hook. "Where the hell have you been!" she demanded as I fell to my hands and knees from the hit. "We've been worried sick, looked for you everywhere, Lucrezia hasn't slept in days waiting for you to return, so what the hell?" She was growling now, eyes glowing red and mouth full of fangs. "And don't you dare say you can't talk about it. Max lost an arm because you refused to talk!"

"It took me two hours to fix the damage," Monica spoke up. "Most of that was arguing the finer points of a metal skeleton, but Max kept saying no."

"Ignoring Monica, we deserve an explanation, Dante. Everyone here, awake, knows that you're the Phantom. So spill." I felt my eyes widen in surprise and pointed at Zoe. "Yes, her too. You tell us what happened, and she'll explain how she knows."

We glared at each other, but I was stuck, literally because Nex had bound my feet, so I told them. Told them what my brother told me, what he did to me, what I was planning on doing and what I had to do, and how Max tried to knock some sense into me but triggered something, and I almost killed him.

"Something is very wrong with me, and I need to find out what," I said, finishing the recap. "This isn't something I'm doing as a Hunter. This is completely for me, and I have to do it alone. That's why I was keeping my distance, to make it less painful when I do leave."

"Less painful for you or us?" Zoe accused, making me hang my head in shame because, either way, I was a coward. "It doesn't matter. You do what you need to." She then released a high-pitched whistle. "Dante, I am Zoe of the Honor Guard of His Majesty Lord Oberon, king of the Fae." I was surprised by this. She was always quiet, but it's usually the quiet ones with the big surprises, isn't it? The Fae was a general term for all magical beings in Europe, a place some believed to be the birthplace of all magic, and Oberon was the lord and guardian of some great magical power. But as far as I heard, he was just a baseless legend made by Shakespeare on the order of the Hunters, just another piece of evidence that I was likely being lied to by the Hunters. "Much like how Monica learned your identity, my king also looked into the future and saw you and what you would do. He charged me with becoming your ally and bringing your steed. A mighty hippogriff," she said as massive equine figure with a bird's upper body cawed had made its presence known while it descended.

"Hippogriff? You only brought that horse Hip…po…and that raven…Griff." Realization hit me like a sledgehammer. "I'm an idiot," I groaned as the hippogriff cawed in the way Griff let me know he was coming to perch, making me extend my arm for him. "I'm usually better than this. I must really be out of it." Griff cawed lightly and went to my shoulder. "Anything else you wanna tell me?"

"My master will be waiting for you in Tír na Nóg. There, your destiny will become clearer." So now I had two things to look for, the angel Lo and how to get to the Fae Kingdom of Tír na Nóg. Nex released my feet, and Saya stood aside. I started walking, but Saya grabbed my wrist.

"After you get your answers and come back, and you *will* come back, you're going to apologize to Max and everyone else for your stubbornness," she ordered before letting me go, going to Monica and helping to carry Lucrezia back to the dorms. "We'll tell her something to explain your absence, but you need to make this up to her." They began walking to the dorms, leaving me to continue to the Gate with Nex and my new hippogriff companion. But when I got to the Gate, I found another surprise in someone I hadn't seen in so long. Hippogriff seemed to sense trouble and flew off my shoulder.

"Rachel?" I asked, not believing my eyes as I saw an old friend from my training days. Rachel was a tall black-haired woman wearing a black shirt, gray hoodie, tight jeans, and brown boots that I'm betting were steel toed.

"Hey, Dante," she greeted with a smile. I know I just said she was an old friend, but seeing her again didn't invite happy memories. Instead, I was back in that torture chamber, and her voice played in my head along with a dozen others saying the same thing, "Hunt, Phantom." Just over and over as I tried to focus. "You haven't been in contact for a while. Wizard got worried about you, you know?"

"Wizard actually caring," I returned while still flashing to my torture and hearing the voices telling me to hunt. "That is something."

"Well, here's our orders." She dropped her smile and looked to the school. "This place has been deemed as a risk and now must be destroyed."

I froze, dozens of thoughts going through my head on what was happening. I said this place posed no threat, that it was a rehabilitation and acclimation center, that it was safe for everyone. How could it change into a threat? Was it because I wasn't keeping in contact with the Order? Or…maybe…

"After all, this is our duty as Hunters. All monsters must die for humanity's safety," she said, though it seemed a bit more angry than she probably meant.

"Why don't I believe that?"

"*Hunt, Phantom*," she suddenly said, making my body seize as I felt something else take over. "*Hunt, Phantom*. You must kill anything inhuman. *Hunt, Phantom*. Only when they're all dead will your work be done. Now do your duty, and *hunt, Phantom*," she kept saying, and I felt my body begin to move against my will.

NEX! STOP ME! I quickly pleaded, screaming at my familiar. Probably the first time I managed to ask for his help as more memories flashed in my mind, some of them being me killing a family of Incruentati. Nex answered my call by shooting bone spikes through my leg, letting me use the pain to get my body back under my control. "I have some—" I started, only to get shot in the throat for my trouble. She had a silencer on a 1911, and I felt the bullet spread out in my throat. RIP rounds and a silencer, tearing my throat to bloody ribbons, and no one would hear as she fired round after round into my neck as I dropped to my knees. I saw her mouth move before her body began to emit a light so bright and pure that any darkness was immediately gone, meaning I lost Nex as even my shadow disappeared. I fell to the ground, paralyzed and helpless though not for long as my body already began to heal.

"Send another of the team and make it quick," I heard her say as my body fixed itself. "The conditioning is wearing off, and I have to restore some of it. It has been an honor. For the supremacy of humanity." She finished as she straddled my body, taking out a glowing syringe that felt like it held some powerful spells in it. Lucky me, though, as I healed enough to regain control of my arms and I grabbed her head, flooding it with enough of my power that her head exploded like a water balloon. The light dimmed, and Nex washed over me like a wave, cleaning off all the blood and the body, except for a strip of muscle that appeared in my hand.

"How nice of you," I said, sitting up and cracking my neck as hippogriff returned to my shoulder. "Sharing my kill." I held up the remaining bit of my enemy for the raven who quickly snatched up and swallowed the meat. This only confirmed two things: that I couldn't trust the Order anymore and that I had to leave this place protected, and there was only one being I could trust with that.

"Nex, leave my shadow and stay here." I ordered, the entity rising from the ground to look at me with concern. "I can't trust the Hunters. This place is doing good, and if I don't leave you to protect it, then I might as well just kill everyone here myself already!" I growled, feeling betrayed, manipulated, and furious with the whole thing. "Do this for me, Nex. You already know I'm coming back," I said, not waiting for a response as I already began marching down the tunnel of the Gate.

This was the real start of my journey. I find out that someone was messing with me. Most of what I knew was a lie. I had to get answers, and I am likely to have a trail of bodies behind me. I started my journey of self-discovery sad and hopeless. Now? I'm just plain pissed.

CPSIA information can be obtained
at www.ICGtesting.com
Printed in the USA
FSHW011823160321
79558FS